Also By Jen McGee

A LOVE TO KILL FOR

A LOVE TO FIGHT FOR

A Meadow Oaks Novel

JEN MCGEE

LilyPad Publishing, LLC

Copyright © 2026 by Jen McGee

ISBN: 979-8-9905168-5-4

Cover Design by Amber Simpson

All rights reserved.

No portion of this book may be reproduced in any form without written permission from the publisher or author, except as permitted by U.S. copyright law.

The characters and events in this book are fictitious. Any similarity to real persons, alive or dead, is purely coincidental.

All brand names, product names, business names used in this book are trademarks, registered trademarks, or trade names of their respective holders. LilyPad Publishing, LLC is not associated with any product or vendor in this book.

Published by LilyPad Publishing, LLC.

jenmcgee.com

"The heart has its reasons of which reason knows nothing."
-Blaise Pascal

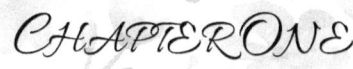

Chapter One

Sadie stared down at the human heart mocking her with its stillness in her patient's open chest cavity. *Beat damnit! Beat!* Sadie screamed inside her head at the idle heart while remaining calm and collected on the outside. The sound of the EKG monitor alerting the medical staff that the patient had flatlined was loud in her ears. Another Friday night in the trenches.

"Dr. Jennings, what do we do next?" the over-eager male resident standing across the surgical table from her questioned.

Sadie raised her perfectly arched right eyebrow at the young doctor. "Well, Dr. Wu, after we have verified there is no pulse, gently reach in," she began as she demonstrated, "being careful to avoid the phrenic and intercostal nerves, and palm the heart with both hands, careful to only use the flat part, and begin to manually massage it." She counted to ninety slowly in a whisper and removed her hands. She mentally willed the heart to beat. *Come on! Come on!*

Finally, the heart began to thump, sluggishly at first, and then stronger.

"We have a rhythm Dr. Jennings!" Dr. Wu exclaimed.

The sounds coming from the monitor coincided with the beat of the heart. It was music to Sadie's ears. The woman on her table had three teenage children and Sadie was determined to make sure that they got to hug their mom again.

"The trick, Dr. Wu, is to know when to keep fighting," Sadie told the resident, like she hadn't doubted the positive outcome for a second.

Sadie took a deep breath. "Alright, let's finish this repair and close her up." Sadie glanced over to the windows that peered into the adjoining scrub room and saw the Chief of Surgery watching her. She gave him a quick nod and got back to work.

"Dr. Wu, how would you like to sew Mrs. Dean up?" Sadie asked. Dr. Daniel Wu might be a rookie, but he had great hands and did beautiful sutures. He was a bit of a brown-noser, but Sadie overlooked that one flaw because his work ethic was unmatched among the surgical residents.

"Yes, of course, Dr. Jennings." He got to work immediately.

Sadie looked on as Dr. Wu's hands moved fluidly, almost like a dance. It was mesmerizing.

"Dr. Wu? Not that I don't enjoy working with you, but I thought I was working with Dr. Madison tonight?" Sadie asked absentmindedly.

"He had a family emergency. Worked out for me," Dr. Wu said while never taking his eyes off of his suturing.

Sadie shrugged and as Dr. Wu pulled together the last bit of Mrs. Dean's surgical site, she exited to the scrub room.

"That was some amazing work back there, Dr. Jennings."

Sadie grinned as she turned to face MUSC's Chief of Surgery at the scrub sinks. "Why thank you, Dr. Richards. I didn't realize I was going to have an audience tonight."

"Don't play coy, Sadie. It doesn't suit you. And I mean that as a compliment," the older gentleman replied as he gave Sadie the side-eye. Dr. Samuel Richards was from somewhere out west in California and did not understand the subtle art of southern banter.

Sadie chuckled as she led the way out into the hallway with Dr. Richards following close behind. "Okay, fine. I knew you were there the whole time, but thank you nonetheless."

Down the hall a ways and around a corner she opened the doors to the doctors' break room and stood to the side, letting her mentor precede her inside. She made a beeline for the coffee to refuel before her next operation. "Honestly, Mrs. Dean was lucky she happened to be sitting near a nurse in the restaurant who recognized she was having a heart attack. The poor woman thought she was just having some serious indigestion."

"Even so, you saved that woman's life when others would have given up. Keep it up and you'll be taking my job someday." Dr. Richards winked and walked out of the break room with a smug look on his face.

Sadie watched him leave wondering what all of the unnecessary praise was about. It wasn't really his style. She took a sip of her black coffee and shrugged, chalking it up to one of the great mysteries of the universe. She turned to go sit on her favorite couch by the window and noticed it was already occupied. *So that's the reason behind Dr. Richard's gushing. Old man trying to start trouble,* she thought. Sadie had to giggle at the sneaky manipulation. On the couch was Dr. Jeff Montgomery, Sadie's colleague, and biggest competition for top cardiovascular surgeon at the hospital. Dr. Richards loved pitting them against each other.

"Yeah, yeah, I heard. You're amazing, blah, blah, blah. I think the old man is going senile," Dr. Montgomery muttered, never taking his eyes off the tv.

There was a very serious looking female news anchor in a dark purple pantsuit reporting on two murders in Charleston that according to the authorities seemed to be linked. Two young women had been stabbed outside of nightclubs only three days apart. When Sadie didn't respond, he looked over at her and smiled. He was also her closest friend at the hospital.

"He doesn't have to convince me, I know you'd wipe the floor with me if it ever came down to it," Dr. Montgomery conceded, waving away the thought with a swish of his hand.

"Aren't you the flatterer this evening," Sadie commented, raising her right eyebrow in question. She had once tried to do her signature eyebrow move with the left one, but it didn't feel right to her.

"What can I say? It's a gift," he answered haughtily, shrugging and patting the cushion next to him. As a native Charlestonian, he definitely understood the art of southern banter.

Sadie finally gave in and cracked a smile and took a seat on the couch next to her friend. "Who are we kidding? He's as sharp as he's ever been and will probably outlive us both."

"Look, I know you are as ambitious as the next guy, literally the guy sitting right next to you," Jeff paused to motion between the two of them, "but are you sure you're ready to give up a packed surgery schedule to have to do paperwork and deal with the bureaucratic side of medicine?"

"Maybe in ten years or so, but it's a moot point anyways. The old man isn't going anywhere," Sadie replied, but started picturing what it would be like to be the chief. She would mentor young surgeons, keep the talented surgeons as happy as she was capable so they wouldn't leave to go to other programs, stay on top of her paperwork at all times, and find time for a personal life. Yeah, right.

After a few moments, she emerged from her daydream to find that Jeff was still looking at her.

"What?" she asked, a little startled.

"Oh, nothing. You're just so dang cute when you are lost in thought," he teased.

"Save your charm for your fancy ladies. It doesn't work on me. I'm immune," Sadie playfully rebuffed.

"Fancy ladies?" Jeff asked, confused. A crease forming between his eyebrows while he tried to figure out what she meant by that.

"Oh, like you don't know what I mean." *Old money mingles and marries old money,* Sadie thought to herself, then chided herself for being unfair to Jeff.

"Are you saying I'm a snob?" he asked, a hint of worry in his tone.

"No, of course not. But your idea of casual is a seersucker suit, and your women are on that same level. You know, when we first met, I didn't think we would have anything in common, but I'm glad to have been wrong." Sadie reached over and squeezed his hand. She didn't want her friend hurt over a thoughtless comment.

"Oh, yeah? What changed your mind?"

"Figuring out that you didn't become a doctor because of money or status. You genuinely feel the need to help people and you take every loss to heart. It moved me," Sadie said softly.

The two doctors from the same city, but two different worlds, stared at each other. When the silence became more than Sadie could bear, she glanced away.

"How is your fancy lady by the way? The one that was at the benefit ball a couple of months ago in that gorgeous Valentino gown. What was her name? Clementine? Penelope?" she asked playfully.

"Her name was Charlotte and even though she wasn't as uptight as some of the others, it didn't work out. She didn't like my hectic work schedule."

"Oh, sorry to hear that. I was only joking," Sadie said, feeling like a complete ass, again. *What is my problem tonight?*

"It's fine, Sadie. You know I don't get too attached. Well, except to you," he replied as he winked at her. "How is your friend Paige? She recovering after her ordeal with that psycho?"

"Nice subject change, and yeah, she's doing better. I wouldn't say fully recovered but making progress. Her and Jake are getting married soon, and her pregnancy is progressing nicely."

"How are you doing with all that?" Jeff asked. Sadie appreciated him checking on her well-being. Even though she hadn't personally gone through the trauma Paige had, the aftermath was affecting everyone close to her.

"I'm better, thank you for asking. I still have nightmares, but not as often. Paige offered to take me to one of her therapy sessions to talk through it, but honestly, we do enough of that with Faith over tea and snacks. It has really helped." Sadie smiled thinking of her two best friends and how they can talk about anything and not feel judged.

Sadie knew Jeff was about to suggest that therapy might not be a bad idea, he'd suggested it more than once before, but he was interrupted by their pagers going off. They looked up at each other and simultaneously stood and rushed to the corridor where the operating rooms for cardiac surgery were located. They were met by their favorite nurse, Pearl, and she started rattling off stats about the incoming emergency surgery while they all scrubbed in.

"We have a twenty-two-year-old female that was brought in by ambulance about five minutes ago. She was found in an alley outside of the nightclub where she works. She is covered in deep cuts all over her hands and arms, defensive wounds, but the concerning injury is the stab wound to her chest," Pearl reported.

Sadie felt a sense of déjà vu and the room started to spin. Jeff tapped her elbow with his, mindful of their freshly scrubbed hands, and asked, "Are you okay to be in this operation?"

When Paige had been brought in after Stacey violently tortured her with a knife, they hadn't let her help treat her friend or even be in the room until they had her stable. Jeff had supervised on her behalf.

Sadie didn't take him questioning her mindset personally; the priority was the patient and getting the best outcome possible. She took a quick moment to think it over and finally answered, "Yes, I am fine. You take lead just in case." Jeff nodded and the three of them headed into the sterile operating room.

As the woman was wheeled in and transferred to the operating table, Sadie looked her over from head to toe. *Definitely defensive wounds on her hands and arms.* The woman had put up a hell of a fight. Sadie was determined to save the brave young woman who had faced such horror and fought back. Jeff started giving orders and they got to work trying to save their patient.

A couple of hours later the trill sound of the EKG monitor alerting them that their patient had flatlined echoed around the room, as it had been for quite a while.

"Sadie, we've done everything we can," Jeff said gently, leaning over to remove Sadie's hand from the bloody surgical field. Looking up at the clock, he announced, "Time of death, one o' seven a.m."

The medical staff went to get cleaned up with their heads hanging down. One of the newer nurses had tears streaming down her cheeks and dripping off of her chin. Sadie could hear the nurse's whimpers as she tried to keep from sobbing out loud herself. Pearl went and wrapped her arms around the younger nurse's shoulders, whispering gentle reassurances. Sadie felt a heavy weight on her own heart at the loss.

Dr. Richards was waiting for Sadie and Jeff when they stepped into the hallway. "There are a couple of detectives waiting to talk to one of you outside of the emergency department doors," he said solemnly. He put a hand on each of their shoulders in commiseration, then turned and walked slowly back towards his office. It was a late night for everyone.

"I'll handle it. I need the fresh air," Sadie said. "You get some rest, Jeff."

"Fine, I'll be in the on-call room. Make sure you get some rest after talking to the police." Jeff squeezed her shoulder as he walked away. Sadie would replay the surgery in her head until she was satisfied that they had done everything they could have before she would be able to sleep, and Dr. Montgomery was the same way.

Sadie made her way outside but did not go straight to where the two suit clad detectives were waiting for her. There were also a few uniformed officers milling around the emergency entrance. She sat down on a hard metal bench, a couple of big bushes blocking her from the view of the group waiting to hear the fate of the poor woman. She put her head between her knees and silently begged the bile she felt rising in her throat to let her be. It was always hard losing a patient, but since the ordeal with Paige a couple of months before, any violence related losses had been even harder to bear. She took slow deep breaths and after a few minutes the bile receded and she was sure she would not fall apart while speaking to the detectives. She owed the young woman her strength in doing her part to help find the murderer.

She made her way over to the law enforcement officers and introduced herself. "I am Dr. Sadie Jennings, one of the cardiovascular surgeons that operated on the young woman who was brought in with the stab wound to the chest and other injuries. How may I help you?"

"I'm Detective Benjamin Jenkins, and this is my partner Detective Maxine Fuller. We have a few questions about the injuries that the victim sustained. First though, did she make it?" asked the older of the two detectives. He reminded her a little of Paige's dad. At first glance, he appeared stern and stiff, but once he spoke it was plain as day that he was a big ol' teddy bear.

"I'm sorry to say that despite our best efforts, she did not make it through the surgery. Her injuries were too severe." Sadie spent the next half hour or so going over each wound on the patient's body, whether she thought the cuts were done by someone right-handed or left-handed, and so on. When she thought she possibly couldn't take anymore, the detectives closed their little black notebooks.

"Has she been identified?" Sadie asked.

"Her name is Birdie Duvall. She worked at Club Oxygen. The manager found her outside in the alley behind the club. He went looking for her when she didn't come back from taking out the trash. The poor man is traumatized."

"I bet," Sadie whispered. Sadie knew that she would never forget Birdie Duvall and what had happened to her.

Sadie was about to say goodbye to the detectives and go back inside to check on her other patients when a thought occurred to her. "Detectives, I saw a news report earlier tonight on a couple of murders that sounded a lot like this case. Two young women stabbed outside of nightclubs within a few days of each other. Is it possible we have a serial killer in our city?"

"Off the record, it's looking that way. I trust you will be discreet, but once word of this homicide gets out it will be all over the news. This killer is escalating at a very quick pace. This attack was during the club's busiest time. There were so many employees working that it's a wonder no one else was out in that alley smoking or taking out more trash. It was a ballsy move." Detective Jenkins sighed wearily. "I have a daughter about the same age. I can't help but think that it could have been her in Birdie Duvall's place."

Sadie gave the detective a sad nod. She knew what he was going through. He was on the outside of the tragedy, but still felt personally affected by it. "Our staff will get all of the physical evidence they can from her body. Then you'll find this monster," Sadie declared. As Sadie attempted to give him her most reassuring look, all she could think was, *here we go again.*

Chapter Two

Officer John Avery leaned back in his chair at his desk in the Meadow Oaks Police Station and rubbed his hands over his face. He was exhausted from working overtime to cover for one of the other officers whose wife had recently given birth to twin boys. Thank goodness Meadow Oaks was a safe small town and the hardest thing he had to take care of that week was a teenager trying to shoplift a six pack of beer. *I can't be nearly as tired as a new dad of twins. I just need more coffee,* John thought.

John made his way to the break room and found his favorite mug in the drying rack. He poured himself a cup from a freshly made pot. He didn't bother with cream or sugar. Coffee wasn't something he necessarily enjoyed; it was fuel to keep him going when he felt sluggish.

"Alice, you outdid yourself on the coffee," John said looking over to the emergency operator sitting at one of the tables drinking from her own cup.

"Why do you assume that I made it?" she challenged. Her hair color this week was jet black with lime green chunks, very Billie Eilish circa twenty-nineteen. Alice dressed in all black most of the time with black and white checkered Vans on her feet. She didn't take shit from anyone. She was John's favorite person at the station. The ten-year age gap only made their friendship more interesting.

"Because you're the only one that can make a decent pot," John replied, unfazed at the implication she might be offended. They had too much respect for each other to get upset over the little things. He knew she liked messing with him for the hell of it.

"In that case, thank you. And I'm supposed to tell you that your friend Officer Sanders from Charleston P.D. called about thirty minutes ago. Wants you to call him back ASAP."

"It's only six a.m. and someone is looking for me," John mumbled, as he started to walk back towards his desk.

"Better than being bored!" Alice shouted after him.

John sat back down at his desk with his coffee and dialed Officer Sander's extension over at Charleston P.D. "Hey man, what's going on?" he asked when his fellow officer picked up the call.

"Hey, John. I overheard something at the water cooler first thing this morning and I wanted to give you a heads up," Officer Sanders began. "There was a homicide last night over here in Charleston. Victim was a young woman from your neck of the woods; her name was Birdie Duvall."

"I know of the Duvalls. Nice family," John lamented. His heart broke for her parents. "The dad is a pharmacist at the local drug store and the mom a music teacher at the middle school. Birdie was their only child."

"I believe your chief went to personally notify the parents early this morning. The reason I'm calling though is that the doctor who spoke with our detectives at the hospital after trying to save Miss Duvall was your friend Dr. Sadie Jennings. I figured with everything she went through with her friend Ms. Collins, it might have been a little rough on her."

John mulled that over for a minute. He felt a tug of worry in his chest for Sadie. Of course, it would have been hard on her to witness more violent bloodshed. He hadn't seen her in a couple of weeks, but they often spent time together with Paige and Jake and it was impossible not to notice the way she hovered over Paige.

"I appreciate the heads up. I'll check up on her. She's a strong lady with a big heart," John paused to switch gears before he went down the Sadie rabbit hole. "Y'all got any leads on the case?"

"We think we have a serial killer on our hands, unfortunately. This is our third victim with the same M.O."

"Dang, that's tough. Let me know if there is anything we can do to help," John offered. His department would go on high alert to make sure none of the violence from the city spilled into Meadow Oaks.

"Thanks, John. I'll let you know when our detectives make some headway in the case. Talk to you soon," Officer Sanders said.

"Yeah, man. Bye," John said and then hung up.

John swiveled side to side in his chair thinking about the world and its harsh realities. He remembered the first time he had to notify a family member that their loved one was dead. A new father had a tire blow on his car as he was going over Muddy Creek Bridge, and he lost control and hit the concrete barrier. He hadn't been wearing a seat belt. As John had walked up to the front door to inform the man's wife, his heart had raced, and his body flushed with sweat. He was so scared he was going to say the wrong thing or not seem empathetic enough. Over time he learned that there was never a right thing to say when someone lost a loved one. The only thing he could do was show that he was there for them. The only downside to being a police officer in a small town like Meadow Oaks was that he knew just about everyone, so it was rare to be delivering bad news to a stranger.

The image of Sadie's face drifted into his mind. He could see her dark brown eyes and the frantic look that was on her face when Paige had been brought into the hospital that terrible night a couple of months or so ago. The tug on his heart was still aching thinking of her trying to save a young woman who had been violently attacked and the unavoidable feeling of failure when her efforts were unsuccessful. He didn't need to know the specifics of the crime to know that it would bring up difficult feelings for Sadie. He spun and spun in his chair debating on the best way to help her. John wanted to be the one to soothe any hurt she was going through but thought that might be selfish of him. What she really needed was her girlfriends.

With a new sense of urgency, John called his buddy Jake to enlist him into figuring out what could be done to help Sadie.

"Hey, Officer John! What's up, man?" Jake said cheerfully when he picked up the call.

"I need your help with something, but I'm not sure how to go about it," John began.

"I'll do whatever I can. What do you need?" Jake asked, immediately concerned.

John quickly explained what Sadie had been through a few hours before. "Do you think Paige is up to going to check on Sadie after all Paige has been through? Will hearing about that young woman cause Paige too much pain? I wouldn't want anything happening to her or the baby."

"I mean, yeah, it worries me a lot," Jake hesitated, "but I know my Paige, and she will kill me if she finds out Sadie needed her and I didn't give her the option to make that decision for herself." With more confidence in his voice Jake added, "Paige knows how much she can handle."

"Faith will want to be there too," John said.

"They are something, aren't they?" Jake murmured.

"They'll hold each other up," John replied.

He'd never seen anything like those three. Him and Jake would joke about how Jake was really marrying all three of them and how Faith's husband Travis was their first husband.

The men said their goodbyes and John felt most of the weight that had settled on his heart lift. The bit that was left still wanted to take care of Sadie himself. He contemplated what would be the best approach. He conceded that it would be best if the women checked up on Sadie at her home where she would be more vulnerable. She wouldn't want him to see her like that. They had gotten closer over the past couple of months and definitely had chemistry, but they hadn't let their guard down around each other yet. He picked his phone back up and dialed the hospital to find out Sadie's schedule.

John's chief would want someone to follow up on Charleston P.D.'s investigation of Birdie Duvall's murder. He would have to make sure the job was assigned to him. It made the most sense, John had the greatest number of connections in Charleston besides the chief himself. He could do his job and keep an eye on Sadie. She was an amazing woman, and he wanted her. The question that had been running through his mind was whether or not the big city surgeon would be into a small-town cop. He also had a pretty clear picture of what he wanted his future to look like, and it didn't include having kids of his own. He liked kids well enough; he simply didn't want to raise any. Would Sadie be okay with that, or was she yearning to be a mother?

His cell let out a ping informing him that he had a text. Jake was letting him know that Faith was on her way to pick up Paige and they would go to Sadie's place. They didn't waste any time. The women would rally around Sadie. John sometimes envied the ladies' bond. To have someone always in your corner like that, no judgement or awkwardness. He wasn't the greatest at opening up to people, preferred to handle things on his own. It was part of being an only child with no cousins nearby he reckoned.

John saw the chief's SUV pull into the parking lot, so he got up to go outside for some fresh air. He walked over to the chief who was sitting in his car, a sorrowful look on his face. When he noticed John approaching, he slowly got out of his vehicle.

"Mornin', Chief. Rough start, huh?" John said solemnly.

"Yeah, I guess you heard about Birdie Duvall."

"Yes, sir. Damn tragedy. I hope Charleston P.D. figures out who did it fast before another young woman gets hurt. They think they might have a serial killer on their hands."

"Me too." The chief took off his hat and rubbed his head. "John, I'd like you to use your connections over there to keep up with the case. I don't want to interfere with Charleston's investigation, but I feel like we need to stay on top of it for the Duvalls' sake. They are heartbroken. No parent should have to go through what they are going through."

"I agree, Chief. I'll get on it," John assured him. John felt relieved that the chief assigned him the job of being the liaison with Charleston without him having to ask.

Together they made their way into the Meadow Oaks Police Station. Once the news spread about the murder a somber cloud settled over the officers and staff. Birdie Duvall would be on everyone's mind for a long time to come. Probably forever.

Chapter Three

Sadie couldn't make herself stop crying. It began in the shower when she got home from her shift at the hospital. Under the spray of hot water, she cried for the young woman who lost her life. She cried for her best friend Paige who had recently gone through something similarly horrible. She cried for the cruelty and violence in the world. She wasn't used to feeling helpless and it had broken something inside of her.

The crying continued way past the point of dehydration and Sadie was beginning to feel sick. She had collapsed on her bed after her shower, barely having enough energy to put on pajamas, and couldn't make herself get up to go drink water. She heard knocking on her front door and was determined to ignore it. She was not fit to talk to a neighbor or someone looking to spread the good word. She felt like nothing would ever be good again. She had lost faith.

Whoever was knocking at the door gave up fairly quickly. Or at least that's what Sadie thought before she heard a key turning in the lock. She tried to sit up, but her arms were too shaky. She couldn't remember the last time she ate. She collapsed back down on the pillows, listening as her front door opened and closed. She could hear her unexpected guests removing their shoes, their footsteps across her carpeted floors too quiet to hear.

"Oh, Sadie, honey," Faith whispered as she came through Sadie's bedroom door and made her way over to the bed.

Paige walked in behind Faith, her bright green eyes glistening with tears. She was carrying two paper grocery bags and set them down by the door. She pulled out a plastic bottle filled with pink liquid and brought it over to Sadie. She sat down on the bed and lifted Sadie's head to her lap.

"You need to drink this, Sadie. It will help you feel better," Paige whispered as she guided her friend up to a sitting position where she could sip from the bottle.

Sadie recognized the slightly salty strawberry-kiwi flavor of her favorite electrolyte drink. She liked to drink them after a long surgery to rehydrate. Her friends didn't rush her into talking or getting out of bed. They took care of her. They were the only people in the world Sadie would let see her fall apart.

When she had had enough of the drink, she laid her head back down in Paige's lap. Her eyes felt so heavy, and they burned. She didn't even try to fight them closing shut. She concentrated on the rhythm of Paige rubbing her hair. It didn't take long for her to fade into a deep sleep.

Sadie woke up in a dark room, daylight long gone. The bathroom light had been left on with the door cracked. There was a delicious smell coming from her kitchen. Faith was working her magic. Hints of garlic had Sadie up and on her way through her condo. She didn't even have to think, she let her nose lead the way.

"There she is," Faith said cheerfully.

Faith was pulling on oven mitts and bending over the oven door to pull out a casserole dish, which Faith must have brought from her own house because Sadie was pretty sure she didn't own one. The timer on the toaster oven on the counter dinged.

"Just in time for some lasagna and garlic bread," Paige announced.

"How long did I sleep?" Sadie wondered.

"A few hours or so. I took a nap with you for a little while. This baby has me so tired," Paige chuckled, rubbing her barely protruding belly.

They worked together fixing plates and iced teas. The three friends gathered around Sadie's little dining table and dug in. Almost simultaneously they let out appreciative moans at the taste of sauce and cheeses.

"How did you guys know?" Sadie asked. No need to specify what it was they knew.

"You know that game from elementary school, telephone?" Faith asked. When Sadie nodded Faith said, "It was kind of like that."

"Our town hottie, Officer John, called Jake and told him about what had happened to Birdie," Paige said, her voice started to tremble. "She used to babysit the kids every once in a while, when me and Matt needed a date night if my parents or Faith weren't available." A combination of hormones and sadness over her late husband's untimely death and Birdie's murder had her on the verge of sobbing.

Sadie reached over and squeezed Paige's hand. Paige sniffled and attempted to pull herself together by breathing in through her nose and out through her mouth.

"John told Jake that you were one of the surgeons who tried to save her," Faith said, her blue eyes full of unshed tears. "Sadie, honey, we can only imagine how hard that had to be for you, especially after everything that happened with Paige and Cora Rae," she continued gently.

They held hands around the table in silence for a few moments, almost like a vigil in Birdie's memory.

"She fought," Sadie said, breaking the silence. "Like you did, Paige. She fought back." Sadie's breath caught on a sob. "I assisted Dr. Montgomery, you know, Jeff. I didn't trust myself to take the lead. When we were in the thick of things, I was able to focus on his directions and do what I needed to. In the end, there was just too much damage already done by whoever attacked her."

"Sweetie, I'm sure you and Dr. Cutie Pie did everything y'all could," Faith insisted.

"Let me get this straight, we have an Officer Hottie and a Dr. Cutie Pie," Sadie said. It felt good to lighten the mood a bit. It took a second, but then all three women started laughing. A little lightness was exactly what they needed.

"It's the pregnancy hormones," Paige joked.

"Yeah, I'm going to blame it on that too since I spend so much time with her," Faith teased. "Or, you know, the fact that I have eyes and those are two handsome men." Faith held a finger up to her chin. "If only I knew an attractive, brilliant, single woman to matchmake with one of them."

"That is a problem," Sadie smirked.

She would never want to complicate her work relationship with Jeff; it was too important to her, and she didn't feel an attraction to him like that. John on the other hand, well that had possibilities. She'd been crushing on him for a couple of months, but between her busy work schedule and worrying after Paige and Cora Rae, she'd tried to ignore the feelings to see if they would go away. Since they weren't, she would need to determine whether or not her not wanting to have kids would be an issue if they pursued a relationship.

"Fine. If you are not going to let me play matchmaker, at least let me plan a fabulous birthday party for you since that's coming up soon. It will cheer you up. It'll cheer us all up," Faith insisted.

"Deal," Sadie conceded. She could play matchmaker herself when she was ready.

They went on eating their lasagna and garlic bread, chatting all the while. The topics varied from Paige's kids to their respective jobs, and men. Every once in a while, Birdie Duvall and what happened to her would come up again.

"Y'all know what got me so worked up I couldn't get ahold of myself?" Sadie asked. When her friends nodded, she continued. "I just felt such earth-shattering despair at all of the cruelty in the world," Sadie confided. "The unfairness of it all was, and still is, so overwhelming."

"I know what you mean," Paige responded. "Everything will seem to be going fine but then out of the blue, panic will rise up in me, and I'm not able to catch my breath," she admitted. She rubbed her belly protectively as she remembered that horrible day in the Hideaway Cottage.

"I went with Cora Rae to her physical therapy appointment yesterday morning," Paige said. "She's doing much better. Her balance and fine motor skills have improved a ton."

Paige's coworker and their new best friend, Cora Rae, never had to go through any of her recovery alone. She had helped Paige overcome Stacey that terrible day they were both tortured in the Hideaway Cottage and since then was loved and cherished by the three women and their families.

"I'm driving her to counseling on Monday," Faith added. "I think she is doing better with all that too. When she first started going, she would look haunted when she came out. Lately I can tell she has been crying during her sessions, but instead of looking haunted she looks like a weight has been lifted off of her shoulders."

"That's great news. She has another CAT scan coming up. I plan on being there for that," Sadie said.

"Should we tell her about what happened to Birdie?" Faith asked.

"I don't think so," Paige replied. "She didn't know her, and Cora Rae has been through enough. It might set her back and have the worst of her PTSD return."

"Agreed," Sadie commented.

"I bet John shows up to check on you in person at some point. He's crushing hard on you, Sadie," Faith said, wagging her eyebrows suggestively.

Sadie averted her gaze but couldn't stop the cheeky grin that spread across her face. "I'll admit a visit from Officer Hottie would be welcome," she said.

"That was awfully thoughtful of him to contact Jake to let us know what had happened. He was so worried about you," Paige said endearingly.

Faith waggled her eyebrows at Sadie some more.

Sadie pictured the handsome police officer in her mind and felt her skin tingle. They seemed to gravitate toward each other whenever they were hanging out at Jake and Paige's house. They ran into each other from time to time at the hospital. John's work in Meadow Oaks didn't bring him to MUSC often, but when it did, he would seek her out. Sadie couldn't deny the chemistry between them, nor did she want to. If Officer John was up to pursuing more with her, she was game.

"Sadie and John sitting in a tree, K-I-S-S-I-N-G," Faith began singing, sounding like the kids at her daycare center. She only stopped when Sadie threw a balled-up napkin at her.

The three best friends laughed until they cried. Sadie felt her heart lighten. Until she had met Paige and Faith, she had never known the feeling of instant relief that confiding in others could give a person.

"Gosh, I love you two," she said on a sigh.

"We love you too, Sadie," Paige and Faith said in unison.

CHAPTER FOUR

Sadie went into work the next day with a renewed sense of purpose. A night talking with her girls was just what she had needed to get through her despair. She still felt grief at the loss of Birdie Duvall, but she no longer felt hopeless. She made her way from the parking deck through the hospital hallways, greeting her colleagues as she went. As she rounded the corner leading to the hall with the break room, and hopefully a fresh pot of coffee, she saw John leaning up against the wall across from the door. He was in uniform. Looking him up and down shamelessly, Sadie admired the way his muscular form filled it out.

"What an unexpected surprise, Officer John," Sadie said to alert him to her presence.

Sadie smiled as he shot off the wall to stand up straight. His light brown eyes gave away his nervousness. His eyes were Sadie's favorite feature on him. They were so open and honest. She liked them enough to have noticed the flecks of gold in them. John was sporting a little stubble on his face which was unusual for him. He normally went for the clean-cut look. Sadie wondered what that stubble would feel like rubbing against her face, her breasts, her inner thighs. She shook off the intrusive naughty thoughts and focused on the man in front of her.

"Hi, Dr. Jennings. I was in the hospital following up on Birdie Duvall's case on behalf of her parents and decided to stop by and say, well, hi," he finished nervously.

"You don't have to be so formal just because we are both on the clock, John," Sadie insisted. "I assisted on Miss Duvall's operation; did you need anything from me?"

"Oh, no. Dr. Montgomery was nice enough to speak with me earlier," John answered.

"Okay, great," she replied smiling coyly.

They stood awkwardly in the hallway. Sadie couldn't believe how silly they were being. They were friends and had been for a few months. Why were they acting so ridiculous? They were adults for crying out loud.

"Sadie," John began, breaking the silence, "I also wanted to make sure you're okay. You know, after everything you went through seeing what happened to Paige and Cora Rae, and now with Birdie, I mean Miss Duvall." John ran his hand over his hair in exasperation at his inability to confidently say what he came to say. "Are you okay, Sadie?" he finally blurted out bluntly.

Sadie took pity on him. She stepped up until they were only arm's length away and put a hand on his shoulder, partly to reassure him and partly because she really wanted to touch him.

"John, I am doing much better, thanks to you. It means so much to me that you took it upon yourself to make sure the girls knew what was going on. If you hadn't called Jake who knows if I would even be out of bed today. I was not in the right headspace to ask for help. Thank you, truly."

"I hope it doesn't bother you that I called Jake instead of Paige or Faith directly. I wasn't sure since Paige is still recovering and being pregnant how she would take it..." John stopped talking as Sadie squeezed his shoulder.

"You did the right thing. It was very thoughtful of you to think of Paige's well-being also. I'll give Jake a hug later for handling it like a gentleman."

"Do I get a hug too?" John asked with a sly grin.

"Sure," Sadie chuckled as John pulled her in for a hug. His arms went around her waist and hers went around his neck. They held on longer than a friendly hug normally dictated, but she couldn't make herself let go. He smelled so good. One day she would have to ask him what product he used for his hair; the scent was divine. His hard broad body pressed against her athletically lean one and she could imagine what it would feel like in bed. They were about the same height, which with other men had made Sadie feel too big, but with John it felt perfect. John didn't seem in any rush to let go either.

A loud, intentional throat clearing broke whatever spell Sadie and John had found themselves under and they pulled apart, slowly. Sadie found herself facing Dr. Jeff Montgomery's shocked and amused expression.

"Jeff, I believe you've already met my friend, Officer John Avery of the Meadow Oaks Police Department," Sadie said as she slid her arms off of John's shoulders.

"Yes, we've known each other a while. Our paths have crossed on other cases, as well as the unfortunate one we spoke of today." Jeff's eyes were still wide open in shock and Sadie wished he'd knock it off.

The two men gave each other a friendly nod. John took it as his cue to start to leave. Sadie wasn't ready for him to go yet.

"I should head back and report to the chief in Meadow Oaks. Thank you for your assistance, Dr. Montgomery," John said as he shook the doctor's hand. "Sadie, I'm sure we'll run into each other again soon."

"Count on it," Sadie said, smiling brightly. She watched John walk away, admiring the view from the back. That was a man with one nice muscular ass.

"Well, well, well!" Dr. Montgomery teased. "You naughty girl. Here I thought you were some lonely spinster, but you got yourself a man in uniform."

"Oh, cut it out. He's just a friend," Sadie argued half-heartedly.

"Uh huh." Dr. Montgomery said as he opened the door to the break room for Sadie. "I know what friend hugs look like and that was not it. That screamed I wish we didn't have our clothes on right now."

"I'm so not talking about this with you," Sadie said as she covered her face with her hands so he couldn't see her smiling.

"We don't have to talk about it. I already know what's up," he replied as he handed over a cup of fresh coffee.

Sadie laughed and shook her head at her friend and colleague. She felt truly happy, but on its tail came guilt. Was it fair for her to feel so much happiness after seeing what had happened to Birdie Duvall? After seeing the violence other women had been through? Her friends would tell her that she did deserve to be happy. She had not caused the suffering that she had witnessed. Still, she felt obligated to be in solidarity with those women, her friend Paige included. Paige wouldn't admit it often, but she was still suffering from the aftereffects of what had been done to her, Cora Rae too. Birdie Duvall's family would be suffering for a long time. How could a world filled with so much pain and suffering have any room for love in it? These were the thoughts that consumed Sadie's mind lately. She couldn't help it. All she could control was to focus on her patients and do her best for them. With each life she saved a little happiness was brought back into the world for the loved ones. Sadie knew her purpose in life and she would do her best to fulfill it.

***

Sadie's spirits were considerably improved when she started rounds with the residents. The young doctors were huddled up together whispering, and she could hear them saying words like "stabbing" and "flatlined". Her steps faltered not wanting to hear what they were talking about and pulling her back down into grief.

Jeff quickly approached the group and snapped them to attention. "Alright, alright, enough blabbing! You're doctors, time to focus!" he bellowed.

The four doctors immediately straightened their posture and stuck their hands in the pockets of their white coats. They had the grace to look embarrassed at least. Sadie joined them and started rapid firing out instructions.

"Dr. Wu, Dr. Madison, Dr. Pope, Dr. Jones, get your iPads. Dr. Montgomery and I will observe you leading rounds today. Think you can handle that?" she challenged, staring them down one by one.

They gulped but nodded that they were ready and Sadie led the way to the first room. She set a quick pace and Dr. Montgomery smirked from the back of the group as he watched them struggle to keep up with her. Sadie winked at the nurse manning the nurses' station and stopped at the closest patient door. She whipped around and gave the residents her most serious face. They skidded to a halt, bumping into each other to keep from invading Sadie's personal space.

"Dr. Wu, since you assisted on Mrs. Dean's surgery last night, you take lead on this one," Sadie proclaimed.

"Yes, Dr. Jennings," he answered nervously, but he held his head up and straightened his scrubs and coat.

Sadie knocked on the door to give Mrs. Dean and whichever family member was sitting with her a heads up that they were about to have company. She moved aside after opening the door to let the residents enter first. She shared a sneaky smile with Jeff when the residents were inside and then the two lost the smiles and joined them in the patient room.

"Hello, Mrs. Dean. I am Dr. Daniel Wu. I assisted on your procedure last night with Dr. Jennings," Dr. Wu stated, as he looked back to Sadie. She gave him a curt nod and he continued. "These are my fellow residents," he said indicating his colleagues, "and Dr. Montgomery has joined us as well."

Mrs. Dean gave everyone a weak wave and then looked over to where a pimple-faced young man was sitting, reading a comic book. "This is my son, Nathan. He's been keeping me company the last few hours."

"I've been telling her to rest, but she insists on staring at me," the teen mumbled.

"Son, I thought I might never get to see that handsome face again. Let me be," she scolded lovingly.

Sadie's heart warmed at the exchange. *This is why I love what I do. This right here is what makes it all worth it.*

Dr. Wu began going over Mrs. Dean's chart, walking his colleagues through the steps taken in the surgery and her recovery plan and prognosis. The more he spoke, the more confident he got. By the end, Sadie and Jeff were both nodding their heads in approval. Usually, the residents will rush through, whether from nerves or the misconception that they needed to get through as many patients as they could as fast as possible. Dr. Wu was very thorough.

"Dr. Jones, you look like you have a question," Sadie said when Dr. Wu wrapped up his presentation of Mrs. Dean's case. Dr. Jones had been fidgeting and biting on her lip since halfway through.

Dr. Jones, shocked at having been called out, dropped her pen on the floor. After picking it up, she said, "Um, I was wondering if over time, would it be possible to lower the dosages of her medication if she made substantial lifestyle changes?"

"Great question, Dr. Jones," Sadie complimented. "Dr. Wu, what do you think?"

Thus began a great discussion and debate amongst all the residents about diet, exercise, meditation, being outdoors, and all things wellness. Jeff nudged Sadie's shoulder and tilted his head towards the hospital bed. Mrs. Dean had fallen asleep amid all of the fuss, and her son was looking over at her, his eyes a bit watery.

"Doctors, " Sadie began to get their attention, "I believe we have worn Mrs. Dean out, onto the next."

Simultaneously, every head turned to Mrs. Dean, her face serene in sleep. They quietly exited, little smiles on Dr. Jones and Dr. Pope's faces.

In the hallway Sadie addressed her residents. "How do we think Dr. Wu's presentation went?"

"Nailed it," Dr. Todd Madison answered, fist-bumping Dr. Wu.

"He was very thorough. I felt like I know the case as well as I would have if I had been on it myself," Dr. Jordan Jones commented positively, if somewhat begrudgingly.

"Any suggestions for improvement?" Sadie asked the group.

Dr. Hailey Pope hesitatingly looked side to side before meekly raising her hand.

"Yes, Dr. Pope?" Sadie questioned.

"I feel like there could have been more personal interaction. Like it felt too clinical, more like she was simply a case, not a person," Dr. Pope answered.

Sadie saw Dr. Wu stiffen out of the corner of her eye, but she ignored it and stayed focused on Dr. Pope. "Give me an example of how he could have made it more personal," she urged.

"Well, a simple, how are you feeling, Mrs. Dean? Or maybe ask her who was with her instead of waiting for her to introduce her son. Something like that," Dr. Pope answered shyly.

"Very good, Dr. Pope," Sadie stated. Turning to the other residents she explained, "Dr. Wu's clinical presentation was flawless, but we must always remember that our patients are more than cases to be closed. They are people who have been through something hard, and they are tired, and maybe even worried or scared. They need to know we care about them as a person. We can't assume that they know that simply because we chose to be healers."

Sadie gave them a moment to take her words in and then turned to Jeff. "Anything to add, Dr. Montgomery?"

"Nailed it," he answered, looking over to Dr. Madison and winking. "Dr. Madison, you're in the hot seat next."

"Actually, I was hoping you would go over the case that came in last night, Dr. Montgomery. The woman that didn't make it," Dr. Madison said, feigning innocence at such a request.

As Jeff's eyes widened in shock and then narrowed in anger, Sadie decided to step in before her friend put the cocky baby doctor in a headlock. "Let's focus on the patient's in our care now. You are more than welcome to review that case and study it on your own time."

For the remainder of rounds, Sadie stayed glued to Jeff's side to prevent any accidental tripping or shoulder checking of the young resident. *Men, ugh* she thought. The absurdity of it all kept her mind from drifting back to the young woman they lost. The one that John was seeking justice for.

CHAPTER FIVE

Sadie had the following weekend off, so Paige and Jake planned a cookout in her honor for Saturday night. Well, Paige planned and Jake did everything his pregnant fiancé asked of him to prepare for it. It just so happened that John was off duty for the weekend as well. Not that Paige and Faith had taken that into consideration when scheming about a get together. No, of course not.

Sadie walked straight to the backyard from the driveway, not bothering to go into the house first. She could hear Henry running around out back, begging his sister to play tag with him. She balanced the veggie tray she brought as her contribution in her left hand and opened the gate with her right. John and Jake were standing near the charcoal grill, both with bottled beers in their hands. John was wearing khaki shorts that showed off his muscular calves and Hey Dudes with no socks, revealing his ankles. She glanced to Jake and noticed he was wearing practically the same thing. The only difference was the color of their t-shirts. Jake had opted for white and John wore navy blue. Both men were built for hard labor. Sadie thought of the power John possessed and what he could do with it. She had to shake away the thought before she got too riled up for a family-friendly cookout.

"Hey, you two! Y'all coordinate your outfits this morning?" Sadie teased as she approached.

John quickly set his beer down and rushed to take the veggie tray from her hand.

"Here let me take that for you," he said, sliding one hand under the tray and the other to hold the side. It teetered a little so Sadie grabbed on to steady it.

Their hands touched around the tray, and they both looked down to where they were connected. Sadie's skin was a smooth dark brown, while John's hands were a lighter brown and callused. She liked the contrast and hoped that someday in the near future she would get to see how their bodies looked entwined with one another.

"I think I have it now," John said after clearing his throat. He looked as unnerved as she felt, in a good way. Sadie smiled at him and let go of the tray.

She glanced over at Jake who was standing at the grill, holding a grill brush and grinning devilishly. Sadie walked over to him to say hello. He was the host after all, and she was raised with proper manners.

"Good afternoon, grill master. What are you cooking up for us today?" she said pleasantly.

"Just burgers and hot dogs. Paige whipped up some potato salad and Faith should be here any minute with whatever delicious side and dessert she decided on. I'll start the charcoal whenever everyone gets here. I was getting my tools ready."

He glanced over to where John was arranging things on the picnic table. "He's a good guy," Jake said simply.

"I know," Sadie replied.

Before they could go any further with their conversation, Henry ran over looking frustrated. "Dad, when is Caleb going to get here? Chloe won't play tag with me. She won't play anything. She's so boring!" Henry complained.

Henry had been calling Jake "Dad" for a little over a month and it made Sadie's heart swell every time she heard it. Looking at Jake's face, it was clear that it had the same effect on him as well.

"Well, bud, I think if you listen real hard, you'll hear his Jeep coming up the road," Jake said looking off in the distance.

Henry leaned his head to one side, lifting an ear to the sky. A moment later his face lit up and he yelled, "YES!" and ran to the gate to greet Caleb when he pulled into the driveway.

"Perfect timing," Sadie exclaimed.

"And not a moment too soon. Henry and Chloe have been butting heads all day," Jake said.

"Caleb is so good with both of them. He excited to have another little brother or sister on the way?" Sadie asked.

"He's thrilled. He loves little kids. Made me nervous for a while until we had a talk and he assured me that while he enjoys playing with and caring for his siblings it doesn't mean he wants to have a kid of his own anytime soon."

"He has a girlfriend?" Sadie inquired.

"Not at the moment, but that changes every other day or so. I guess you could call them summer romances, but school starts back in a few weeks, so we'll see if any of them stick." Jake replied.

Sadie watched as Caleb came through the back gate and put his arms around Henry's shoulders. He guided his soon to be little stepbrother over to a picnic table and listened attentively to him as he complained about his big sister. When Henry paused to take a breath, Caleb interjected and whatever he said calmed the little boy down. The smile Henry was sporting was so precious. Her friend's family had had their world shook up, first with Matt's death and then with Paige's abduction. Jake and Caleb were like a balm to their burned hearts. It made her acutely aware that she was alone. She may not want kids of her own, but a man to snuggle with through good and bad times would be pleasant.

Speaking of which, John was making his way back over to her. She hadn't been able to stop thinking about their lingering hug at the hospital and the look in his eyes told her that he had been thinking about it too. She tried to think of an excuse to touch him again. Jake was busy getting his grill ready, so maybe she could get a few minutes alone with John to flirt openly without being watched too closely by the others. As he approached, he smiled and reached out to put his hand on the small of her back. He pressed gently so they were walking away from Jake. When they were a good distance away, he leaned over, bringing his lips dangerously close to her ear.

"I've been dying to tell you how good that dress looks on you. There's nothing like a beautiful woman in a flowy dress to make a man's imagination go wild," he whispered.

Sadie's blood began to pump earnestly, a rush of heat overcoming her body. They had been dancing around each other for a couple of months and John had taken the dance from an innocent jive to a sensual rumba. She slowly turned her head until his lips were only an inch away from hers. She quickly changed her mind about caring who saw them, she was finally going to taste him after so much speculation. She could feel his breath on her and it made her light-headed with burning need. He placed his hand firmly on her waist, squeezing once. Sadie wasn't sure if it was a sort of question, but she answered anyway, "God, yes." It came out almost like a plea, but Sadie felt no shame. She brought her hand to the back of his neck to pull him to her.

"We're here! The party has arrived!" Faith yelled as she opened the gate.

Sadie burst out laughing to keep from crying. She pulled back from John and gave him an apologetic look. Even though she was eager to kiss him, she didn't want an audience. Faith's arrival would have brought everyone's attention away from what they were doing, and they would have definitely noticed Sadie and John in a passionate lip lock.

"And that's why I call her the little blond tornado," Jake smirked from behind them.

Jake's accurate remark brought another chuckle out of Sadie. John laughed a bit also. He gently rubbed his hand down her back before completely breaking contact. The absence of his touch made her skin feel too light.

"We'll find time to pick this back up later," John promised quietly.

They walked together to greet the new arrivals. The kids were racing over to Faith to see what goodies she brought for dessert. Travis was the one actually carrying all of the food Faith cooked, so she scooped Henry and Chloe into her arms before they could get a hold of her husband.

"You rascals! You have to wait for dessert like everyone else," she teased them.

Sadie watched as Faith turned to her husband and took the top container off of the stack he was carrying. She handed it to Chloe and said to her and Henry, "Don't tell your mother and make sure to share with Caleb."

The kids took off running in the opposite direction, eager to see what treat Auntie Faith had brought them. Sadie and John stepped up to say their hellos and to help Travis with the food.

"And look who I brought," Faith said.

Cora Rae stepped up from behind Travis and Sadie let out a shriek of excitement. "I'm so glad you decided to come! Paige will be so happy to see you! Why didn't you call me? I could have picked you up on my way over!"

"Faith came to Charleston earlier and took me shopping. It was a nice surprise," Cora Rae answered.

They were joined by Jake who hugged Cora Rae tightly and guided her over to a comfortable chair to sit down. She could walk but still lost her balance sometimes. The damage done to her brain was healing, but it had been a long process. Sadie sat down across from Cora Rae and began asking her about the next wedding she would be covering. Nothing got Cora Rae in a joyful mood better than a big showy wedding. Paige, as her editor-in-chief, allowed Cora Rae to go back to work on the condition that Paige help her with her assignments by attending the weddings with her. Paige, as Cora Rae's friend, was concerned for her mental health and would do anything to help keep her in high spirits, hence being her wedding date over and over.

Sadie watched Cora Rae's animated face as she described the elegant gown with sewn in pearls that would be worn by the bride and how the groom had family in Scotland that would be flying to the States for the ceremony. The doctor in her was evaluating Cora Rae's speech and movements, the friend in her was pleased that her friend was happy doing what she loved. Cora Rae no longer stumbled over words or had spasms in her hand movements. Sadie laughed when Cora Rae relayed the drama around the bride declaring that if the Scots insist on wearing kilts to the wedding, then they better damn well wear undergarments or she would put tacks on their seats.

"You'll definitely have to let me know how that one goes! Sounds like it will be a fun reception with that bunch," Sadie said.

"I'm looking forward to it. If Paige can't make it, you can see it firsthand as my handler. I haven't done one alone yet," Cora Rae said a little sadly. "But I've enjoyed the company, don't get me wrong," she added frantically, worried she had offended Sadie.

Sadie reached over and held Cora Rae's hand. "I know what you meant and you're almost there, Cora Rae. And I'll be there with you this week at your CAT scan. I'm thinking it's going to be your last one for a little while. You are doing better than you think, I promise," she reassured her.

Paige and Faith came over to sit with Sadie and Cora Rae. Paige propped her feet up on a gardening stool and sighed. "My legs swell so much more this pregnancy than they did with my other two. Doctor says to put my feet up as much as possible." At seeing the worried look on her three friends' faces she quickly added, "All my tests are coming back normal, but the doc and I have an agreement to be extra cautious. So, don't worry, we're on it."

"Glad to hear it," Sadie replied sternly. "Maybe I should go with you to your next appointment?"

"There's barely enough room in the little exam room for Jake's huge self. You're on my HIPPA form, so feel free to call and ask all the questions your heart desires."

Sadie nodded and made a mental note to do exactly that. Her new niece or nephew already held a special place in her heart. She knew how much the pregnancy meant to Paige and Jake. She wondered what that was like. Sadie loved Paige's kids and spending time with them. She loved Paige's unborn child. The desire to have one or more of her own completely alluded her for some reason. Glancing over at Faith, her best friend who would give anything to have a child of her own but couldn't, Sadie wondered why things happened the way they did. She found herself wondering that type of thing a lot lately.

"So, Sadie," Faith began, cutting off Sadie's wandering train of thought, "what do you want to do for your birthday? You know we have to have some kind of celebration."

"I'm turning thirty-six. What's so special about that?" Sadie asked, caught off guard by the shift in subject.

"We're getting old and need to party while we can," Faith answered, half-jokingly. "Plus, you already promised that I can plan something."

The ladies giggled and Cora Rae said, "Y'all are not old! That would mean I'm old!"

"What about a night out in Charleston?" Faith suggested.

"You have heard there is a possible serial killer on the loose, right?" Cora Rae exclaimed.

Sadie, Paige, and Faith quickly glanced at one another and averted their gazes. "We'll have a big group and as long as no one goes out into an alley alone, or a stairwell, PAIGE," Faith fake coughed and shot wide eyes at her pregnant friend then continued, "then it should be perfectly safe. Charleston P.D. ramped up patrols around the clubs and bars last week."

"What should be perfectly safe?" Jake asked as he walked over with John and Travis bringing the ladies plates laden with appetizers.

"Going out in Charleston for Sadie's birthday in a couple weeks. Cora Rae is concerned about some of the things we have been hearing on the news," Paige said, giving John a meaningful look.

"Am I invited?" John asked, looking over at Sadie with a mischievous grin.

"Of course," Sadie replied, smiling coyly.

"Well then, it will be perfectly safe. Plus, I'll have Jake and Travis for back-up. Normally, I would include Paige and her Buffy moves, but she's knocked up," John said.

"You're really lucky you added that last part. I was about to call you a sexist pig," Faith said, giving John a bit of side-eye. "Don't forget Dr. Cutie Pie needs an invitation," she added, smiling over at Sadie.

"Who is Dr. Cutie Pie?" John asked anxiously.

"Dr. Montgomery," Sadie answered.

"Oh, okay. He's cool, I guess," John shrugged. Faith snickered behind him.

Sadie could only shake her head and laugh. She loved this group of people so much.

"That settles it then, my birthday in Charleston. Faith, I'm leaving all the planning in your capable hands. Good luck coordinating mine and John's work schedules to make it work." Sadie couldn't imagine it being much of a celebration without the hunky officer there. She always had fun with her girlfriends, but she was looking forward to ending the celebration wrapped up in John's arms and whatever other body parts got caught up together. She decided right then and there that she would take him home with her after her party. Until then, she would flirt and build the anticipation for both of them.

After their bellies were full and the sky began to darken, the guys built a bonfire, a small one since it was hot and muggy out. They really liked to burn stuff. Henry begged for smores, and Paige brought out the graham crackers, chocolate, and marshmallows. Caleb and Henry were the only two to eat any of it. Everyone else was full from the tarts and pies Faith had brought. The young boys seemed to have bottomless pits for stomachs.

Sadie sat well away from the fire. It was pretty to look at, but it was hot and she didn't want her hair and her dress to smell like smoke. She was more of a city girl than her friends. The peace and quiet was hard to get in the city, so she appreciated both worlds. Faith made her way over to where Sadie was relaxing with Cora Rae in tow.

"We're heading out, going to take this one home," Faith declared.

"I'm sorry to cut out early, I just get tired," Cora Rae said apologetically.

"No need to apologize, Cora Rae," Sadie replied before turning to Faith. "Why don't I take her home? Her apartment isn't but ten minutes from my condo. Seems silly for you to drive all the way out there and back when I already have to go that way," Sadie insisted.

With it all settled, Sadie and Cora Rae made the rounds saying goodnight. When she got to John, Sadie asked, "Walk us to the car?"

John all but hopped at the chance to escort Sadie to her car. In an attempt to not seem too eager, he offered Cora Rae his arm to help her walk over the uneven ground in the dark.

"Ooh, such a gentleman," Cora Rae exclaimed, winking at Sadie over John's shoulder.

"What can I say, my mama raised me right," John quipped.

The three walked to Sadie's car chatting and laughing. A gentle breeze picked up, ridding the air of some of its mugginess. Sadie looked up at the moon and stars in the clear night's sky and thought to herself, *this is the life*. She opened the passenger side door so John could ease Cora Rae in. He said goodnight to his charge and gently shut the door.

Sadie made her way over to the driver's side with John following behind. She turned and leaned her back against the driver window, blocking the view from inside the car. John didn't even hesitate; he put a hand firmly on Sadie's waist and kissed her with everything he had. She willingly opened her mouth to him, inviting his tongue in to explore. He tasted like a breath mint and rendered Sadie breathless in seconds. Her head spun and she wondered how in the world she was going to be able to hold out for a couple of more weeks without fully giving in to him. Images of them taking it further right there on the car played in her head. She imagined opening the back door and dragging him inside the backseat. At first the image got her even hotter, until she remembered Cora Rae was presently sitting in the front seat. It was the reminder she needed to be able to pull back from John's intoxicating kiss.

"I've been waiting all night to do that," John said breathlessly.

"I've been wanting you to do that all night," she replied. Her voice was husky, so she cleared her throat to try to speak normally. "Cora Rae is waiting. I should get her home."

"See you soon, Dr. Jennings."

"Yes, you will, Officer John."

Sadie turned and opened her car door before she could change her mind and pounce on John. She plopped heavily in the seat. It took her a couple of tries to get her seatbelt on and then she cranked the car. With her hands gripped tightly on the steering wheel, she turned her head to the right to start backing out and looked right into Cora Rae's smiling face.

"Not one word," Sadie said, grinning shyly.

"Wasn't going to say anything," Cora Rae answered. She simply turned in her seat to face forward, but the smile never left her face.

The smile on Sadie's face remained all the way home as well.

CHAPTER SIX

Sadie entered the hospital Monday morning with a travel coffee mug in one hand and a smile stretching her cheeks. The steamy kiss with John was living rent free in her head and had her feeling optimistic and giddy. Her feelings for John had moved past the crush phase into full on pining. She couldn't wait to spend more time with him. Unfortunately, as she made her way into the doctors' lounge the neon orange flyer on the notice board reminded her that the next two weeks at work were going to be hell.

"Ready to put the surgical residents through their paces, Dr. Jennings?" Dr. Montgomery asked, walking over to stand next to her in front of the notice board.

"The question is, Dr. Montgomery, are they ready?" Sadie questioned back.

"True enough, Sadie. We are about to give these rookie surgeons a shot at really proving themselves." He paused. "Remember those days when we were baby surgeons? Dr. Richards almost made me cry. I swear!" he exclaimed when Sadie looked over at him in disbelief. "If Pearl hadn't been there to keep me straight, I'd be waiting tables at my parents' country club right now."

Sadie chuckled. "You were born to be a doctor, Jeff. I remember constantly feeling like I had to prove myself. To be better than the guys."

"That's right, you were the only female in our residency that wanted to specialize in cardio. All the others went into obstetrics," he replied, thinking back to the early days of their careers.

"Yup," Sadie responded simply.

Sadie thought back to her residency days and the loneliness she felt at first, before her and Jeff became friends. She never told him, but before she figured out that he wasn't like the other residents, she would go to the gym and knock around a punching bag, picturing their faces with their barely veiled racist and sexist remarks. She had unfairly lumped Jeff in with the others, but he quickly separated himself from the pack, in skill and in manners. He treated her the same way he treated the experienced surgeons they were learning from, with kindness and respect. Jeff got her through the toughest of times and she liked to think that she did the same for him.

"You were smiling pretty big when you walked in here," Jeff commented.

Sadie realized he had been talking to her while she reminisced about the first year of her career. Turning to face him, she took in his handsome face and his friendly smile.

"Uh, yeah. I had a great weekend," she stated with a huge smile.

"Did that have anything to do with a certain small town police officer I caught you embracing in the hallway last week?" he asked with a knowing grin.

"Yeah, actually it did. I like him. Like, really like him," she admitted.

"It's about time, Sadie," Jeff replied, sounding only a little disappointed. "I don't know Officer Avery in a personal manner, but what I do know of him tells me that if I had to lose you to someone at least it's to a good guy."

Sadie rolled her eyes at him while blushing and grinning happily.

She changed the subject back to their residents and they got down to business getting on the same page about skill levels and expectations for the weeks to come.

"The ever-eager Dr. Daniel Wu is this year's front runner in terms of skill. I'm worried that the trials of the next couple of weeks might kill his spirit. It will be challenging and there will be far less handholding since these baby surgeons have to prove what they have learned and what they are capable of," Sadie began as she made her way to the coffee pot to refill her travel mug.

Jeff followed her over to the counter. "He idolizes us, and his performance over the next couple of weeks will determine whether or not he gets to follow in our footsteps like he hopes. I think he's got what it takes."

Sadie nodded and moved on to the next resident. "Dr. Jordan Jones is a bright young woman that reminds me a lot of myself. She has a drive to prove herself, and she is crazy smart. Her hand is first up in rounds, and she isn't scared to take on new responsibilities. Her only downfall is she doesn't know when to ask for help." Sadie had to tell her on more than one occasion to never be afraid to ask a question or for assistance. It wouldn't be weakness; it would be putting a patient's well-being before one's pride.

"Dr. Haley Pope shows great promise as well," Jeff stated. "Maybe not for cardiovascular, but she is definitely a surgeon. She is showing the most promise in neurosurgery. Even though she hasn't technically specialized yet, the neuro doctors have their eyes on her. Her hands are quick and sure, an important trait for someone to have if they are going to be cutting people's brains."

Jeff and Sadie moved over to the couch and took a seat facing each other.

"Lastly, there is Dr. Todd Madison," Sadie said.

"I must admit that I feel conflicted when it comes to Dr. Madison," Jeff replied.

"Me too," Sadie agreed.

"He is smart, a bit on the cocky side, and he has a temper," Jeff began. "It isn't necessarily anything new in the medical field where stakes are high and the losses hurt, but I prefer to work with doctors with a more level-head." Sadie nodded in agreement and Jeff continued. "He has missed a few shifts here and there for family emergencies. He is a local who lives with his mom and sister. The mom holds down two low paying jobs, while the sister apparently has a drug problem."

"While I can empathize with his familial situation, his absences put him at a disadvantage," Sadie lamented.

"I guess we will know soon enough if these four have what it takes. I'm rooting for them," Jeff grinned devilishly.

"You're going to enjoy putting them through their paces, aren't you?" Sadie asked, swatting Jeff's arm.

"You know it," he laughed.

There had been a few more residents, but one by one they had switched fields. The first one dropped on the very first day. As soon as a scalpel had sliced through skin and muscle the young man fainted. There hadn't even been any blood yet. He decided to be a pharmacist. One young woman transferred to another hospital to follow her boyfriend. The final one had not even a month before decided to be a pediatrician. Dr. Richards had tried to convince that one to go into pediatric surgery, but to no avail. So, they were down to the final four and they were about to see what the young surgeons were made of.

***

"I'm so exhausted," Sadie groaned as she set her hospital cafeteria tray down on the table in front of Paige and Faith. It was Wednesday, day three of what the residents were calling hell week, and Sadie couldn't argue with them. On the bright side, they were performing brilliantly, and the patients were benefiting from all of their hard work.

"Honey, you don't have to come with me to my appointment. Why don't you go take a nap in the on-call room instead?" Cora Rae said as Sadie plopped down next to her.

"They'll just call me into help the residents with another surgery. At least at your appointment I can sit down," Sadie mumbled.

"We're here eating this hospital slop in support of you, Cora Rae. Speaking of which, where is your lunch?" Faith asked.

"I'm too nervous to eat," Cora Rae admitted.

Sadie reached over to Cora Rae the same time Paige and Faith did. "Everything is going to go fine today, Cora Rae. You've made considerable progress.

I'm only going because I want to as your friend, not because I'm worried about anything," Sadie assured her.

A tear escaped out of Cora Rae's left eye. She sniffled and shook her head. "You're right. I need to get it together." Before the other ladies could fuss over her, she added, "Did Sadie tell you she made out with John?"

Sadie felt her face heat up as her two oldest friends looked at her with wide eyes and identical excited smiles. She had been eager to tell them all about it but wanted to do it in person. The thought of John filled her with such happiness; she could gush over the details all day. She had never felt this way about a guy before, and her friends knew it.

"He kissed me at the car when I was leaving the cookout the other night," she began. "I can't wait until these two weeks are over and I can spend time with him again. I was thinking that after my birthday party I could take him home with me for an adult sleepover and a little pillow talk if you know what I mean."

"Oh, I have a feeling there is nothing little about it," Cora Rae teased.

"I got a feel when he was up against me at the car the other night and you are completely right, Cora Rae," Sadie confided in a whisper.

All three women squealed, catching the attention of the tables around them. Some of the people did not look happy to see the women celebrating. Remembering where they were, the friends attempted to make their faces look more somber and lowered their voices to a whisper.

"That will be perfect, Sadie!" Faith said. "Paige and I have been working on your party. It is going to be flapper themed, which I know is a little overdone around here, but it's just so much fun to wear the dresses and the hair pieces. Paige has a call into a couple of the bars near the magazine, and I've already told John to take that Saturday night off."

The four women quietly discussed the party, what they would wear, and who else they would invite. When Sadie's twenty minutes were up and it was time to go to Cora Rae's appointment, Paige and Faith gave her big hugs. Their words of love and reassurance lifted Cora Rae's spirits and Sadie walked a much calmer Cora Rae over to the neurology department for her CAT scan. The technician gave her a hospital gown to change into and had her lay on the slab to be put into the machine.

Sadie entered the adjoining room to watch the scans on the monitors as she had times before for Cora Rae. Her specialty was the heart but had become reacquainted with the brain over the last few months. As the first scans started showing on the monitors, the door opened and a doctor Sadie was not familiar with walked in. He was an extremely handsome man, a little on the lean side, but striking, nonetheless.

"Hi, I'm Dr. Raj Patel," he said, holding his hand out to Sadie. "I'm the new staff neurologist."

"Oh, yes. I read about you in the newsletter. I'm Dr. Sadie Jennings, cardio," she said, shaking his hand in return. "You were at Duke, right?"

"Yes, I loved it there, but my parents are here, and they are getting older, so I decided to move closer to them."

"That is really admirable," Sadie replied.

"So, if you're cardio, is this a mutual patient of ours?" Dr. Patel asked, looking over at the monitors.

"Oh, no. This is a dear friend of mine. I'm here for moral support," she explained.

"My first VIP," he said sweetly. "Okay, tell me about her."

Sadie went on to tell him Cora Rae's medical history. In the beginning she kept strictly to the medical facts, but Dr. Patel's kind face had her opening up about the more personal facts of what had happened to Cora Rae. She hoped her friend wouldn't mind.

"She was kidnapped, along with my best friend Paige, and suffered a lot of physical abuse as well as witnessed what had been done to Paige. She was so brave though and ended up saving Paige's life. Cora Rae is a very special lady, and I'll have her back for the rest of my days."

"Sounds like your friend has been through more than her fair share," Dr. Patel said when Sadie was done with the story. "Try not to worry, she's in good hands with me."

When the scans were all done, Sadie walked Cora Rae over to an exam room to get changed and meet her new doctor. Sadie told her she would be seeing a different doctor than usual but left out how attractive he was. She was going to let her friend form her own opinion of him. The look on Cora Rae's face when Dr. Patel walked in the room was priceless. Cora Rae had always been one of those people whose face clearly showed what she was thinking and, in that moment, she was thinking, *hot damn!*

"Hello, Ms. Summers. I'm Dr. Raj Patel," he said, holding out his hand to Cora Rae. "Dr. Jennings brought me up to speed on your case. It sounds like you have been through a lot."

"Yes, Dr. Patel," was all Cora Rae managed to say. She had a look of wonder on her face as she stared at him dreamily and Sadie had to hide her smile behind her hand.

"Well, I have good news for you. My initial review of your scans show no evidence of bleeding or swelling. There is some scar tissue, but it is minimal. It shouldn't cause you any troubles. I'll review the scans again to work up an official report. In the meantime, I am officially clearing you to drive," Dr. Patel stated happily.

"Thank you, Dr. Patel," Cora Rae replied, still dreamy eyed. Sadie wasn't even sure Cora Rae comprehended anything he had said.

Sadie also thanked the doctor and put her arm around Cora Rae's shoulders and squeezed her tight. When the door closed behind him, Cora Rae said, "That is one smoking hot man."

"Yes, he is," Sadie laughed and walked Cora Rae out of the room. She texted the good news to Paige and Faith.

"You think he might want to come to your birthday party?" Cora Rae asked, finally coming out of her trance.

"I'll ask him. Maybe I won't be the only one to get lucky that night," Sadie teased.

Sadie walked Cora Rae to the parking lot where Paige was patiently waiting to take Cora Rae back to work. Paige took one look at Cora Rae's dreamy face and looked over at Sadie confused. Sadie shook her head and chuckled. She would let Cora Rae tell Paige all about the handsome new doctor. She had to get back to work. With the last hugs given, she turned to go back into the fray.

CHAPTER SEVEN

J ohn rolled over in his queen size bed. He was feeling restless and couldn't fall asleep even though he was exhausted. He couldn't get Sadie off his mind. Looking over at the time on his phone screen, he debated texting her. It was two a.m.; he had gotten home from his shift an hour ago. If it was anyone else John wouldn't dare text at that hour, but she worked crazy hours like he did.

> John: You up?

He hoped she was up. He wanted to be on her mind as much as she was on his. He'd never felt so strongly about a woman before. A couple of the guys at the station had gotten wind of his feelings for the sexy surgeon and had given him shit. He didn't care; he was man enough to know that a good woman was worth putting in the effort. No amount of teasing would have him backing off of Sadie. She was smart, funny, and sexy. John squeezed his phone, mentally willing her to answer him. When he saw those three magical dots appear on the screen that indicated she was typing, he moved around, getting comfortable. His blood pumping in anticipation.

> Sadie: Yes, just got home

> John: We can talk tomorrow if you're tired

> Sadie: I'm exhausted but doubt I'll fall asleep anytime soon

> John: Rough day?

> Sadie: Something like that. What are you doing up?

> John: Thinking about you

> Sadie: Oh really?

> John: Can I call you? It would be nice to hear your voice. Texting isn't really scratching the itch.

> Sadie: Yeah, I know what you mean

John didn't hesitate in pressing the call button. He couldn't wait to hear her sweet voice.

"Hey. So, you've been thinking of me, huh?" Sadie said, answering the call on the first ring.

"Oh, yeah! Have you thought about me?" he asked, his voice husky.

"Maybe," Sadie replied coyly.

"Maybe, hmm? Work keeping your mind occupied? Too busy to pine over me?" John questioned, lying in the dark making him bold. Not that he was a shy guy by any means, but Sadie was a formidable woman. She wouldn't fall for games; directness was the way to go with her.

"Well, it's what the surgical residents are calling hell week, so they are doing their best to keep my mind off of you, but you've snuck in there a time or two."

"Glad to hear it. When can I see you?" he asked eagerly.

"Unfortunately, I'm basically living at the hospital right now. I only came home tonight so I could water my plants. The night of my birthday celebration will be my first night off. Faith says you're coming to that."

"Wouldn't miss it for anything."

"Good. I got big plans for us that night."

"Us as in our whole group or us as in me and you?" he asked hopefully.

"Me and you. Definitely just me and you," she answered, her voice seductively silky.

John immediately felt his blood travel south. He got a visual of him and Sadie horizontal, and he let out a growl. He couldn't help it.

"Sounds like you're on board for that. I'm going to try to get a couple hours of sleep. Sweet dreams, John," Sadie teased.

"Oh, I'm sure they'll be the best dreams I've ever had. Goodnight, Sadie."

John reluctantly hung up the phone. The need to touch Sadie was unbearable. How was he supposed to wait ten more days? The answer was that he couldn't. As he took care of the raging hard on her voice gave him, he visualized all the ways he would please her. When he was done and he settled in his blankets to try to sleep, thoughts of a more innocent nature filled his head. He didn't want Sadie only for her body, he wanted her as a partner. Someone to wake up next to, someone to share his day with, to make a home with. He knew that her intelligence level surpassed his own, but he admired that about her. He wanted to be the person she wanted to share her day with, her wins and her losses. He made the decision right then and there that he was going to make Dr. Sadie Jennings his wife someday.

***

John woke early the next morning to the screeching of his alarm. He had the day off, but he liked to do his daily run before it got unbearably hot. He reached for his phone and saw that he had missed messages from Alice the dispatcher telling him that there was another woman murdered in Charleston.

He made a quick call over to Charleston P.D. for an update and found out that while he was on the phone with Sadie, a twenty-one-year-old woman lost her life outside of the bar she was at with friends. John hung up and sat on the edge of his bed with his head in his hands. He was so tired of the violence.

Thoughts of the family that were mourning the loss of the latest victim flooded his mind but also worry for the women in his life that were trying to recover from their own trauma. What he wouldn't give to let them have peace. With a heavy heart, he rose from his bed and got dressed in basketball shorts and a white tee for his run.

With his earbuds in, blasting the soulful voice of Chris Stapleton, he ran along his street towards town. He made his way down Third Street and was about to turn onto Main Street when he caught sight of the bright yellow and blue sign for Faith's daycare center, Happy Littles Learning Center, on the corner. John had a sudden stroke of genius and made his way inside the white picket fence to knock on the window of Faith's office. Faith swiveled around in her chair ready to chew someone out but smiled and waved when she saw it was him. He walked over to the front door to wait for her to let him in. He had the code to get in for emergencies, but since he wasn't on official police business, he figured he could wait to be let in like any other civilian.

"John! What a pleasant surprise! Come on in," Faith urged as she held the door open for him.

John followed her down the hall and around the corner, smelling disinfectant, crayons, and the slight hint of dirty diapers that someone not used to the smell can always pick up on, no matter how clean the facility. When they entered Faith's office, he took a seat and smiled at the adorable pictures she had hanging on her walls.

"How is everything going around here, Faith? Kids keeping you on your toes?" he asked conversationally.

"You know it. These little darlings are always up to something. They are so cute and creative. I can't tell you how many containers of glue we go through a week," she says, laughing happily.

"You have truly found your calling," John said, admiring the glow exuding from Faith as she spoke of the kids.

"For sure. But I know you didn't come here to talk about kids, John. What's up?"

"Well, I'm sure you've noticed that I have a thing for Sadie," he began, "and we've spoke on the phone some this week, but I'm dying to see her. She says they are busy at the hospital with the residents, so I was thinking about maybe taking her lunch or something. An excuse, really, to see her without imposing too much."

"I think that is a great idea!" Faith exclaimed. "She loves those poke bowls that they sell pre-made at the fancy grocery stores. Packed with protein or some such nonsense. Bird food if you ask me, but she loves 'em." Faith shrugged and shook her head like there was no accounting for Sadie's weird food preferences.

"That's what I'll do then," John said with a smile. "Thanks, Faith. I owe you one."

"Honestly, I'm hoping to get a juicy story about it out of Sadie later. They have broom closets at the hospital, right?" Faith joked, winking at John.

John could feel the color rise in his cheeks. He considered himself a gentleman and didn't kiss and tell, but the image Faith's words put in his head had him grinning mischievously.

"You're a bad influence, Faith," he teased.

"Oh, you know you want to get with Sadie. Don't even play," she teased back.

"Wish me luck," John said as he turned and left the daycare center. He decided not to finish his usual route and jogged a bit faster than normal back to his house to get cleaned up. He wanted to look sharp when he went to see the impressive Dr. Sadie Jennings.

Chapter Eight

John ran into the first fancy grocery store he saw upon entering Charleston and like Faith had said, there were poke bowls in the refrigerated prepared food section. He had never heard of a poke bowl before, but it didn't hurt to learn something new. He bought one for himself as well, in case he was lucky enough to get Sadie to sit down somewhere for a quick meal with him.

Luck was with him as he walked into the main entrance of the hospital, he recognized the police officer on duty by the door. John walked over to the guard station and greeted the officer. After a moment of small talk, the officer made a call to the cardio nurses' station and found out where Sadie was.

"Turns out she just finished a surgery a few minutes ago and is cleaning up. The nurse said for you to head on up," the officer told him. "Good luck with your lady, man!"

John hurried upstairs to wait for her in the hallway outside of the operating rooms. The look of gleeful surprise on her face when she spotted him lit him up on the inside. Lifting the grocery bag, he smiled and shrugged his shoulders in question. The door behind Sadie opened up and two young female doctors came out into the hallway. He assumed they were Sadie's residents. They looked from John to Sadie, smiled, and then took off down the corridor whispering to each other and stealing glances back at him.

"I'm afraid I may have given your residents some gossip fodder," he said, sauntering over to her. When the two women went around the corner and were out of sight, John stole a quick kiss.

"Follow me. I know where we can go away from prying eyes," Sadie whispered conspiratorially.

"It wouldn't happen to be a broom closet by chance?" he asked. When Sadie gave him a quizzical look, he chuckled and shook his head. "Something Faith said."

"A little bigger than a broom closet but not by much," she said, opening the door to a small room with a tiny bed and a desk.

Sadie flipped on a light and made her way over to the pitiful bed and sat down. John looked from the bed to the one chair at the desk and back to the bed. He closed the door, walked across the small room, and sat down on the bed across from Sadie. She gave him a flirty smile but remained silent. The ball was in his court.

"A little blond birdie told me that you like poke bowls," John said, pulling the two bowls out of the grocery bag along with plastic forks and a couple bottles of water. "I brought two different kinds. You pick first and I'll eat the other."

"Yum! I'll take the tuna, if you are okay with the salmon?" she asked.

"I like salmon. I'll give it a try." he answered.

"Have you never had a poke bowl before?" she questioned, mildly shocked.

"No, this is my first," he admitted.

"Well, I am honored to be the one to expand your palette," she declared.

John didn't know why that sounded suggestive to him, but as soon as the words left Sadie's gorgeous mouth, the blood in his body started heading south; a common occurrence where Sadie was concerned. He gulped and dipped his plastic fork into his bowl. They ate in silence for a few minutes. The poke bowl was tasty, and he hummed appreciatively as he ate.

"Jake does that too," Sadie commented between bites.

"Does what?" he asked, covering his mouth with his hand while he spoke.

"Hums while he eats," she replied.

"Means the food is good. Manly thing, I reckon," he grinned and shrugged.

Sadie swallowed the bite of food in her mouth and asked, "Any exciting plans for this evening?"

John nodded his head as he chewed, not wanting to show Sadie a mouth full of food. He took a sip of water and answered. "Actually, I do have plans tonight. Once a week I go visit my elderly neighbor, Ms. Joyce. She records The Great British Baking Show so that we can watch it together when I have a night off. We drink sweet red wine with ice cubes in it. It's really quite tasty."

Sadie set her bowl on her lap for a moment. She was pleasantly surprised and moved by his plans.

"That's awfully sweet of you, John," she praised.

He shrugged. "Yeah, well, she used to babysit me way back in the day and she lost her husband last year. I felt it was the least I could do. She was always really nice to me when I was a kid."

Hot, compassionate, and sweet! Sadie cheered to herself.

They finished their lunches quickly, which was not surprising as the bowls didn't contain the hearty servings John was used to, but he felt full, so he was satisfied. John gathered up their trash and threw it in the container by the door. He looked back over at Sadie on the bed and saw that she was checking her phone.

"Do you have to go back to work right away?" he asked.

"I have about ten minutes until I need to meet up with the residents and go over our next case. I wonder what we could get accomplished in ten minutes?" she queried coyly.

John didn't waste a second pretending he didn't know what she was implying. He made his way quickly over to the bed, and in one swift movement sat down and took Sadie's face in his hands and kissed her deeply. She moaned in pleasure and put her hands on his shoulders and pulled his body closer. They made out like horny teenagers, until breathlessly, Sadie pulled away.

"I have to go before someone comes looking for me," she said, struggling to calm her raging libido. "Thank you so much for bringing me lunch. That was very thoughtful of you," she added sweetly.

"It was actually very selfish of me. I couldn't stand the thought of having to wait so long to see you," he admitted. He was laying his cards on the table. There was no way he was letting such a magnificent woman slip through his fingers by trying to play it cool. He wanted there to be no doubt in her mind about how he felt about her.

"I was dreading that, too," Sadie said. She sidled up to him and kissed him gently, wrapping her arms around his neck. John was in heaven. She pulled away and gave him one last smile before walking out of the small on-call room to return to work.

John waited a few minutes to let his heart rate reset back to normal and then he exited the on-call room, made his way through the hospital and to his car. It was only when he was starting his car to head home to Meadow Oaks that he recalled Sadie's words from their phone conversation the night before about what she had planned for them the night of her birthday celebration. *Hmmm...something to look forward to, for sure,* he thought happily to himself.

Chapter Nine

Early Saturday morning, a couple of days later, Sadie walked into the resident's locker room and was surprised to find it empty. She heard a loud thud coming from the bathroom and went over to check it out. She looked in and saw Hank the janitor coming out of one of the stalls with his mop and bucket.

"Good morning, Hank. Have you seen my residents?" she asked.

"I kicked 'em out so I could clean," he grumbled. Then he turned his back on her and went about his work.

Sadie chuckled to herself. Hank was a fixture at the hospital. A bit grumpy for a guy only in his thirties, but he did an amazing job keeping up with the constant cleaning demands of a busy hospital.

She made her way down the maze of hallways to the second place she could think of to look. The largest of the on-call rooms had multiple bunks, a couch, and a flat-screen tv. Sure enough, that is where she found them. The four young doctors were scattered around the room, fast asleep. Sadie couldn't blame them for their exhaustion. They had been worked to the bone, but it hadn't been in vain. Their decision-making skills had quickened tenfold under the pressure. She had to admit that she was impressed. They were going to make it as surgeons, and she couldn't be happier for them. She decided she could give them thirty more minutes of shut eye. After debating whether or not to turn off the tv, the local news station blaring louder than necessary, she chose to leave it on and not risk the sudden quiet waking them up.

John was a contributing factor to her generous mood. She couldn't stop thinking about him and the kisses they shared the day he brought her lunch. Her birthday celebration could not come fast enough. She was eager to touch him again. After flirting for months, she was ready to seal the deal. She was confident that they could work through any speed bumps along the way. He was kind, thoughtful, and smart. He didn't give himself enough credit when it came to how smart he was. After working with cocky doctors, finding a humble man seemed like finding a unicorn.

"What's got you all smiley, Dr. Jennings?"

Sadie jumped in surprise. She had been too busy daydreaming about John to notice that she had walked into the doctors' lounge on autopilot. Looking into Dr. Montgomery's eyes, she decided to be evasive for the time being, just for fun.

"I walked in the big on-call room a minute ago to find all of our baby surgeons fast asleep. They are so adorable when they snore. I'm going to give them a little longer to rest. We have a full schedule, so they'll need it," she said.

"So, it doesn't have anything to do with a certain small-town police officer we both know?" he asked teasingly.

Sadie shrugged coyly.

"Fine, woman. Keep your secrets," he said with faux sternness. "Since we have a few minutes, let's discuss our baby surgeons. I think they have really stepped up these past few days. I've already spoken with neuro, and they have their eye on Dr. Pope. They are convinced she'll declare her specialty as neuro when the time comes. Dr. Wu worships you and I can't say that I blame him."

Sadie shook her head in disagreement. "He doesn't worship me; he worships cutting into people and fixing them. He has that sense of wonderment and hope that doctors who get into medicine for all the right reasons have. I believe Dr. Wu genuinely wants to help people. He has the skill, but he is going to need to find a balance emotionally so that when he loses a patient it doesn't ruin him. Know what I mean?"

"I know exactly what you are saying. What about Dr. Jones and Dr. Madison? I think they are hooking up," Jeff whispered conspiratorially.

"You are so crazy. We're supposed to be talking about their medical skill development, not locker room gossip," Sadie replied. "But I may have seen them sneak a steamy kiss in a stairwell."

"I knew it!" Jeff exclaimed, pumping a fist in the air.

"We really need to get lives outside of this hospital," Sadie groaned. "Anyway, back to the subject at hand, Dr. Jones is going to be a top cardiac surgeon someday. I wasn't sure cardio was the right track for her at first, but she has really performed well this week and shown an enthusiasm specifically for the heart. Dr. Madison has surprisingly impressed me too. He hasn't had any family emergency distractions lately and he's really been able to show what he can do with a scalpel. He thinks fast on his feet and is more careful and precise than he was at first. He's paid attention and it shows. I think he'll make a great general surgeon if he can keep his personal life from interfering."

"Good. We are on the same page. Let's go wake them up and give them their assignments. Can I bring a pot to bang like a gong?" Jeff asked eagerly.

"If you can find one," Sadie answered, shaking her head. They really needed to get more of a social life.

Jeff didn't find a pot in the doctors' lounge, but he did manage to find an empty glass bowl with a lid. He filled it with ice cubes and off they went to wake the residents. Sadie stood by the doorway as he went around from baby surgeon to baby surgeon and shook the bowl of ice right by their ears, ripping them from sleep. They all muttered and moaned but obligingly got up and straightened their scrubs and ran fingers through their messy bed heads.

"Y'all should be counting your lucky stars that I didn't dump the ice on you!" Jeff said over his shoulder as he left the on-call room.

"You enjoyed that way too much," Sadie whispered as she followed him out.

A few minutes later, the residents made their way to the hallway where Jeff and Sadie were waiting for them. Dr. Patel, Cora Rae's hot new neuro doctor, was conferring with his fellow surgeons. He stole Dr. Pope away to assist him, leaving the other three residents waiting anxiously to see what they would be doing.

"Dr. Jones, Dr. Richards has requested that you assist him with a liver transplant," Sadie told the young surgeon. The smile that spread across Dr. Jones face reassured Sadie that the doctor was going to rise to the challenge of operating with the Chief of Surgery. She didn't show a bit of nerves.

"Dr. Wu, you are with me. Dr. Madison, you are with Dr. Jennings. Let's get to it," Jeff said, and they headed to their respective areas to get prepped for their surgeries.

Sadie went over the plan for the upcoming procedure with Dr. Madison. They were both familiar with the patient as it was someone they had been monitoring for a couple of days. At the scrub sink, Sadie was quiet, performing the surgery step by step in her head, anticipating any complications and how she would adjust accordingly.

"Dr, Jennings?" Dr. Madison began, breaking Sadie's concentration. When she looked over at him, he went on, "I want to say thank you for never giving up on me. I know I wasn't the most reliable resident at first, but I am fully committed to being the best surgeon I possibly can be."

Sadie gave him a reassuring smile, "You are very gifted, Dr. Madison. I'm glad those gifts are not going to waste. Now, let's go repair Mr. Henderson's heart so he can get back to flirting with all of the pretty nurses."

Dr. Madison chuckled and they made their way into the operating room, the nurses and surgical techs already in there, ready to go. Throughout the surgery, Sadie gave Dr. Madison every chance to prove his skill. With a sure hand, he wielded the scalpel like it was an extension of his hand. With a confident voice, he recited step by step what to do as Sadie had done in her head. She was starting to understand what Dr. Jones might see in him. His temper seemed to have mellowed a bit, and he was in complete control. He was going to make it as a surgeon after all.

Back at the scrub sinks after the successful surgery, Sadie asked, "How are your mom and sister doing?"

A pained look came over Dr. Madison's handsome angular face. "Same ol', same ol'."

"Dr. Madison. Todd, look at me," Sadie insisted, waiting for him to make eye contact with her. When he finally lifted his bright blue eyes, she went on, "We all have our burdens, some more burdensome than others. I think you stepping up to the challenge of a surgical career and not using your family situation as an excuse to give up is extremely admirable. Hang in there."

He nodded and gave her a slight smile. Sadie figured she had said enough regarding his personal life and turned the conversation back to work.

"You are with me for the rest of the day, so buckle up. We have a full schedule," she instructed.

Sadie spent the rest of the day observing Dr. Madison operate on patients, stepping in when needed. Every once in a while, when she had a moment or two, she'd daydream about what was going to happen between her and John the night of her birthday party. She was counting down the days.

Chapter Ten

The smartly dressed newscaster was mocking him. She was telling everyone that the extra police presence around the clubs and bars of Charleston were preventing him from "striking" again. Ha! They did not understand him at all. He was not striking out. He was exterminating. His inactivity had nothing to do with the laughable presence of the boys in blue, it was a consequence of his other life. The life he showed the world. No one knew he had been chosen to save the world from those that do not deserve to inhabit it. Those lowly women that spend their time in irreputable places. Sluts, all of them. He made plans to sneak out of his other life and assure the world he was still committed to fulfilling his true purpose.

Chapter Eleven

Paige, Faith, and Cora Rae sat around Paige's dining table, simultaneously putting together the final touches for Sadie's birthday party and planning Paige's wedding to Jake, after work the following Wednesday night. One half of the table was covered with cutouts from every bridal magazine known to man and on the other half sat Faith's laptop and papers with guest lists and to-do lists. Working together, the women were making significant progress on both events. Jake had wisely chosen to take the kids out for dinner and ice cream to stay out of the ladies' way.

"It's a bummer we are doing this without Sadie," Cora Rae mused.

"It is, but her birthday party will be a fun surprise after having to basically be at the hospital for two weeks straight," Faith responded.

"And she'll still get to help with whatever is left to do with the wedding since it's not until next month," Paige added cheerfully. She laid out pictures like a collage as inspiration for decorating the local park where her and Jake were to marry. There would be lights strung from tree to tree overhead where the reception would take place after the ceremony by the waterway. A simple, yet charming celebration with their closest friends and family.

"If she were here," Faith began, "I bet we would be getting a visit from a certain hunky cop." She smiled as she looked over her final list of RSVPs. "He's been by the hospital a couple of times to visit her. Once he took her lunch, then I heard there was a late-night snack." Faith waggled her eyebrows at the other two ladies.

"I bet there was a super steamy on-call room encounter that night too," Cora Rae said gleefully.

"Cora Rae! You are so bad," Paige teased. "And probably so right," she added.

"Y'all know her better than I do. So, you think this a fling, or could it be the real thing?" Cora Rae asked, already picturing covering the wedding for the magazine. Sexy big shot city surgeon and a hunky small-town cop? The article would practically write itself.

Paige and Faith both looked up at Cora Rae and tilted their heads, almost identically. They pondered her question a moment before trying to answer.

"With Sadie it's hard to tell. She's never been one to get serious about a guy, but John is different for a few reasons. For one thing, he's a friend of the whole group. I don't think she would risk causing a ripple in our collective friendship if she wasn't really into him," Faith stated.

"I agree," Paige commented. "I believe it's a good sign that she is taking their courtship relatively slow. She's excited about him. There is definitely long-term potential between the two of them."

"He's absolutely crazy about her. I've never seen him put so much effort into wooing a woman. John has always been a good man, just not one to dwell on romantic relationships. At least not that I know of," Faith said.

"Jake told me there was a girl a long time ago. They were in their early twenties and John fell hard, but she didn't want to be with a small-town cop. She wanted bigger and better things. John has always wanted to be a police officer and stay in Meadow Oaks. Apparently, she was really nasty about it, trying to make him feel silly for not wanting more," Paige explained.

All three women shook their heads in disgust.

"It's one thing to know what you want and get out of a situation that doesn't meet your needs, but to be cruel about it is plain rude and ugly," Cora Rae said passionately. Paige and Faith agreed wholeheartedly.

"What about Sadie?" Cora Rae asked.

"What do you mean?" Paige questioned, confused.

"Well, John has a disappointing heartbreak to explain why he's never settled down. You said she never gets serious about guys, so I wonder, why not? Was there a heartbreak, some kind of childhood trauma, or something else?" Cora Rae questioned.

"No, nothing like that," Paige said, looking to Faith for confirmation. When Faith nodded in agreement, Paige continued. "She's always been goal oriented. First with school and her extra curriculars, and then with her career. She dates occasionally, but no one made it past the first couple of dinners. I don't think there was anything wrong with any of them, but with her work schedule, they never really ever got to know each other deeper before the initial attraction wore off."

"So, John is special because their attraction has been allowed to bloom over time?" Cora Rae deduced.

"Yes, I guess so. And because John is the literal best guy ever. He's chivalrous, the type to help old ladies cross the road and get kittens out of trees, protective, secure enough in his manliness to be able to be with a strong woman," Faith explained.

"Basically, he's the perfect modern man," Paige concluded. Faith smirked at her.

"I can see that. I know when he walked me to the car after the barbeque it was an excuse because he wanted to say goodnight to Sadie more privately, but he was still so attentive to make sure I didn't stumble. I felt perfectly at ease with him," Cora Rae stated.

Paige and Faith muttered to each other about missing all the good stuff.

"Did y'all hear that another girl was killed in Charleston last week?" Cora Rae asked, abruptly changing the subject to a darker one.

Paige and Faith nodded their heads solemnly.

"I hope they catch him soon," Paige said quietly.

"Or her," said Cora Rae. "We all know firsthand that women are just as capable of that kind of violence as men are."

"Unfortunately, we do," Paige agreed, covering her belly protectively with her hands.

***

The following afternoon John strolled through Under the Oak Tree, a boutique store on Main Street in Meadow Oaks. The store carried an eclectic collection of vintage jewelry, handmade decor, metal art, and the kind of stylish clothing one would wear to brunch in Charleston. He wanted to find the perfect gift for Sadie's birthday. She spent most of her time in scrubs, but he noticed that when she was not working, she favored bold and bright colors. He would never dare buy clothes for a woman so early in the relationship, so he was leaning towards getting her a unique jewelry piece or an interesting knick-knack for her home.

He didn't think Sadie would decorate her home with something that had frogs or roosters on it, so he bypassed those items. There were a couple of nice things with fireflies and dragonflies, but he knew that was more Paige's style. John pondered over how it was that he already knew so much about Sadie, but at the same time there was still so much more to learn. He had considered asking Faith for help in picking a gift. The need to be able to show Sadie the thought he put into choosing something for her on his own had stopped him from asking for any assistance.

He walked away from the decor section, hoping to have more luck in jewelry. He knew a ring was out of the question, but maybe a nice pair of earrings or a bracelet would be appropriate. He looked over the choices carefully, trying to picture Sadie wearing the pieces and what they would look like against her dark smooth skin. His eyes scanned the displays until they landed on exactly what he was looking for. Nestled in a square box lined with navy blue velvet was a gorgeous art deco gold and sapphire hair pin with a solitary pearl in the center. It was bold and beautiful like Sadie. He hoped it would go well with the gold flapper dress she had described to him for her party.

The saleswoman saw him eyeing it and came right over to get it out of the case for him.

"Officer Avery, you have exquisite taste. Is this for your glamorous mama or do you have a special lady friend I don't know about?" she questioned as she handed the pin over to him for his inspection.

"As a matter of fact, Shirley, I do have someone special. I plan to give this to her as a birthday present," John answered, his heart swelling with joy.

"She sure is a lucky lady. There are going to be hearts breaking all over Meadow Oaks when word gets out that you are off the singles market. There isn't a woman alive who doesn't love a handsome man in uniform," she cooed in her thick southern drawl.

"You flatter me," he said as he eyed the unique hairpin. He ran his fingers over the piece and tried to picture it in Sadie's hair. It was going to look gorgeous on her. "I'll take it, Shirley. Would you mind gift wrapping it for me? I'm terrible at that sort of stuff."

"Sure thing, hon," she answered with a wink.

John watched as she closed the velvet box and wrapped it in gold tissue paper. She placed the wrapped box in a dark blue gift bag and artfully arranged more of the tissue paper to fill the bag. He handed over his card to pay as he buzzed with excitement at having found the perfect gift for Sadie, and on his own too.

Something unique for a one-of-a-kind woman, he thought with pride.

Chapter Twelve

Finally, he could continue his work unencumbered. No one from his other life would be expecting to see him for a couple of days. Hear from him, yes. See him, no. He had managed to sneak in one quick job the other night for his true calling, but it had been rushed and sloppy. He did not get to take his time as he would have liked; to make sure the sinner understood there was only pain and misery waiting for her on the other side. That it was her fault she would no longer be walking the Earth. He wasn't sure why he was chosen to receive the calling, the one that spoke to him about his true purpose. Nevertheless, he knew what must be done.

He would resume his responsibilities that evening. He would find another undeserving woman. Another one that was not worthy of inhabiting the Earth. He hoped his work would send a message to other such women, so that they may repent their wicked ways. If not, they would learn the hard way. He was fine with that, preferred it even.

CHAPTER THIRTEEN

Sadie took one last glance in her bathroom mirror as her doorbell chimed. Satisfied with what she saw, she rushed to the door to answer it. Paige, Jake, Faith, Travis, Cora Rae, and John were meeting her at her condo so they could all go to the bar together. She had her shiny gold sequined flapper dress on, a headband with three gold straps and a black feather, and her hair and makeup were flawless. She opted for strappy flat sandals versus high heels for once. She didn't want to be taller than John. As it was, their lips lined up nicely if she didn't add extra height.

Paige and Faith were the first through the door, carrying garment bags containing their own flapper dresses. Their hair and makeup in a similar style as Sadie's. They went into the guest bedroom to change. They hadn't wanted the costumes to get wrinkled on the drive over from Meadow Oaks. The men followed the women inside the condo and looked very dapper in their trousers and vests. John was the last to cross her threshold, a gift bag in one hand and a small duffel in the other.

Sadie raised her right eyebrow at him, but when he flashed her an open and genuinely happy smile, she couldn't help but be charmed.

"Follow me, Officer John, and I will show you where you can stow your bag," Sadie said quietly.

Jake and Travis made themselves at home on the couch and wisely started talking about sports, pointedly not making a big deal out of John having brought an overnight bag with him.

As Sadie got to her bedroom door, she stepped aside and motioned for John to enter first. Once he was inside, she followed and closed the door gently, trying not to make a sound. She leaned against the closed door and watched as John looked over her most private space.

"It's not much, I'll admit. One day I'll make it homier, but for now it's a place to sleep," she commented, feeling a little self-conscious.

"The bed looks comfortable," John replied, smiling. He turned and stared at her tempting body leaning against the door. He set his bags down on her deep purple comforter atop the bed and made his way over to her.

Sadie watched as his eyes went from playful to heated. He looked her up and down, appreciating every inch of her. He brought his body flushed to hers, pinning her between the door and his hard body. He brought his hands to her waist and squeezed.

"I hope you don't think I am being presumptuous by bringing an overnight bag. I do recall you saying that you had plans for us tonight after the celebration," he whispered huskily in her ear.

"I like a man who comes prepared," Sadie said on a sigh.

John brought his lips to her neck and kissed his way down to her shoulder and then across her collar bone. She let out a moan of pleasure as she gripped his shoulders. Making his way to the other side of her neck and back up to her ear he whispered, "I'm dying to kiss you right now, but it would be a shame to mess up that alluring lipstick. There will be plenty of time for that later. But trust me, Dr. Jennings, I will be kissing every single inch of you when we are finally, completely, alone."

He stepped away from her and Sadie felt like her legs would no longer hold her up. To keep herself from sliding down the length of the door and onto the floor, she gripped the door handle while she struggled to regain her equilibrium.

"I got you a birthday gift," John said, his voice still husky. "I know everyone else is planning on giving you their gifts at the bar, but I want you to have this now. It kind of goes with the theme of your party."

He brought the bag over to her and she took ahold of it with the hand that wasn't death gripping the doorknob. The earnest look in his eyes as he handed the present to her touched her heart and she was able to marshal the strength to stand up straight. She removed the delicate tissue paper from the top and reached in and gripped a square box wrapped in more tissue paper. John took the bag from her so she could use both hands to uncover the velvet box wrapped within. She opened the box and gasped with pleasure as the beautiful hairpin was revealed.

"John! It's absolutely gorgeous!" Sadie exclaimed. She was overwhelmed by the thoughtfulness of his gift. She went over to her vanity and sat down to put it in her hair. It perfectly complemented the pieces she had already chosen. She carefully placed it on the side with the feather so that it looked like the headband, pin, and feather were one piece.

John came up behind her and bent down to make eye contact in the mirror. "You're the one that's gorgeous," he commented, running his fingertips up her neck, sending shivers down her spine.

"We should go back out, before they think we've decided to skip the party," Sadie said, reaching her hand behind her and holding John's for a brief moment as she admired the reflection of them together in the mirror.

They made their way out to the living room where Paige and Faith had joined their men. Paige's little baby bump was noticeable in her dress, and she looked adorable. Sadie was excited about a night out with all of her favorite people after being stuck at the hospital for two intense weeks.

"Where's Cora Rae? I thought she was meeting us here too?" Sadie questioned when she realized there was someone missing from their group.

"Oh, she texted me while you were in your room," Paige smirked. "She's having trouble getting her hair to cooperate, so she is going to meet us there."

"Well then, we best get going," Sadie insisted, gesturing towards the door to distract everyone from guessing what her and John had been up to alone in her room.

The group filed out one by one and as Sadie locked up, she couldn't help but feel giddy at the thought of John's overnight bag on her bed.

***

The friends walked down the sidewalks of downtown Charleston, waving to residents out on their balconies on the humid late August evening. It was too muggy for the tourists from up north, but those native to the south were used to it. Sadie, Faith, and Paige had accessorized with a folding fan, and they were fluttering away to keep the sweat off of their necks.

"Hey, hit me with some of that breeze," John said to Sadie. She obliged, fanning his face for a moment as they walked. She enjoyed flirting with him. It was nice to have some carefree moments instead of the constant life and death ones like at the hospital.

Travis held the door to the bar open for everyone to pass through and Faith led the way to the tables she had reserved near the back. John took Sadie's hand in his as they followed. He leaned in and gave her an affectionate kiss on the cheek. She closed her eyes as she felt herself blush. John was one of the manliest men she had ever been around and at the same time so sweet and affectionate. She kind of hoped she brought the sweetness out of him. She wanted to be special to him.

Sadie was happy to see that Dr. Jeff Montgomery was already seated at one of the tables dressed in what looked to be a tailor-made Gatsby inspired outfit. The man was stylish; Sadie had to give him that. Jeff was chatting away enthusiastically with Cora Rae as she sipped on champagne. Jeff was on call and had to abstain. When Cora Rae saw them approaching, she hopped up and ran over to hug Sadie.

"Happy Birthday!" Cora Rae squealed.

Sadie let go of John to wrap her arms around her friend. "Cora Rae, your hair looks amazing!"

"Oh, thank you, Sadie. I couldn't get it to curl the way I wanted. I actually just got here a moment ago and met your colleague over there."

"Jeff is my favorite person at the hospital. He's a stand-up guy. Definitely worth getting to know!" Sadie encouraged.

"He is lovely," Cora Rae hesitated. "Do you know if Dr. Patel is coming? I told Faith that you extended an invitation to him but last I heard he hadn't RSVP'd."

"I spoke to him at the hospital yesterday and he wasn't sure if he was going to be able to make it or not. I do know that he got an outfit for the occasion just in case since I made sure to stress to him that my friend Faith expected everyone to dress up and that there would be hell to pay if someone showed up underdressed. So, if he is able to make it, he'll be here."

"Ok, good. I was only wondering. No reason," Cora Rae stumbled over her words and spun around to greet everyone else in their group.

Sadie smiled at Cora Rae's back and went over to say hello to Jeff. John was already in conversation with the other doctor and put his arm around Sadie's waist as she joined them.

"You two look awfully happy together," Jeff commented.

"We are," Sadie and John replied simultaneously, then both broke out in shy laughter.

"I'm happy for both of you," Jeff conceded, raising his glass of sparkling water to them.

Paige brought over a glass of champagne for Sadie. "Cheers to the birthday girl!" she exclaimed. She handed Sadie the flute and clinked her glass of Shirley Temple in celebration.

Surrounded by her closest friends Sadie danced, ate, drank, and chatted like she didn't have a care in the world. She held John close as they danced, both of them getting acquainted with the other's body. Sadie saw it as a precursor to later in the evening and she was liking how things were shaping up.

"Sadie, Dr. Patel is here!" Cora Rae whisper screamed in her ear as she walked by as fast as her heels would let her.

Sadie turned to see her new colleague entering the bar and an eager Cora Rae rushing over to greet him and bring him over to their tables. Sadie let John in on Cora Rae's crush and for a minute they watched their friend flirt with the handsome Indian man as Dr. Montgomery looked on, his face a little crestfallen. Sadie was about to leave John's warm arms to go check on Jeff, but John tugged her back to him and nodded towards a hot leggy blond that was making her way over to talk to the lonesome doctor.

"I think he is going to be just fine," John whispered in her ear. "Why don't we go outside and get some fresh air?"

Sadie answered with "Screw the lipstick," and hit him with a steamy kiss before pulling him out of the front doors of the bar. On the sidewalk, back in the balmy night air, John put his hands on the sides of Sadie's face and kissed her hard.

"I'm not going to be able to wait much longer to take you home," he moaned against her mouth.

"I know exactly what you mean," she whispered back breathlessly.

They resumed their steamy kissing until a group of younger women walked by and snickered. John slid his arm around Sadie's waist and led her into the entrance of the side alley by the bar. He backed her up against the building and gripped her hips firmly. Sadie thought he was about to kiss her again, but instead he stared at her with his expressive brown eyes, smiling wide.

"Sadie, I want to make sure you know that tonight is about more than getting you into bed. I care about you deeply and when I think about what my future is going to look like, I see you in it. I'm not saying that to pressure you into a relationship if you don't want to be in one, but in my mind, you're mine."

Sadie hesitated. No man had ever said anything like that to her. Sure, she had heard about how sexy or how smart men thought she was, but nothing so sincere and heartfelt; nothing that had spoken of past that moment of trying to get physical with her. She touched her forehead to his and closed her eyes.

"I see you in my future too, John," Sadie whispered, her heart full of emotion.

Their next kiss was slow and sweet, hugging each other close. *So, this is what falling in love feels like,* Sadie thought to herself. Before she could think anything else about it, the lovers' intimate moment was interrupted by a bloodcurdling scream.

Chapter Fourteen

John kissed his woman slow and deep, letting the love he felt for her come through the kiss. He wouldn't say it out loud yet, but it was what he was feeling. He had fallen for her. Sweat started dripping down the back of his neck from the sultry South Carolina heat, so he was about to suggest they go back inside and say their goodbyes. He wanted her all to himself as soon as possible. As his mouth started to form the words against hers, he heard a woman's terrified scream from nearby.

John pulled away from Sadie and after a quick glance, they both took off running toward where the scream came from. They exited the alley they were in and crossed the street to the alley diagonally across, car horns blaring in their wake. John looked behind him to tell Sadie to stay back, but she was right by his side, even in sandals she was fast. The look of determination on her face told him that she wasn't going to back off for anything. If he hadn't been so scared for her, he would have been impressed.

They entered the alleyway, and it took a little time for their eyes to adjust to the sudden darkness after the bright lights from the street. For a split second, John thought they might be in the wrong alley until a movement towards the back of the alley caught John's attention. Somebody was bent over dragging something heavy around the corner onto the narrow lane behind the buildings that lined the main strip.

"Over there!" John blurted and took off running again.

Willing his legs to go faster and swearing the hard bottomed shoes he wore with his nineteen-twenties getup, he tried to close the distance between himself and who he was pursuing. He could hear the slap of Sadie's sandals keeping up with him in the quiet alley. John rounded the corner and saw the silhouette of a man leaning over what he had dragged out of the alley. At the sound of John's footsteps fast approaching, the man snapped around, his face hidden in shadow. Upon seeing John, he cursed and pulled something out of a holster on the side of his pants. John could see that it was a knife from the moonlight reflecting off the blade.

"NO!" John yelled in despair as the man leaned back down and stabbed the unmoving woman in her chest before running away down the back street.

"I've got her! Go!" Sadie called as John started to slow down at the woman's body.

He picked up his pace and followed after the man. He pulled his cell phone out of his pocket as he ran and dialed nine-one-one. After giving Sadie's location with the victim and which direction he was following the assailant, he hung up. The man was fast, and John was not dressed for a long foot chase. The man veered left off of the street and ran through a grassy area, gaining speed. Up ahead there was an eight-foot chain-link fence blocking a construction zone and the man's trajectory was taking him right to it.

"Damnit," John muttered, knowing the guy in his tennis shoes wasn't going to have a problem getting up and over the fence. Exactly as he thought, John watched helplessly as the guy scaled the fence with ease. The man hit the ground on the other side and took off running again as John hit the fence and pulled himself up. His slippery dress shoes kept him from getting any purchase on the fence. Knowing he wouldn't be able to catch up to the assailant, he called Charleston P.D.'s dispatch again and gave them the direction the man was running, hoping a squad car would catch up to him on the other side.

"Perpetrator is in dark jeans, dark long sleeve shirt, dark gloves and black sneakers. Wearing a ball cap. Didn't get a good enough look to see if there was a logo on it," John reported. "Not sure about skin color, it's pretty dark out here, but I would say Caucasian or possibly light skinned male."

Once the perp was out of sight, John hurried back to where he had left Sadie with the victim. He could hear the sirens growing louder as they sped to the back street. A crowd had since gathered around Sadie of people who had also heard the woman's scream. Sadie was down on the ground, her sparkly gold dress covered in blood as she tried to keep the victim from bleeding out. John looked over the woman on the ground. She was young, early twenties if he had to guess. She had long blond hair and a short curvy body. There was a purple goose-egg on her temple. The man must have knocked her on the head after she got out that ear piercing scream.

"Everyone, clear out!" Sadie yelled.

John helped clear the scene so the EMTs and police could do their jobs. The medics ran over and crouched down next to Sadie and she started barking out orders. John went over to talk to the approaching officers. While the first responders taped off the area, he walked the senior officer on site through what had happened from the time he heard the woman scream until he lost sight of the man. John's phone started ringing and he took it out of his pocket to see Jake was calling him.

"Jake, send everybody home," he said when he picked up.

"John, what's going on? There are cops taping off the opening of the alley down the street and ambulances went flying by. Where are you and Sadie? Are y'all okay?" Jake asked, his voice frantic.

"Sadie and I are fine. We were talking outside when we heard a woman scream. I'll tell you more later, just get everyone home safe," John insisted. "Tell Jeff to get to the hospital and be ready," he added.

"I got it man. Call me later, no matter what time," Jake said. John could hear Paige, Faith, and Cora Rae freaking out in the background, asking a million questions.

When he made his way back over to Sadie, she was helping transfer the young woman from the hard ground onto a stretcher. Sadie's hands remained on the woman's bloody chest as they moved towards the ambulance. John walked next to her, worried about how witnessing a stabbing was affecting her. She looked over to him and he saw steely determination in her eyes. She was competent and in control Dr. Jennings, not a woman about to fall apart.

"I have to go to the hospital with her, John," she said as she passed him.

"I'll catch a ride in a bit and meet you over there," he said loudly to her back. He hated being separated from her after what they saw, but if the man he chased was the same guy who murdered Birdie Duvall, he was going to find out everything he could from the crime scene.

***

Sadie held her hands tight over the woman's bleeding chest wound applying pressure to try to slow the bleeding. The ambulance was on its way to MUSC, and she was praying that they made it there in time. As she expected, there was a trauma team waiting for them when they arrived at the hospital. One of the nurses helped Sadie down from the ambulance so she could keep her hands on the patient. She'd never thought she'd be so relieved that she chose to wear flats instead of heels to go out partying. They got the young woman to a trauma bay and once they were set up, Sadie stepped away from the patient and let the nurses and doctors do their work.

"Dr. Montgomery is prepping in O.R. two right now," Dr. Richards said to her as he joined her at the side of the bay. Sadie hadn't even realized he had walked into the room.

Dr. Richards put his arm around her shoulders and led her out of the trauma bay and over to one of the staff elevators. As they rode up a couple of floors to the doctors' locker room, Sadie looked down at her dress. It was ruined.

"I'll get cleaned up and go in to assist Jeff," Sadie said to her boss.

"Sadie," he began, "if I remember correctly, you are off tonight and you were going out to celebrate your birthday. You aren't on call, so I'm assuming you were drinking alcohol. You can't assist," he reasoned gently.

"Oh, right," she replied.

"Dr. Jones will assist. After you get cleaned up, you can stay and watch from the scrub room if you'd like," he offered.

"Yeah, I'll do that," she murmured.

In the locker room, she changed into green scrubs and went to O.R. two as fast as she could.

Jeff was an artist with a scalpel. Sadie watched as he worked tirelessly to save the young patient's life. Her assailant had stabbed her in a hurry and didn't go as deep as he had no doubt meant to. Jeff was able to repair all of the damage in her chest cavity. Sadie breathed a deep sigh of relief a few hours later as the patient was being closed up. When Jeff entered the scrub room to get cleaned up, he walked Sadie through what he had done. She had seen most of it, but it was reassuring to hear his opinion on the extent of the patient's injuries and her prognosis.

"I think it's the same guy," Jeff stated.

"What makes you think that?" Sadie asked. She agreed with him, but she hadn't voiced it to anyone yet.

"It's what my gut is telling me. We'll hand over the pictures and notes to the police and they might be able to tell us for sure after the experts review it all. You and John interrupting him saved her life," Jeff declared.

"Jeff, it was terrible." Sadie's defenses finally broke down, and she collapsed against him and sobbed.

Jeff quickly dried his hands and pulled her into a tight hug. "Shh, shh, I've got you."

Jeff held her as the sobs wracked her body, and she let go all of the fear and sorrow she had been holding in since hearing the woman scream. He gently lowered her down and they sat together on the scrub room floor wrapped around one another. As the rest of the operating room nurses and technicians came in to get cleaned up, Jeff looked up to make stern eye contact and tell them without words that no one was to hear about Sadie's breakdown outside of that room.

What felt like hours, but was only fifteen minutes, passed before Sadie could catch her breath. Jeff rubbed soothing circles on Sadie's back as she settled down.

She lifted her head and swiped at her cheeks under her eyes. She could only imagine how rough her face looked.

"So," Jeff hesitated, "I don't think your friend Cora Rae was into me. She dropped me like a hot potato once that new pretty boy, Dr. Patel, got to the bar."

Sadie giggled, then broke into full out laughter. Leave it to Jeff to know what to say to erase any awkwardness there might have been after her crying jag. That was how Dr. Richards found them when he came to tell Sadie that Officer John Avery had arrived and was looking for her.

"Be right there," Sadie said around giggles. She had to avoid direct eye contact with the confused looking Chief of Surgery so she didn't lose it in hysterical laughter again.

"Here, let me help you up," Jeff insisted as he took her elbow and pulled her up with him. "You're going to be okay, Sadie," he said when they stood up face to face.

"Thank you, Jeff. For everything," she replied and gave him one final tight squeeze.

Together they walked out into the hallway and followed Dr. Richards to the breakroom. "He's in there. I'm going home. I haven't seen my wife all week," he nodded at them and walked away.

Sadie and Jeff entered the breakroom to see John nervously pacing. Jeff immediately went over to shake hands with the officer who was still in his celebration attire.

"Any news from the scene?" Jeff asked, knowing that Sadie was curious too.

"They got a shoe print from the chase, but so far that's it. Forensics is still doing their thing, but after a couple hours, I was eager to get here and check in," John said as his gaze shifted over to Sadie.

"Of course. I'll give you two some privacy," Jeff said, shaking John's hand again and squeezing Sadie's shoulder on his way out.

"Come here," John whispered as he opened his arms for Sadie.

She gladly went into his embrace and laid her head on his broad shoulder. She took her first deep breath since coming in with the victim as he held her up.

"How are you?" he whispered in her ear.

"I'm fine," she answered, out of habit.

"You've been crying, Sadie. Talk to me," he insisted gently.

Sadie took her head off of his shoulder and leaned back. She led him over to the couch and poured her heart out to him. If anyone else would understand being on the sidelines of the ordeal with Paige and Cora Rae and then witnessing the violence inflicted on that poor woman, it would be him. He listened without interrupting. He simply held her hands as she bared her soul, nodding occasionally to let her know he understood.

"I'm sorry our special night was ruined," Sadie said as she snuggled into John's chest when she was done.

"Me too. We'll have to reschedule soon. But I can wait until the time is right, Sadie. We've been through so much. I want things between us to be perfect, not rushed."

Sadie closed her eyes and stretched out on the couch next to John. She didn't think she was going to be able to nap, but exhaustion from all of the emotional turmoil dragged her under and her heart knew she was safe with John.

Chapter Fifteen

"Sadie. Sadie."

Sadie came awake to find Jeff standing over her, shaking her shoulder. John stirred behind her on the couch as she started to sit up groggily.

"The patient wants to see you," Jeff said urgently.

"Huh? Why me? She was never conscious when I was around her. How does she even know about me?" Sadie asked, confused.

"When she woke up from surgery, she asked what happened and the female police officer who is stationed in her room told her. So, she asked to see the woman who saved her life," Jeff explained.

"What's her name?" Sadie asked, still trying to clear the fog from her head.

"Her name is Leann. Leann Rivers"

Sadie gave John's hand a squeeze and left the couch to make her way to the patient's room. She made sure her scrubs were straight and that her hair wasn't sticking up, then knocked gently before opening the door. On the hospital bed was a young blond woman, her hair spread over the pillow she laid upon. Sadie glanced at her chart and saw that she was twenty-two years old. Her eyes darted nervously to Sadie and her big brown doe eyes looked so sad and scared. It made her seem even younger. A sudden protective surge went through Sadie as she went over and sat on the edge of the bed. She grabbed the girl's hand and patted it reassuringly.

"Dr. Jennings?" Leann asked, her voice shaking. She had a musical lilt to her voice that added to the impression that she was younger than her years.

"Yes, I'm Dr. Jennings," Sadie replied softly.

Leann immediately started crying, fat tears streaming down her pretty face. Sadie held her tight, or as tight as she could without adding to her physical pain. The young woman squeezed Sadie with all her might.

"I'm so scared. I'm so scared," she said, pulling back and looking frantically at Sadie.

"You're safe now. We aren't going to let anyone hurt you," Sadie urged. She would give anything to take the fear away from Leann. Pulling the girl back to her, Sadie rocked her to try to soothe the pain away.

There was a loud knock on the door and Jeff stuck his head in the room. "Dr. Jennings, there are some detectives here that need to speak with Miss Rivers."

"NO! NO! NO! I can't talk about it! I won't!" the patient started screaming and flailing her arms and legs.

Sadie tried her best to calm the patient down, but nothing worked. Jeff ran into the room to help, but the woman became more and more agitated with him there. Her blood pressure and heart rate were rising and the alarms on the machines started ringing loudly.

"Dr. Montgomery, we have to sedate her. She'll open her chest wound up," Sadie said in her steady doctor voice, looking over at Jeff.

"Do it," he nodded.

Jeff held down the patient the best he could without hurting her. Sadie quickly ran to the door and shouted out orders to a nearby nurse. The nurse ran in with a cart, withdrew a syringe and quickly filled it with a liquid from a vial she took out of a locked drawer. The nurse put the filled syringe on a small sterile tray and handed it to Sadie. Then the nurse rushed to the hospital bed to help Dr. Montgomery subdue the patient. A few seconds after Sadie pushed the sedative into the IV, Leann stopped flailing and eventually fell asleep.

Sadie watched over her, analyzing each rise and fall of Leann's chest. Her heart hurt over the suffering the poor woman was going through. Her eyes filled with tears as she thought of how Leann's life would never be the same. She would be scared of the dark, of leaving the house, of other people, men in particular. The amount of therapy she was going to need and doctor appointments she would have to go to during recovery for heart surgery would dominate her life. Sadie couldn't help but to compare Leann to Paige and Cora Rae.

"How's our patient?" Jeff asked quietly when he reentered the room a while later.

"Respiration is normal. She's sleeping," Sadie whispered even though there was no way the patient would hear her.

"You need to sleep, Sadie," Jeff said. "John is still here. Let him take you home. I'll text you if anything happens with Miss Rivers."

"Okay. Take good care of her, Jeff," she pleaded.

Sadie and Jeff made their way out into the hallway and hugged goodbye. She felt so grateful for her friendship with Jeff.

John was waiting for Sadie in the closest waiting room and stood up as soon as he saw her. She immediately went into his arms and took comfort in his warm touch.

"John, take me home and hold me. I need this awful night to end," she mumbled into his shoulder.

"Of course," John replied. "How is Miss Rivers?" he asked as he took Sadie's hand and started out of the waiting room and into the hallway.

"She became very agitated when she heard that the detectives wanted to talk to her. She had to be sedated. She's sleeping soundly now," Sadie answered.

She liked the feel of her hand in John's. They weren't getting the ending to the evening that they had hoped for, but at least they were together. It gave Sadie a small bit of peace to know that at least she had John.

"The detectives will try again when she wakes up," John stated off-handedly.

Sadie snapped out of her daydreaming about snuggles with John and turned to face him.

"What?" she asked.

"The detectives will have to talk to her when she wakes back up. She has to be questioned," John replied.

Sadie pulled her hand out of John's and took a step back.

"They can't! She went through a trauma! You didn't see her in there, John. She can't handle it," Sadie exclaimed frantically.

Seeing that he was upsetting her, John pulled Sadie gently away from where doctors and nurses had stopped to stare at them and led her into a quiet room.

"I understand that what Miss Rivers went through was terrible, traumatizing to say the least. I was there too, remember? I saw it happen. But if Charleston P.D. is going to catch this guy, they have to find out what she knows. She has to be questioned, Sadie. There is no stopping it," John explained in what he thought was a reasonable manner.

Sadie didn't like his haughty tone. She felt herself hardening as the impulse to protect her patient overtook her. She pulled herself to her full height and crossed her arms over her chest.

"If the patient says no, then I will stop it," Sadie said firmly.

"Sadie, you can't stop an attempted murder investigation. We are looking at a serial killer for crying out loud," he retorted.

"And if the police are any good at their job, they can catch him without her having to relive the most traumatic moments of her life," she snapped back.

"Sadie, calm down," John said, holding his hands out like he could physically lower her rage with a hand gesture. It only served to increase her ire.

"Don't tell me to calm down. You didn't see her in that room, John. You didn't see us having to hold her down and sedate her when she absolutely lost it over thinking she was about to have to talk about what happened."

"I'm very sorry for her. I am. I don't want it happening to anybody else, that's why she needs to be interviewed. I can't believe you don't understand that," John said, absolutely bewildered. "What about Birdie Duvall?"

"Understanding has nothing to do with it and how dare you throw Birdie Duvall in my face. I tried my damnedest to save her. Miss Rivers is my patient now and therefore my priority. I'll do whatever I have to do to protect her physical and mental health. Including keeping anybody from making her talk about what happened if she is not ready. Figure out another way to catch him," she demanded.

Sadie stormed away, mad as fire. She could hear John calling out to her, but she didn't look back. She walked as fast as she could without actually running and got onto the staff elevator so he couldn't follow her. She rode up one floor and went into an on-call room. This one had a set of bunk beds in it and Jeff was curled up on the bottom bunk. He wasn't quite asleep and looked up when she opened the door.

"I thought you were going home. Whoa, who pissed you off?" he asked, sitting up to get a better look at her.

"Nobody. I'm fine," she said. She bent down to untie her shoes.

"Sadie, I can see the steam coming out of your ears. What happened?" Jeff persisted.

"Jeff, I really don't want to talk about it," she answered as she climbed up to the top bunk. "And try not to snore," she added as she settled in.

Luckily, Jeff left it alone and Sadie was able to fume in private as she stared at the ceiling a couple of feet above her. How dare John talk to her like that. She didn't appreciate him getting so high-handed with her. Admittedly, she could understand where he was coming from. Trouble was, he didn't even try to see her side. If he really knew her and cared for her, then he would know that her patient would come first to her over anything and everything else. The investigation could be solved without the patient's cooperation. The patient's mental health could suffer more from being forced to talk about what happened before she was ready. If she ever gets to that point at all. Who could say if she could ever bring herself to talk about it? Maybe with a therapist, but with the cops, maybe not.

Eventually, Sadie's anger subsided and was replaced with disappointment and heartache. Her chest hurt as tears filled her eyes. She clutched her hands over her heart and rolled onto her side. Her tears made salty trails down her face as she tried to cry in silence so she wouldn't wake Jeff.

After a few hours of restless sleep, Sadie awoke with only one thing on her mind, protecting her patient. She went and checked on Leann, who was asleep. The nurse reported that she woke up from sedation and was able to get down some broth and was now sleeping on her own, not because she had to be put back under. Sadie left strict instructions that no one outside of hospital staff was to talk to Miss Rivers without Sadie's permission. With that settled, Sadie left the hospital and returned to her condo. Technically, she was off until Monday.

On autopilot, she turned her keys in the lock and entered her place, still thinking of Leann. Sadie thought over the proposed treatment plan, specialists that needed to be called in, even the possibility of added hospital security outside of her room. At least when Paige and Cora Rae had been brought in, their assailant was dead. There had been no chance of Stacey coming back to get them. Leann didn't have that assurance.

As she walked in her bedroom, something on her bed caught her eye. It was John's overnight bag. All at once the thoughts and feelings of John that she had so carefully locked away that morning when she woke up came flooding back. She had such high hopes for their future, and he had let her down. She laid down on the bed next to his bag and let herself be sad. She would get it out of her system so she could be strong for her patient. Even if it meant butting heads with John again. That thought brought a stabbing pain to her sternum. *How did things go so wrong?* she thought over and over.

Chapter Sixteen

John knocked on the door to Sadie's condo Sunday afternoon with a shaking fist. He hadn't been able to sleep thinking about how things had gotten out of hand at the hospital. The guilt at raising his voice to Sadie when she had been so distraught haunted him. He believed he was right in what he said, but he should have handled it better. Exhaustion after the adrenaline rush of chasing the perp had his system all out of whack. That was no excuse, but he definitely had not been his best self.

Footsteps approaching the door from inside had his heart racing as nervousness got the best of him. The door didn't open as he had expected. After a moment of waiting, he leaned his forehead against the door.

"Sadie?"

When there was no answer, he continued, "Sadie, I'm so sorry about last night. I should never have spoken to you like that."

He heard a big sigh and then the sound of the chain lock being undone, followed my the click of the deadbolt. Sadie stood before him as beautiful as ever. She wasn't wearing any makeup and didn't look to have slept any better than him, but the relief at seeing her made her appear like an angel to him.

"Hey," he said cautiously.

"Hi," she replied, her voice a little gravelly.

"May I come in?" he asked hopefully.

Sadie seemed to think about it for a moment, finally stepping aside to let him in. John could see the reluctance in her eyes, and he kicked himself again for upsetting her. She was a tough woman, and he had been honored that she had let her guard down around him and because of his behavior last night, it might all be ruined. He watched as she sat on the couch and steeled herself, drawing her shoulders up and back.

John sat on the couch next to her and took her hands in his. He rubbed his thumbs over her knuckles, waiting patiently for her to make eye-contact with him so she could see in his eyes how sincere he was. When her dark brown eyes finally rose to meet his, he began his plea.

"Sadie, I am so sorry for how I spoke to you last night. There is no excuse for it. Tensions were high after everything that happened and I did not handle things well."

John held Sadie's gaze as he waited for her to speak. He could see the hurt and disappointment in her stare. When she remained silent, he tried again.

"Sadie, please tell me I didn't mess things up here. I don't want us to end before we really get started. We are too good together," he insisted.

She cleared her throat and finally spoke. "Have your views from last night changed?"

John knew he had to tread carefully. It was no secret that Sadie was a compassionate doctor on a normal day, add in everything she'd witnessed with Miss Rivers, and it made Sadie protective as well.

"I still believe that speaking to Miss Rivers will be the best path to catching this madman. What I didn't say last night that I should have, is that I understand where you are coming from in wanting to protect your patient's well-being," John explained. "I want that too and I think putting this person behind bars will at least give her some peace of mind."

Sadie took her time mulling over his words.

"Thank you for that. I also want to apologize for how I spoke to you last night. It was," she hesitated, "inappropriate," she said robotically.

John felt discouraged by how closed off she was acting, but he wasn't ready to give up. He scooted closer to her, needing to feel more of her against him.

"Sadie, don't shut me out. I know what we saw last night was extremely traumatizing. If there was a way I could go back and stop him before he hurt her, I would in a heartbeat. We need to be there for each other. I need you, Sadie," he pleaded.

Sadie's eyes started to tear up, so he pulled her into a hug. He rubbed her back comfortingly as he whispered, "I need you, Sadie," in her ear.

She let him hold her a few minutes before she pulled back and cleared her throat again. She brushed her fingers under her eyes to clear away the tears that had quietly fallen. Sadie took a few deep breaths.

"What makes a person do something like that? How can a human being viciously, brutally, attack another human being? He could have run off as soon as he saw us behind him, but no, he had to make sure he hurt her before running. It was worth risking getting captured to make sure he hurt her. I just can't wrap my head around it, John," Sadie cried, her shoulders heaving from heavy sobs she could no longer hold back.

John held her tight and rocked her through her tears. "I don't know, darling. Some people think it's because they have no sense of remorse or even no soul. Sometimes it's because they get some crazy idea in their heads and it gives them an excuse to act on their darkest impulses. It makes absolutely no sense to good people like me and you. Especially you, Sadie. A person that saves lives would never consider senselessly taking a life, it would go against who you are."

Sadie nodded her head against his chest as the tears continued to flow. John was relieved that she was letting him help her through processing what they had seen. In his line of work, he had seen too many people try to act like witnessing violent crimes was no big deal, like they could separate from it. But it's not normal to be unaffected by horrible things. Eventually, the emotions bubble to the top and they have to face their feelings. Holding Sadie was helping him deal with the inner turmoil he was experiencing from the previous night's events.

Eventually, Sadie lifted her head, sniffled and wiped the tears off of her cheeks. "I guess I should have gone to therapy with Paige and Cora Rae after all, huh?"

"It's not too late," John answered.

He looked down to where he was holding her hand and felt an overwhelming swell of emotion at the physical representation of their connection.

She stayed silent for a few minutes, also staring down to where their hands were joined. John eventually looked up to her face, pleading with his eyes for her to look up at him. When she didn't, he gently lifted his free hand to cup her face and tilted her chin up.

"Sadie, are we okay?" he asked.

She didn't answer him right away, which seemed to be par for the course since he'd arrived at her condo, so he tried to not let it dishearten him. He waited patiently, letting her gather her thoughts.

"John, I like you. Like, really like you," she began. John's heart perked up.

"I think what we have together is promising and it is important to me," she continued. John sat up straighter.

"And it is for that reason, I think we need to take a step back until this case is solved," she finished.

John's heart flipped. She wasn't ending things with him for good, and that should have pleased him, but she was asking for a break, and that made him sad.

"Sadie, I understand that this has all been really difficult, but I think that gives us more reason to be closer, to be there for each other," he said.

"I feel like it's too much pressure right now. Making a relationship work is hard enough but throw in dealing with a serial killer and PTSD from witnessing said serial killer stabbing a young woman, not to mention it hasn't been that long since the whole Paige and Cora Rae thing. I feel like my heart can't take anymore..." Sadie hesitated to try to find the right word, "feelings."

John wanted to argue with her, he really did. To keep from saying anything stupid like he did last night, he took some time to process her words. He understood that she felt she needed to cope and to focus on mentally healing from the trauma before she would ever be able to be in a romantic relationship. He didn't like it, for selfish reasons of course. He craved her when they weren't together, but he would just have to deal.

"Promise me you'll make an appointment with Paige and Cora Rae's therapist. It really does help. I already made an appointment for tomorrow morning with the one the county provides for police officers and firefighters."

"You did?" Sadie asked.

"Yes, I did. You don't have to go through and figure all of this out on your own," he insisted.

"Okay, I'll set something up tomorrow. Thank you, John, for not pushing, for understanding," she acquiesced.

"I'm not going to lie and say giving you space is going to be easy for me, Sadie. I've never felt this way about another woman before. I respect your reasoning, and I want this to work, so I'll do whatever you need."

John reluctantly let go of Sadie's hand and stood up from the couch. She stood as well and pulled him in for a hug. She cried softly into his neck and it about broke his heart. He squeezed her tight, memorizing the feel of her in his arms and her scent. He would hold the memory close as he spent every waking second searching for the madman that upset his woman.

"Goodbye, John," Sadie whispered into his neck, then she turned and walked to her bedroom and shut the door.

John, with a heavy heart, picked up his overnight bag she had put by the door and let himself out of her condo, turning the lock on the door handle before pulling it shut. He stood in the hallway for a few minutes, gathering his wits. Once he could breathe steady again, he set off, determined to bring Sadie closure in the Miss Rivers case.

Chapter Seventeen

The dream started pleasantly enough. It always did. Sadie was approaching the cutest little cottage in the woods. Through the trees behind the cottage, she could see the water of the sea, or maybe an inlet, glimmering in the sunlight. She felt light and airy, like she was having the best day ever. Then she opened the door and went inside.

Her dream quickly became a nightmare.

Straight ahead of her, Paige was tied up and appeared unconscious. There were cuts covering her body, her belly rounded with pregnancy. Blood was pooling at her feet.

Sadie ran to her, screaming, "PAIGE! PAIGE!"

But Paige did not wake up, and Sadie didn't make it to her because she tripped and fell over something she had not noticed before in the middle of the floor. She fell hard onto her hands and knees and the pain echoed through her bones. She lifted up and looked at her hands; they were covered in blood. Sitting down on the floor in disbelief, she saw that her legs were also covered in blood. Sadie turned over the hump on the floor and gasped at seeing Cora Rae's pretty face.

Sadie's doctor instincts kicked in, and she frantically felt for a pulse on Cora Rae's neck. There was none. Cora Rae was dead. A primal scream ripped out of Sadie's throat as she pulled her friend's torso into her lap and cried out in agony.

Remembering Cora Rae wasn't her only friend in the cottage, Sadie gently laid Cora Rae's body back down on the floor and crawled her way over to Paige. Slowly rising, she examined Paige. As sobs still racked her body, Sadie put her ear against her best friend's chest. Paige was also dead.

Sadie slumped to her knees and screamed at the ceiling. Her heart broke into a million pieces.

When she thought she would die from her broken heart, Paige and Cora Rae's eyes opened and they began to scream.

Sadie jolted up in bed, clutching her heart and covered in sweat. She couldn't catch her breath and felt like she'd ran a marathon. *When will these nightmares end?*

Chapter Eighteen

Monday morning, Sadie met Jeff and the two male residents for rounds. In her left hand was an extra-large travel mug of coffee. Sleep was alluding her. Coffee was her best friend at the moment. Being under the harsh hospital lights helped her stay grounded in reality. Jeff had texted her the night before to say he would cover her patients if she wasn't up to working yet after what she went through Saturday night. She felt like missing work would mean the bad guy had won by keeping her away from her normal routine. It didn't hurt that she was on the day shift and not the night. She wasn't sure she could handle going to work in the darkness yet.

"Good morning, Dr. Montgomery. Hello Dr. Wu, Dr. Madison," Sadie greeted the men. "Where are Dr. Jones and Dr. Pope?"

"They have today and tomorrow off since we had the weekend off," Dr. Wu reminded her, looking over at Dr. Madison.

"Oh, right. Of course," Sadie said, sipping more coffee to wake her brain up.

"We'll be back to normal rotation on Wednesday," Jeff added, looking Sadie over carefully. "You all did very well during hell week, or more accurately hell weeks, so the short time off was well-deserved," he said, directing his attention back to the residents.

"Absolutely," Sadie added. "I hope the ladies stay away from the bars and clubs while they are off," she said absentmindedly.

"Oh, I wouldn't worry about that, Dr. Jennings," Dr. Wu replied. "They aren't what you'd call party girls. They are probably just catching up on their sleep."

"They might have been able to actually sleep in the on-call rooms over the weekend since Hank wasn't here to kick them out so he could clean," Dr. Madison commented. "That other janitor is nicer and lets us sleep. He just comes back when we leave."

"Alright, let's get back on track," Jeff interjected. "You two will round with me while Dr. Jennings checks in on Miss Rivers. After that, Dr. Madison will be with me for a double bypass and Dr. Wu will be with Dr. Jennings for a heart valve replacement and then we'll switch for the following surgeries. Better be ready boys, you'll be taking the lead. We will be there for guidance and assistance."

Everyone nodded that they understood the game plan and while Jeff took the residents in one direction, Sadie made her way to Leann's room. When she entered, Leann was fast asleep on the bed. To the right of the bed was a rolling table with a covered tray on top. Sadie quietly lifted the lid and was happy to see that other than a couple of grapes, Leann had eaten the entire breakfast. *The madman isn't going to beat this girl,* she thought to herself. To give Leann a few more minutes of sleep, Sadie checked her chart and the readouts on the machines before waking her up to check the surgery site on her chest.

"Good morning, Leann," Sadie said softly.

Leann stirred and it took her a few seconds to remember where she was. Sadie watched as the emotions played over her face. First confusion, then fear, then recognition as her gaze landed on Sadie.

"You're in your doctor coat," Leann commented, her voice still sleepy.

"Yes, I'm on rotation today," Sadie replied. "How was your evening?"

"A bit boring. I slept a lot and watched TV," Leann shrugged. "I ate half of what they had tried to call fiesta chicken for dinner. I don't think you can really call something 'fiesta' if it's as bland as cardboard."

Sadie chuckled at Leann's spirit. "You seemed to enjoy breakfast."

"It was fruit and oatmeal," Leann said, rolling her eyes a bit. "At least they put brown sugar on it, so it actually tasted like something."

"I agree, the food is not the tastiest, but eating will help your recovery. Mind if I check your surgical site?" Sadie asked.

In answer, Leann untied the strings of her hospital gown and pulled the sides apart to give Sadie access to the wound.

"On a scale of one to ten, with ten being the worst, what would you rate your pain?" Sadie asked.

Leann nibbled a little on her bottom lip before she answered. "If I'm being honest, seven or eight, but I don't like to take too much pain medicine. It makes me feel woozy and I don't like to feel out of it, especially if you're not here," she admitted.

Sadie's heart broke a little for her. "I completely understand, Leann. I'm here now though, so why don't I give you something. It doesn't have to be super strong."

Leann nodded in agreement. Sadie walked over to the desktop on the counter and started typing in her orders. Out of the corner of her eye, she could see Leann fumbling with the blankets, and she looked really nervous. Sadie finished her entries and walked back over to sit in the chair next to the bed that was meant for visitors.

"Leann, is there anything else bothering you?" Sadie asked.

Leann continued fumbling with her blankets as she spoke, "I've started remembering some things. Well, not remembering really because it's not like I had amnesia, more like things are getting clearer in my head."

Sadie nodded but was uncertain about what she should do. "One of the detectives assigned to your case is a woman. Her name is Detective Maxine Fuller. Do you want to talk to her?"

"Can't I just tell you?"

"Of course, you can tell me anything. I think it would be beneficial to talk to the detective as well. She'd know what kind of questions to ask to help find the guy that did this to you," Sadie explained as delicately as she could. She didn't want to spook Leann.

"But what if I can't answer her questions?" Leann asked.

"Then you just tell her that you don't know. It's okay to do that," Sadie reassured her.

"Is it okay if I tell you first?"

Sadie nodded that it was okay, and Leann began her story.

"I went with five of my friends to The Palmetto Bar to celebrate my friend Mary turning twenty-one," she explained. "We took an Uber to the bar so that nobody would have to be the designated driver. Even so, I only had one drink before I went outside to answer a phone call from my mom. She's in Tennessee, that's where I moved here from."

Leann paused and took a deep breath to steady her nerves before she went on.

"I couldn't hear very well in front of the bar; there were too many people outside talking loudly. The alley was empty, so I walked a few feet in and talked to mom for a couple of minutes. When I hung up and took a step to go back in, someone grabbed me from behind. There was one gloved hand over my mouth and one around my stomach. He started pulling me back further into the alley. I struggled and squirmed, and I guess since it was so hot and muggy outside, my face was all sweaty, and his hand slipped off of my mouth. That's how I was able to scream so that hopefully someone would hear me and come help. Next thing I could remember was waking up in the hospital."

"Has anyone called your mom? I should have asked earlier, I'm sorry," Sadie said when Leann's story concluded.

"Yeah. The officer that was in my room when I woke up called her. She should be here sometime this morning. I guess my phone was lost somewhere in the alley and my purse was inside the bar with my friends, so they had to wait until I woke up to get her number."

"Have you spoken to any of your friends that were at the bar with you?" Sadie wondered.

"Oh, yeah. Once. They were all pretty out of it that night, so it took a while for one of them to realize that all the commotion outside was because of me. They thought it was for some other bar down the road since the ambulances passed by to go to the back street."

"Are they coming to visit you?" Sadie asked.

Leann looked down and started picking at the threads on her blanket. "I told them not to. I just want my mom."

Sadie couldn't think of anything else to say, so she squeezed Leann's hand and stood from the chair.

"I've got a surgery in about ten minutes, but I'll come check on you right after," she promised.

"I want you to be here when I talk to the detective, is that okay?" Leann pleaded.

"Yes, I'll make the arrangements," Sadie agreed.

A nurse entered the room with the medication Sadie had ordered, so Sadie left the room to go do surgery. Leann's story had her wide awake.

News about Leann's attack and talk of a serial killer in Charleston was circulating around the hospital. Sadie's role in being at the scene of the crime was also known to the staff, which Sadie was not thrilled about. Both Dr. Wu and Dr. Madison questioned her about the circumstances surrounding Leann's ordeal.

"I heard you saw the woman get stabbed and Dr. Jones told me she assisted Dr. Montgomery on the woman's surgery," Dr. Madison said. "Was it a close one?"

"Yeah, I heard it was gruesome! Did you see his face?" Dr. Wu added. "How did she even survive? Dr. Montgomery is badass!"

Sadie huffed out a frustrated breath. "I'm only going to answer questions that are relative to Leann's medical treatment."

The details of her attack were for Leann to tell the detectives, not for gossip among the medical staff. Both of the residents asked for detailed descriptions of her wounds and confirmed what Dr. Montgomery had done in the operating room to save her. While Sadie admired and understood their scientific curiosity, talking about it was exhausting her.

It wasn't only reliving the ordeal and her part in it that was tiring her, it was how it brought up thoughts of John. Saturday should have been a romantic and magical night for them, but instead she ended up covered in blood while he chased a dangerous criminal. Then they fought and hurt each other. It made her sad to be apart from him, but she thought it necessary. It occurred to her that even though she was being logical about the situation, it didn't make it any easier. The heart sure was a funny thing.

Chapter Nineteen

Wednesday night, after her shift at the hospital, Sadie found herself in Meadow Oaks putting the finishing touches on Paige's wedding that was to take place in a couple of weeks. Sadie and Faith were finalizing the seating chart, while Cora Rae confirmed the menu with the caterer. Paige was in her room trying on her wedding dress for the tenth time since she had gotten it back from the seamstress. It would be her friends' first time seeing it on her.

"Who had the bright idea of getting married outside in September in the south?" Sadie asked. "The mosquitos are going to eat us alive. That is, if we don't melt first."

"Don't forget it's hurricane season too and there are plenty of storms brewing in the Atlantic right now," Faith added.

"I have faith that Mother Nature will look kindly upon us that day," Paige said as she entered the room donning her maternity wedding dress.

The three women let out appreciative gasps as Paige twirled. She looked breathtaking. Her dress was tea-length, covered in delicate lace, a sweetheart neckline, and lace cap sleeves. The white of the dress set off the glow of her summer tan and her pregnancy. The roundness of her small baby bump added to the picture of femininity that was Paige.

"Oh, Paige! Honey! You're so beautiful," Faith squealed with delight.

"It's not too precious looking? I feel like I'm too old to wear this," Paige wondered.

"Of course not. You are pregnant with the cutest little baby bump. You are allowed to be precious," Cora Rae, the expert on weddings, replied insistently.

"Okay, good! Because I love it!" Paige exclaimed happily. "I'm going to go hide this in the back of the closet, so Jake doesn't get a peek at it, and I'll be right back."

Sadie watched as her friend left the kitchen and was humming to herself as she went up the stairs. Sadie was happy for Paige, but it made her current lack of romance more evident. Being in Meadow Oaks, in Paige's house, had her wishing that John was there with her. She could ignore the ache while she was working, or even at home in her condo, but not here where there were so many memories of them spending time together. When she had parked in the driveway upon her arrival, her eyes had started watering at the memory of their first steamy kiss in that very spot. Even as she sat at the kitchen table with her friends, her eyes kept wandering to the front door, waiting for him to come through it with Jake at any second.

"He's not coming," Faith commented.

Sadie briefly considered denying knowing who Faith was talking about, but she knew it would be a waste of time. Faith was tenacious when she wanted to be. Her friends had guessed that something had gone wrong between her and John, but not exactly what. They had let her off the hook so far over the phone, but she knew that they would be expecting the full story since they were all together in person.

"I'm guessing you're waiting for me to tell y'all what happened with John, huh?" Sadie said, never taking her eyes off of the table.

"Yes, but wait until Paige gets back, so you only have to say it once," Faith said, squeezing Sadie's hand until she looked up with a sad smile.

"You know me so well," Sadie sighed.

While they waited for the pregnant bride to come back down the stairs, Faith puttered around Paige's kitchen, at home there as much as in her own kitchen. Cora Rae typed away on her laptop sending one final email to the florist, every few seconds peeking up at Sadie. Faith set down a fresh pitcher of lemonade on the table and began pouring glasses for everyone.

"Making sure my throat doesn't dry up while I tell my tale?" Sadie joked.

"You know me too well," Faith answered, reiterating the bond between them.

Paige practically skipped back into the kitchen, her joyous energy radiating off of her. "Okay, what are we talking about down here?" she asked in a pleasant sing-song voice.

"I was waiting on you to come back down, so I could tell y'all at the same time about what happened with John," Sadie said before Faith could say anything.

"Stole my line," Faith muttered under her breath.

Sadie grinned at her friend. Paige sat down at the table next to Cora Rae and gave Sadie her undivided attention. Sadie took a sip of the lemonade and began her story.

"Y'all know that another woman was attacked while we were at the bar celebrating my birthday, and that John and I were outside and heard her scream and ran to her." When her friends gave nods, she continued, "When the woman woke up in the hospital, the police wanted to talk to her, but it upset her so much that she had to be sedated. Out in the hall, John and I got into an argument about whether or not she should be made to talk to the police. We were both overtired and stressed about what we saw, angry words were said," Sadie looked down, shaking her head.

"John feels terrible, Sadie. He was freaking out on the phone to Jake about it," Paige said.

"I know. He came over the next morning to apologize and to be honest, I was as much to blame for it getting out of hand as he was. He is forgiven, that's not the issue," Sadie stated.

"So, what is the issue? I know by the way you keep glancing at the door and the way John is moping around town that everything isn't exactly worked out," Faith questioned.

Sadie hesitated to try to explain to her friends that she was most certainly struggling with some sort of PTSD after what she had seen done to Paige and Cora Rae, and then Birdie and Leann. The image of Leann being stabbed flashed through her mind and she shuddered. She knew that what she had been through was nothing compared to the trauma Paige and Cora Rae had experienced and felt guilty for her weakness. The therapist she saw Monday had said it was common for empathetic people to compare their trauma to other people's experiences and rate their own lower; therefore, causing guilt about feeling upset, like they had no right to feel that way. The therapist went on to explain that there wasn't a ranking system to trauma and Sadie knew she was right, but her emotions were not getting on board with that way of thinking.

Faith reached over and held Sadie's hand. "You know you can tell us anything, right?"

"Yeah," Cora Rae agreed, "no judgement here."

Sadie cleared the lump in her throat, "It's just that I seem to be having a hard time, emotionally, with everything that has been going on lately. You know, Birdie and the woman I saw stabbed."

"Well, that is completely understandable, hon," Cora Rae said, reassuringly.

"And what else?" Paige asked gently, knowing that her friend had more on her mind.

"I am experiencing PTSD and the feelings I had about what had happened to you two, the feelings I thought I had been dealing so well with, have been exacerbated by these recent attacks. I feel so overwhelmed, and my heart feels like it weighs a thousand pounds." Sadie paused to take a few deep breaths so she could stop the tears she felt pooling in her eyes. Looking to Cora Rae and then to Paige, who both had tears running down their faces, she continued, "I feel guilty because what you two went through was so much worse than anything I can even imagine and here I am, physically unharmed, and I can't deal."

Paige jumped up and came around the table to throw her arms around Sadie's shoulders. "Oh no, sweetie, no! You have nothing to feel guilty about. You've been through so much too. You fight every day to save people's lives and you have every right to feel the way you do. Oh, Sadie! We love you so much. Don't ever think that we wouldn't want to know what you are going through and be there for you," Paige exclaimed.

"Trauma isn't a competition, sweetie," Cora Rae added gently.

"I know, that is what my therapist said. I can't seem to get my heart to listen, though," Sadie replied.

"I'm glad you are talking to someone about it," Faith said, reaching over to squeeze Sadie's hand.

"Yes, well, John insisted when we spoke Sunday, and I knew he was right."

"Care to tell us the rest of what happened with John?" Paige asked as she went to sit back down.

Sadie nodded and continued her story, "When John and I got in our argument, I don't know, it felt like something cracked inside of me. My feelings for him are so strong. I've never felt like this about anybody. You guys already know that. I want to have a future with him. Things got so messed up, and I don't think I can handle a romantic relationship with the ups and downs that go with that and make it work while I feel so bogged down. I explained that to John, he didn't seem to like it, but he respected it. So, we're not over, we're on pause," Sadie said glumly.

"You don't seem so happy about it yourself," Faith commented.

"I miss him," Sadie admitted.

The room grew quiet as the women each contemplated how crazy their lives had been the past few months. The ding of a timer broke up the silence and Faith hopped out her chair.

"Nothing feeds the soul quite like a pot roast. Hope y'all are hungry!"

"Always," Paige replied, rubbing her belly theatrically.

The friends giggled as the mood was lifted a little bit. Paige's pregnancy was a bright ray of sunshine in the gloom that had overtaken Sadie. The child growing inside of Paige, the spark of life that had survived despite Paige's psycho stalker's attempt at snuffing that spark out, was a reminder that good can win and love can endure. Sadie felt a sliver of hope in her chest and her heavy heart felt a little bit lighter.

Chapter Twenty

That same evening, John sat at his desk in the police station staring at his computer screen but not really taking in anything he was looking at. He missed Sadie. It hadn't even been a whole week yet and he was going crazy. They were getting no closer to finding the serial killer. The fact that it was a male and his shoe size was an eleven were all they had so far. It was so damn frustrating. He hadn't struck again since Leann Rivers. It was almost like his failure to complete his task had halted him. John had been speaking with criminal psychologists, trying to get in the guy's head. He wanted to get justice for Birdie Duvall and Leann Rivers, but at the heart of it, he wanted Sadie back in his arms.

His cell phone rang, pulling him out of his wallowing. A picture of his mother lit up the screen. The smile that spread across his face was his first that week and a welcome change to all of the doom and gloom.

"Hey, Mom," he said when he answered the call.

"Bonjour, Cher! Ça va?" she asked in her Cajun French accented voice.

"Just working, Ma," John replied.

"What's wrong my darling? You sound like you've lost your joie de vivre?" she asked, alarmed at her son's tone.

John internally debated how much of the situation to tell his mom about, not wanting to expose her to the uglier parts of his job. She was so happy that he was a small-town cop and not a big city one. He'd have to tell her something though, she knew him too well to try to play it off as nothing.

"Ma, I think I'm in love," he sighed.

"Think?" she asked.

"Know. I know I'm in love," he corrected.

"What is the problem? Does she not return your feelings? I don't know if I'd want my son pining after a woman who doesn't know a perfect man when she sees him," she scoffed.

"I think you are a bit biased, Ma. But to answer your question, yes, she does return my feelings. It's complicated."

"Love is only complicated if you make it complicated, my son," she replied confidently.

Abella Boudreaux Avery considered herself an expert on love and her son knew there would be no arguing with her.

"I know. I just have to wait for her heart to heal and then it will all work out like it should," he explained.

"Is she heartsick over another man?" Abella asked in disbelief. Her son was her stars and her moon, and she would go to her grave believing that he was the best man in the world.

"No, Ma. Sadie is a doctor; a cardiovascular surgeon to be exact. I mentioned her to you before. She is Jake's soon-to-be wife's best friend. She works at MUSC in Charleston and anyways, that's not really the point. To make a long story short, Charleston has a serial killer on the loose and while out celebrating Sadie's birthday this past weekend, her and I witnessed a young woman get stabbed. She helped the victim while I chased the guy. Afterwards, we got in a disagreement about the victim talking with the police. We made up, but Sadie is still processing what her friend Paige went through and on top of that she lost one of the killer's prior victims in surgery and is feeling protective over the young woman we saved. She is heartsick, Ma, but not over a man, over this world we live in."

"Ah! Pauvre bêtes! How horrible for both of you! Why didn't you call me right away? You know me and your Papa would have come!" she exclaimed.

"Y'all didn't need to come here, Ma. I'm fine." John insisted, even though he felt anything but fine. His heart felt so heavy.

"Nonsense! You don't need to be so strong all the time, my son. Let your Mama take care of you every once in a while!"

"That's really not necessary."

"We'll be there tomorrow."

"Ma, really, I'm fine."

"We've been discussing coming to see you soon, so now is the time. I'm going to hang up and book a hotel room right away. I love you, Cher. We'll see you tomorrow."

"I love you too, Ma."

John hung up the phone and let out a small chuckle. His mother was a force of nature. It reminded him of Faith since Jake liked to refer to her as the little blond tornado. Abella Boudreaux Avery could be described as a class five hurricane, without all of the destruction and devastation.

***

Sadie was barely in the door to her condo, returning from her time at Paige's house, when her hospital pager went off. She wasn't on call that evening, so she knew it had to be something with Leann. As she was reaching for her cell to call into the hospital, it rang with Jeff's name flashing on the screen. Sadie turned right around and headed out her door as she answered the call.

"Jeff, what happened?" she asked, skipping the usual pleasantries.

"She coded. It came out of nowhere, Sadie. We've resuscitated her, but we had to put her in a medically induced coma. Sadie, I'm so sorry. I don't know how this could have happened," Jeff said, practically pleading for understanding.

"I'm on my way," Sadie replied and hung up the phone. She ran down two flights of the stairs in her condo building, not bothering to wait for the elevator. She sprinted to her car and sped the few blocks over to the hospital. She was standing next to Leann's hospital bed, reviewing her chart with Jeff, ten minutes later.

"I did rounds at nine p.m. and she was fine. Vitals were great, incision site healing nicely, no infection. Her bloodwork came back normal this afternoon. I was planning on speaking with you about discharging her tomorrow. Her mom was begging to take her home with her to Tennessee and continue outpatient treatment there," Jeff explained in a quiet voice.

Sadie looked over to where Leann's mom was sleeping. She had pulled the chair as close as she could to Leann's bedside and her head was resting on the bed, her hand on top of her daughter's. Sadie had spoken with Leann's mom multiple times. Each time the woman hugged her over and over, thanking Sadie for saving her daughter. Sadie felt like she was failing her.

"Was her mom here when she coded?" Sadie questioned.

"No, she had gone outside to call Leann's dad. They are divorced and he is stationed in Alaska at Fort Greely. They are four hours behind us there, so that is about the time he gets home. She said Leann was sleeping and breathing normally when she stepped out. She lost it when she came back in and couldn't see Leann while we worked on her. The guilt she felt for going outside to make a phone call was written all over her face. Poor woman," Jeff lamented.

"Have we drawn more blood since she coded?" Sadie asked, flipping to the orders sheet.

"Yes. She coded at ten-seventeen p.m., and it took about eight minutes to revive her. I ordered every test under the sun to try to figure out what could have caused this. That was about an hour ago, so results should start showing up in the system soon. I have the residents keeping an eye out," Jeff said.

"Who is on tonight?" Sadie asked out of curiosity.

"Dr. Wu, Dr. Madison, and Dr. Pope. Dr. Jones comes back on rotation at six a.m."

"Okay, good. We'll have extra hands if we need to go back in and operate. I'm hoping that isn't the case." Sadie looked over at Leann and hoped to the Good Lord above that she would be okay.

"I want to know as soon as those results start coming in," Sadie whispered to Jeff before walking out of the room to go in search of some clean scrubs.

Chapter Twenty-One

An hour later and most of the blood tests results were in and everything was coming back normal. Sadie was baffled. They were waiting on a few more random tests to finish up, but she didn't think those results would tell her anything either.

Sadie looked over Leann as she slept and noticed a sheen of sweat on Leann's forehead and upper lip. Glancing up at the monitors, she noted that Leann was still experiencing tachycardia. She went through the medical encyclopedia that was her brain searching for an answer. Hell, even a tiny clue to lead her in the right direction of figuring out what had happened to her patient would be a blessing.

"How is she?" Jeff whispered upon entering the room. He walked over to stand next to Sadie to examine Leann with her.

"She's sweating and tachycardic. All of the blood tests so far came back normal," Sadie murmured, still lost in thought. Pages of medical texts flipped through her mind, she knew the answer was right in her reach and she was angry that it eluded her.

Jeff began to pace, his mind also working. He made his way to the cart with the laptop and looked over the blood tests he'd ordered. "CBC normal, no sign of infection, potassium levels normal, bicarbonate levels normal, magnesium..." he paused as Sadie's head shot up to look at him with wide eyes.

"Please tell me you ordered an insulin to c-peptide test! I know it's random, but it might have our clue," Sadie exclaimed urgently.

"I told you, I ordered everything under the sun," he said as he scrolled through the chart. "Yes! It's one of the ones we are still waiting on the official report, but the preliminary numbers show an abnormality."

"Jeff, I could kiss you!" Sadie shouted.

Sadie watched in amusement as a blush crept across his face. Jeff cleared his throat and said, "Yes, well I had no clue what had caused her to code, so I was covering all possibilities."

Together they looked over the preliminary numbers on the test results. "Her c-peptide levels came back above normal limits," Jeff said, pointing to the screen.

"Insulin poisoning? That's the only explanation since she doesn't have diabetes," Sadie commented.

"So, someone waited for her mom to leave the room, came in and injected insulin in her IV? Sadie, that's crazy," Jeff replied.

"We are so lucky we didn't lose her, not knowing about this," Sadie said.

"Maybe they got interrupted when dosing her, or maybe there was some sort of mistake?" he debated.

"She's on a morphine drip and we were weaning her off of it, and her antibiotics are in a bag, so nothing was ordered to be injected into the IV line. Jeff, someone tried to kill her. Think about it, that test would not normally be ordered, it was lucky you even thought of it in that situation. Whoever it was almost got away with murder," Sadie explained.

"I'll call security right away and have them contact Charleston P.D.," Jeff moved to the phone next to the patient's bed.

"She needs to be moved to a more secure room asap," Sadie added.

They got to work making arrangements to transfer Leann to another room and calling in the police. They woke up Leann's mom and filled her in on what they had figured out. A half hour later Detectives Jenkins and Fuller walked into the hospital and into Leann's room. It was obvious by the bags under their eyes that they had been pulled from bed, but the detectives were used to being called in the wee hours of the night. Sadie had not left Leann's side since discovering someone had tried to kill her, again. The overnight staff was still working on getting a secure room ready for her, so Sadie was standing guard. She explained to the detectives what she believed was going on. Detective Jenkins took notes and asked questions while Detective Fuller looked around the room.

Jeff entered the room and shook hands with the detectives. "Her new room will be ready in ten minutes," Jeff told Sadie when he was done with the greetings.

He looked over to the hospital bed. Leann had slept through all of the commotion.

"May I see the room she is going to be moved to?" Detective Fuller asked. "We will have an officer outside of the door, but I want to make sure the inside will be secure, check windows, that kind of thing."

"Of course, I'll take you up," Jeff replied. "The door has a keyless entry lock on it. Only necessary staff will have the code."

Sadie nodded a thank you to Jeff as he led the female detective from the room. She zoned out, lost in her thoughts when Detective Jenkins came to stand beside her, shoulder to shoulder.

"She looks so small in that hospital bed," he said. "There is a place in Hell waiting for the person responsible for harming her."

"I'm dreading having to tell her when she wakes up that someone tried to take her life again. I had promised her that she was safe here. I've failed her," Sadie said, her voice like steel, hard and unbending. She was never going to forgive herself for not having Leann in a secured room from the get-go.

"Cut yourself some slack, Doc," Detective Jenkins said. "Who could have guessed he'd have the balls to try something in a hospital with cameras everywhere, security guards, police officers in and out all the time."

Sadie didn't say anything. She stood there quietly, watching Leann's blanket move up and down with her breathing.

"Is her mother in the waiting room?" Detective Jenkins asked.

"Uh no, take a right out of here and through the double doors. We put her in a counseling room, third door on the left," Sadie directed.

The burly detective patted Sadie on the shoulder and went to speak with Leann's mother. Left alone, the first thought that crossed Sadie's mind was that she wanted to call John. Not only to tell him what had happened to Leann for investigative purposes, but for comfort. She yearned to have his strong arms wrapped around her, warming her, keeping her grounded. She had never been that type of woman, to need or desire comfort from a man, but she couldn't deny feeling that way at that moment.

Using her surgical training and her natural gift for compartmentalization, she pushed the feelings to the back burner and focused on the matter at hand. With security being beefed up around Leann, she felt a tad better but still could not make herself leave her patient's side. Not yet. She also knew that there would be no sleeping in her own bed for a while; good thing there was an on-call room on the floor Leann was being moved to.

Dr. Wu and Dr. Madison poked their heads in the room.

"What's going on Dr. Jennings? Do you need our help?" Dr. Wu asked eagerly.

"Miss Rivers will be changing rooms. I have it handled. Please see to our other patients." Sadie rattled off patients' names that needed their surgical sites checked and bloodwork followed up on. Without having any inkling as to who tried to kill Leann, she wasn't taking any chances, not even with her own residents. Sadie learned from Paige's ordeal that you never know what the people around you are capable of.

Chapter Twenty-Two

A few days later, on a sunny Saturday morning, Paige and Faith went to the hospital to check on Sadie, knowing their friend hadn't left the hospital since her patient was poisoned. John was being kept in the loop by the Charleston Police Department, so he was aware of what had happened to Miss Rivers. He had passed that information onto Faith on one of his morning runs so that she could be there for Sadie since he couldn't. Faith had heard the unmistakable heartache in his voice as he told the tale.

The women found Sadie at the nurse's station directly across from a patient room with an officer stationed outside the door. Faith assumed that it must be the girl who had beat death twice within a short amount of time in the room under guard. Sadie looked like she hadn't slept for days and was sipping coffee from a mug that said, "If you steal someone's heart, do you get cardiac arrested?"

"You are such a dork," Faith teased as she walked up to the counter, breaking Sadie out of the tired trance she had been in.

"Huh?" Sadie asked, still kind of out of it.

"Your mug," Faith replied.

Sadie looked down at her mug, not having the slightest clue what was on it. "Oh," she chuckled, "it was a present from one of the nurses during Secret Santa last year."

"Cute," Paige said. "How are you doing, Sadie?"

"Hanging in there," she answered.

"When was the last time you got some sleep? Or left this hospital?" Faith asked, hand on her poked-out hip.

"I can't leave," Sadie quipped.

"Yes, you can," Faith retorted.

"And you should," Paige added. "You won't be any good to anyone if you burn out."

Before Sadie could open her mouth to disagree, Dr. Richards, looking distinguished in his Chief of Surgery white coat, walked in on their conversation and proceeded to add his two cents. "Dr. Jennings, I agree with your friends. You need a break from this hospital. Actually, I insist on it since you worked on your scheduled days off," he said in an authoritative tone.

Paige and Faith smiled in victory as Sadie gave them the side-eye.

"You know what, we will take her home right now and personally make sure that she gets some sleep," Faith chirped, smiling at Sadie's boss.

"That would be much appreciated, ladies," he replied charmingly. "Dr. Jennings," he began, turning to face her, "I will be here at the hospital, along with Dr. Montgomery until you return on Monday. We won't let anything happen to your patient. You have my word," he vowed.

Sadie looked into his eyes and saw that he meant every word. She knew they would protect Leann as best they could. She would have to be okay with that. Her friends weren't wrong that she needed rest and a break from the fluorescent lights and the hospital smell. She nodded her assent to her chief and pushed herself slowly out of the chair. With one friend on each side of her, she went to her office to get her personal belongings and walked out of the hospital doors for the first time in days.

When Faith and Paige had told her boss that they would make sure she went home and got some rest, Sadie hadn't realized that they were being literal. She had wrongly assumed that they would walk her to the parking lot where she would get in her car and drive herself home. Nope, they had other plans. They had carpooled from Meadow Oaks, so Sadie sat in her passenger seat while Faith chauffeured her home and Paige followed behind. Her friends then proceeded to follow her up to her condo, where they came in and made themselves at home.

"Not that you two aren't welcome here, but I didn't expect you to actually tuck me in when you promised my boss to make sure I got some rest," Sadie stated as she closed her door when she realized they weren't leaving anytime soon.

"Well, we have something we need to talk to you about. I'm just going to make you some chamomile tea first," Paige answered.

Sadie worried that they were going to try to have some sort of intervention about how obsessive she had become over protecting Leann. She started lining up her arguments in her head, but then Faith broke her concentration.

"You don't need to look so flustered, Sadie. It's about something potentially fun. You need some fun. We all do," Faith said.

Sadie had been unaware that she had tensed up so much that her shoulders were up by her ears until she let out a deep breath at Faith's words and her whole body relaxed.

"Sorry guys, I feel like I'm always on the defensive lately. I can't seem to compartmentalize on this one," she explained.

"No need to apologize, sweetie. You have been through some serious shit," Paige stated as she came back into the living room. She handed a hot mug of tea over to Sadie and they all took a seat on the living room furniture that only got used when they came over.

Faith shifted her butt around on the couch cushion, "You know, I think I just about have my spot broken in over here," she joked. The ladies laughed at her childlike silliness and Sadie felt lighter.

"I always feel so much better around you two. When I'm at the hospital I get so caught up in the tension. I used to be better about finding balance, but lately I can't seem to get my bearings. Does that make any sense?" Sadie asked.

"Of course it does, Sadie," Faith replied. "We are here to help you get some balance with some good ol' Meadow Oaks fun."

"Oh yeah? What kind of small-town trouble are you planning?"

Faith and Paige exchanged a knowing look. "You tell her, Paige. She won't say no to the pregnant lady."

Paige shrugged and squared her shoulders towards Sadie. "John's parents are in town and we were all invited to a show at Frankie's Jazz Club with them tonight."

Sadie was on the verge of telling them no way was she going to meet John's parents while they were on a break and was already shaking her head no when Faith bounced in her seat, begging her to come.

"Come on, Sadie! You can't miss this. John's mom was a famous jazz singer in New Orleans before she had John and still sings from time to time when people beg her. She was that good! Please! Please! Please!"

"And it's kind of a pre-wedding celebration for me and Jake. So, you kind of have to come because you are one of my bridesmaids," Paige added.

"Not to mention, the weatherman is predicting that Tropical Storm Ivey will be a full-blown hurricane by next weekend and Paige's wedding might get rained out," Faith exclaimed. Paige nodded her head vigorously in agreement.

"This is entrapment," Sadie half-heartedly argued.

"This is two friends getting their best friend out of the funk she is in. You would do the same for us," Paige insisted. It was Faith's turn to nod her head up and down vigorously in agreement.

"Fine. I'll go," Sadie reluctantly agreed.

"Yay! Now go get some sleep and I expect you at Paige's house at seven sharp, dolled up and ready to celebrate the union of two people getting their second chance at love. Okay?" Faith insisted.

"How am I supposed to sleep when my mind is racing about meeting John's parents tonight?" Sadie asked incredulously. "Not to mention that John and I are on a break from each other!"

"Like I tell the kids at the daycare at nap time, lay your head on the pillow, snuggle in your blankie, close your eyes, take deep breaths, and think happy thoughts until you fall asleep," Faith answered. "And you and John are both miserable without each other.

Sadie thought that Faith's solution to falling asleep was easier said than done but wasn't about to argue. If she was seeing John later, she needed to not look like a zombie, so she would try to sleep. After her friends left, she rinsed out her mug in the sink and made her way to her shower. She stood under the hot spray, letting it massage her tired body. She toweled off and didn't bother with clothes; she climbed into her bed and followed Faith's directions.

As she closed her eyes, John came to her mind. She was nervous about seeing him, but also hopeful. The ache in her heart reiterated what her brain already knew, she missed him. Her thoughts played through what might happen when they saw each other at the jazz club later. Would he take her hand in his when they greeted each other? Or maybe a hug? Would he touch her at all? She hoped he did. Her skin was crying out to feel his. She wanted to hear his voice, to smell him. She hoped his feelings for her hadn't faded. Her heart would break if they had. Hers had only gotten stronger.

Chapter Twenty-Three

When John stepped into Frankie's Jazz Club with his parents in tow, he couldn't stop himself from looking around to see if Sadie was already there. A quick sweep of the tables in the dimly lit space told him that they were the first to arrive from their group.

The owner, Frankie, greeted them at the door with a huge smile. The man was always there. He had a small apartment above the club. He lived and breathed for jazz music. His passion was contagious and probably the only reason his club was able to survive in such a small town. People came over from Charleston to visit his place. The authentic vibe so much more alluring than the generic copycats in the bigger city.

"Abella! So good to see you again, darling. It's been too long since you graced us with your exquisite presence," Frankie cooed to John's mom. Abella held out her hand regally and Frankie placed a chaste kiss on the back of it. He turned and flashed John and his dad warm smiles. "I'm glad to see that you got our Officer John here to take a night off. He works so hard for our little town."

"Yes, my son is a good man, is he not?" she replied proudly.

"He is indeed. Is it the three of you tonight or are we expecting more to join your party?" he asked, always the ideal host.

"My friends are joining us, nine of us total," John answered after quickly doing the math in his head.

They followed Frankie to a big round table off to the side of the small dance floor. Most people enjoyed the music from their seats, but there were always a few couples who would get swept up by the romance of the slower jazz songs, moving them to get up to dance cheek to cheek. An off-white linen tablecloth covered the table and a group of small flaming tea lights in the middle provided a warm glow. The Meadow Oaks Fire Department chief had begged Frankie to switch to candles with an artificial flame, but he insisted that a real flame, even a small one, added a special ambience to his club.

Once they were settled, Frankie left to attend to his other guests. John absentmindedly tugged at the collar of his button-up shirt, feeling restless. His mom placed her hand over his as it gripped his shirt and gently squeezed. He stopped fidgeting and looked over at her. Both of his parents were giving him knowing looks. Earlier, when Jake had texted him that the girls had convinced Sadie to come, he had stared at his phone so long that it caught his mom's attention; she knew it had something to do with Sadie and asked for an update on their courtship, as she put it. He told his parents how much he missed her, how nervous and excited he was to see her again. He told them that he loved her. There was no point in holding back to his parents, they knew him too well. Plus, his parents had always been open about their love for one another. Their happy ending was hard-earned, and they never took it for granted. They had a love story for the ages. He wanted that with Sadie desperately.

John stopped messing with his shirt and took a deep breath. He looked to the spotlit stage to watch the musicians as they strummed their instruments. A man in a blue suit crooned away at the microphone, his voice soulful and deep. He let himself get lost in the music so he wouldn't turn around and watch the entrance. After a minute, he started to sway along to the music, finding a bit of peace for the first time since the night of Sadie's birthday. The feeling was brief.

A few moments later, a movement caught his attention out of the corner of his eye, and he looked over to see Jake and Travis shaking hands with his dad. His chest tightened as Faith, Paige, and Cora Rae passed by him to take their seats. Their mouths were moving, but he didn't hear what they were saying. He held his breath as he waited for Sadie to appear. He would not turn around to make sure she actually came. He couldn't let himself be that vulnerable, because if she wasn't there, if she had backed out, there would be no hiding his disappointment.

He was put out of his misery not a moment too soon. As soon as he caught a glimpse of her, he was out of his seat, pulling the chair on his left out for her to sit. It was an unconscious act, his body moving of its own accord, craving to be near her. He could almost swear his heart stopped beating as she hesitated, luckily it was only for a second before she whispered, "Thank you," and began to sit down in the offered chair. He gently eased the chair in to meet the back of her knees and returned to his seat, never taking his eyes off of her. She looked tired and beautiful. It was the first time he had seen her since she'd asked for space. It had only been a week, but to him it had felt like a lifetime. There were many times he'd had to stop himself from going to the hospital to check on her. Especially when he had heard that another attempt had been made on Miss Rivers' life.

She held his gaze, which was promising, so he bravely swallowed his nerves and spoke, "Hi."

"Hi," she answered.

Having gotten over the first big hurdle, he decided to brave another one. He placed his hand on the table towards her, palm up. She tentatively placed her hand in his. At the contact, the room went quiet and everything else faded away for him. She had his undivided attention. The feeling of peace he had earlier while getting lost in the music came back and all felt right in the world. He ran his thumb over her soft skin, and she closed her eyes and took a deep breath. When she opened her eyes, they shimmered with unshed tears, but the look of utter relief in them told him they were happy tears. He knew exactly how she felt. Before they could get too lost in each other, his mom interrupted.

"Aren't you going to introduce us, *mon cherie*?" Abella asked.

John reluctantly looked away from Sadie to smile at his mom who was sitting on his other side. "Ma, this is Dr. Sadie Jennings." He looked back to Sadie, "Sadie, this is my mom, Abella Boudreaux Avery."

"Pleasure to meet you, Mrs. Avery," Sadie said cordially.

"Please, dear, call me Abella," his mom insisted enthusiastically.

John smiled as the two most important women to him greeted each other warmly. A not-so-subtle throat clearing had him chuckling and nodding his head towards his dad. "And that handsome devil over there is my dad."

"Sebastian Thomas Avery, but you can call me Bash. It's nice to finally meet you," his dad said with a sly wink.

"Watch out for him," John joked, "he is a charmer."

Sadie laughed good-naturedly and with the first impressions out of the way, the group ordered drinks, listened to the music, and enjoyed good conversation in between songs.

"Abella, tell us the story about how you and Bash fell in love. It's such a romantic story and I don't think Sadie or Cora Rae have heard it," Faith urged during one of the breaks.

"*Oui*, of course! I will never say no to telling our story!" Abella exclaimed. "I'm a real-life Louisiana Cinderella, you know!" she said looking from Cora Rae to Sadie. "I was born in a wooden shack out on the bayou. My *papere* had rebuilt it with his own hands after a hurricane before I came along and it was nicer than most out there, which isn't saying much. My *maman* was musical like me. She taught white children in the big houses how to play the piano. When they realized I had a unique singing voice, *maman* taught me the notes and how to read music. They encouraged me to sing as often as possible and eventually I ended up singing in a New Orleans night club when I turned eighteen. That is where I met my Bash," she paused to smile lovingly at her husband.

"He came in with his rowdy friends one night. I recognized him from the papers, son of the wealthy sugar tycoon, Mr. Jeremiah Avery. *Maman* had taught his sister to play piano. His friends were so rude, hooting and hollering while I sang my songs, but not Bash. He stared and stared at me while I was on stage."

"Most beautiful girl I had ever seen with the voice of an angel," Bash said, leaning over to kiss his wife's cheek.

Abella looked down demurely and smiled before continuing her story. "He waited for me outside of the club, which these days might get someone tasered, but he wasn't aggressive. He was very earnest and sweet. He asked if he could call on me sometime. I told him that I didn't live in the city and only came there to sing. He said he would go anywhere I was, just to talk to me. The first time he came to see me in the bayou, this city boy got his boat stuck in the hyacinth! He's lucky the *cocodril* didn't get him!" she joked.

Her face grew serious, and she held onto her husband's hand. "He came out to visit me as often as he could. We would walk on the dock and talk about our future. He would help my *papere* repair what needed fixing and he would lift heavy things for my *maman*. They grew to love him as much as I did, but they warned us that our love would not be easily accepted by others. They were right. His parents caught wind of our relationship, and all hell broke loose. It was not only the color of my skin that they objected to, but also my lack of money and my profession as a club singer. Never mind that everyone else in the city revered me for my voice, to them I might as well have been a harlot. I was sure he would leave me and end up with someone they deemed more suitable. He didn't. Bash showed up in the bayou with a suitcase and a diamond ring. He got a job here in South Carolina, so we moved and I sang when I could in clubs in Charleston. We had John a few years later and raised him in Meadow Oaks in the home he lives in now. When he became an adult, we started to travel and fell in love with Savannah and made it our home base. We've been living our happily ever after."

Abella and Bash shared a deep kiss and when they finally separated, Abella said, "See? I really am Cinderella!"

The whole table clapped and a few wiped away tears. John had been holding Sadie's hand under the table, and he squeezed it, wanting to be closer to her. He was about to ask her to step outside with him so they could have a moment alone, when Frankie took the stage.

"Ladies and gentlemen! We have a special guest with us tonight. The renowned jazz singer, Abella Boudreaux, is in the audience tonight. I bet with the right encouragement we might be able to tempt her to sing us a song!" Frankie exclaimed.

The crowd burst out into applause.

John's mom looked to be shocked, but John knew she was absolutely delighted. She gracefully made her way to the stage and embraced Frankie in a friendly hug. She took a moment to speak with the band and made her way to the microphone.

"I have asked the band to play a song that is very special to me. I hope that my son will take this opportunity to ask his beautiful lady friend to dance," she said, grinning at John slyly.

John shook his head at his mom for her less than subtle maneuvering and smiled at the realization that he was about to hold Sadie in his arms. Well, if she said yes. He stood up and held out his hand to her. She took it with no hesitation and let him lead her to the dance floor. They held each other close, dancing cheek to cheek as Abella sang a romantic ballad. Other couples joined them on the dance floor, but as far as John was concerned, the only person there was Sadie. The feel of her body under her silky dress, the delicate scent of her neck, and the beat of his heart was all he knew in that moment.

Chapter Twenty-Four

The following Saturday was the day of Paige and Jake's wedding, and Hurricane Ivey was on her way up the East Coast. According to the weatherman on T.V., they would have just enough time to get the ceremony in and maybe a bit of the reception before having to hunker down. It was the calm before the storm and Paige was going to get her big day.

They hadn't done the whole bachelor and bachelorette party thing; the night at the jazz club had served as their big night out. The men were all over at John's house getting ready, while the women had taken over Paige's place. The ceremony was to be held in the evening, so the women had all day to spend together and get ready. The bridesmaids, the mother of the bride, and the mother of the groom sipped mimosas while Chloe had plain orange juice. Paige drank ginger ale; she didn't want to risk being nauseous on her special day.

Sadie tried to focus her attention on the bride, but her mind kept wandering. Leann was going to be released from the hospital on Tuesday and Sadie was worried that without the police protection she was getting at the hospital Leann would be in danger again. Leann's mother was planning to take her home with her to Pigeon Forge, Tennessee, and Sadie hoped that was far enough away to keep her safe.

"How are you doing, Sadie? Need a refill?" Paige's mom, Sherry, asked lifting the pitcher of mimosa up.

"Oh, yes, please," Sadie answered, her attention returning to the present.

"Something on your mind, dear?" Sherry inquired as she topped off Sadie's champagne flute.

"I bet I know what's on her mind," Faith teased from across the room.

"Me too!" Cora Rae added. "He's handsome, kind, smart, has a smoking hot body, and looks at Sadie like she is the most wonderful woman in the whole wide world," she cooed.

Sadie rolled her eyes but couldn't hold back her smile when Sherry beamed at her. "Paige mentioned that sparks seemed to be flying again between you and John the other night when she came by to pick up the kids. Could this mean you guys are officially together now?" she asked.

"Yes, do tell, Sadie. We are all dying to know!" Paige exclaimed.

"Nothing else has happened since the jazz club. I slept all day Sunday and was back at work Monday. There have been some texts, so it's not radio silence anymore. Baby steps," Sadie said.

"Hmm...maybe that will change after the wedding tonight. Romance will be in the air. Jake and Paige are so lovey-dovey it's enough to make anyone want to puke," Faith joked.

Paige threw an empty orange juice bottle at Faith as everyone had a good laugh.

Sadie wasn't sure if she was ready to get into a full-blown relationship with John quite yet. She was still dealing with all her feelings from the ordeal with Leann. The man John chased the night Leann was attacked had still not been caught. There weren't even any leads. Somehow the cameras at the hospital had gone on the fritz the day Leann was poisoned. The argument she had with John over the police talking to Leann was a non-issue since Leann herself had opened up about what had happened to her after bravely deciding she needed to face her fears.

Sadie still didn't feel settled though. Therapy had helped some and she continued to go once a week. If she was honest with herself, she had to admit that she was scared; not that John wasn't the right guy for her, she knew he was. She was worried that if she jumped back in too soon that she would screw it up somehow.

Maybe she would start an argument over something stupid. Maybe overwork herself like she had been lately, and he would get tired of waiting around for her. She needed more time.

"Did Cora Rae tell y'all she has a date for tonight?" Paige asked the room, bringing Sadie out of her daydreaming, again.

Everyone turned to Cora Rae with expectant faces as Paige walked over and put her arm around their friend.

"Who?" Faith asked.

"Well, I tried to set her up with Mason as her date tonight," Paige began, "but sneaky Miss Cora Rae here had already asked Dr. Patel!"

Sadie started at the news. "What? When did y'all become a thing?" Sadie asked, excitedly.

Cora Rae looked shyly down at the ground but then let out a huff and straightened her shoulders. "If this last year has taught me anything it's that life can be short and tomorrow isn't promised. So, when I couldn't get him off my mind after the one appointment I had with him and seeing him at your birthday, I went to the hospital on my lunch break one day. Luckily, he was available to talk for a minute, and I gave him my number," she explained. "We've been talking on the phone a lot, meeting for lunch often, and been out to dinner twice."

"Good for you, Cora Rae!" Sadie exclaimed. She was super impressed by Cora Rae's boldness. "You deserve someone amazing, Cora Rae, and I think Dr. Patel is great," she said earnestly. "Man! I wish I had known, I would have been...I don't know, maybe tried to talk to him more since he is dating one of my best friends."

"We just made it official, like you know, had the talk. We are exclusive, not that I wasn't the whole time. Turned out he was only seeing me too. He makes me so happy," Cora Rae gushed.

Everyone simultaneously converged on Cora Rae, wrapping her up in a bear hug and telling her how thrilled they were for her. She had been through stuff most people only see in horror movies and here she was, finding love. It gave Sadie a boost of hope that everything was going to work out.

The hairdressers and makeup artists started showing up in the afternoon to get everyone ready. At six p.m., the women slipped into their dresses, the bridesmaids wearing a dusty rose color, each in a different style of dress that was flattering to their individual body types. The mothers wore shimmering silverish grey dresses, and of course the bride glowed in her ivory maternity dress. The flower girl was the five-year-old daughter of Paige's cousin. The little girl had wanted a princess dress, so Paige had gotten her an ivory ball gown style dress. It was adorable.

The ceremony was to start at seven p.m., right around sunset, at a park not too far from Paige and Jake's home. There was a section of tall, old oak trees that formed a sort of walkway that had come to be known locally as The Bridal Walk. The waterway ran alongside it, turning it into one of the most beautiful views nature had to offer. There was a wrought iron fence running alongside the water to keep any nosy gators out, but it didn't take away from the ambience.

The tricky part about The Bridal Walk was walking along the grass in high heels. Some people were able to do it without a problem, but Paige hadn't wanted to risk anyone tripping or twisting an ankle, so the groomsmen were escorting the bridesmaids down the aisle instead of waiting at the altar with the groom. They lined up with their escorts; Sadie was paired with John. With her heels on, Sadie was a couple inches taller than him.

"You look absolutely gorgeous," John whispered to her.

"Looking pretty good there yourself," she whispered back.

She looped her arm in his and waited for their turn to walk down the aisle. She could feel his warmth and the outline of his muscles through his navy-blue suit. His tie matched her dress, and it felt like they were a couple. They fit together like two pieces of a puzzle.

When the music began to play Cora Rae went first, escorted by Jake's dad who was one of his groomsmen. From her spot in line, Sadie noticed Dr. Patel in the second to last row smiling brightly at Cora Rae as she walked past him. She waved her flowers at him as she went by, her other arm holding on to Jake's dad to keep herself steady.

After Cora Rae had made it most of the way down, Faith and Travis began to follow. As a couple that had been together many years, their walk was perfectly in-sync. Faith was fully confident in her high heels, holding on to Travis while she waved at everyone, knowing Travis would never let her fall.

"Ready?" John asked when it was their turn to start walking. "I got you," he whispered when Sadie squeezed his arm and squared her shoulders, raising her bouquet in front of her chest.

"I know you do," she whispered back, and they took their first steps down the aisle towards the altar where Jake was waiting. They waved at people they knew in the crowd as they made their way to take their places.

Sadie reluctantly let go of John and took her place next to Faith and turned to watch the maid of honor make her way down with the best man. Chloe and Caleb looked so happy walking arm in arm towards where Caleb's dad was standing. Jake took a step forward when they approached and pulled Chloe into a big hug. She had happy tears in her eyes. Sadie heard Jake whisper to Chloe that he loved her, and she said, "I love you too, Dad." Sadie had to wipe a tear off of her cheek and she could hear Faith and Cora Rae sniffling beside her.

Caleb took his place next to his dad, and everyone watched as Henry came down holding a tiny white pillow with the rings on it, his navy-blue suit matching Jake's and he was grinning from ear to ear. The flower girl in her poofy ball gown walked next to him, tossing pink flower petals with a flourish. Everyone "Oohed" and "Aahed" over how cute they both were.

When the wedding party was assembled at the altar, the music went quiet and a violinist that was sitting off to the side, picked up her bow and started to play. As the bow slid gracefully across the strings, the notes of John Legend's "All of Me" flowed through the air.

Paige appeared and everyone stood. She looked gorgeous! The dress hugged her curves in all the right places and flowed prettily at the bottom. Her hair was styled like a classic movie star, big waves and curls framing her face. She was glowing and her smile made it clear that she was over the moon with joy.

Sadie heard Jake's sharp intake of breath as he saw her, and she looked over to observe his face at seeing his bride in all her glory. His hand was on his heart and his eyes were watering. Caleb reached over and put a hand on his dad's shoulder and squeezed. He whispered something that Sadie couldn't hear, and Jake smiled.

Paige's dad was holding on to her with two hands, guiding her down the aisle. His face was stoic as usual, but Sadie could tell he was clenching his jaw extra hard, trying to hold back tears. Sadie loved the family so much and she felt like she was watching a sister find her happy ending.

Her head turned back towards Jake, but John caught her eye instead. He was watching her, the intense look in his eyes made her heart do a flip. The yearning and love he felt for her written all over his face.

With the sun setting over the horizon, Sadie watched Paige finally marry Jake.

"I, Jake William Bennett, take you, Paige Hawkins Collins, to be my lawfully wedded wife. I promise to love and cherish you and our children for the rest of my days. I promise to rub your feet when you get home from work and to bring you snacks when you're feeling hangry," Jake vowed.

Sadie giggled along with the rest of the crowd and listened intently as Jake continued to describe the epic love he felt for Paige and his anticipation for a future full of family and happy times.

When it was Paige's turn to say her vows, Sadie braced herself for seeing her friend cry happy tears while she declared herself in front of all their friends and family.

"I, Paige Hawkins Collins, take you, Jake William Bennett, to be my lawfully wedded husband. I promise to never take our love for granted and live everyday as a special one. I promise to not nag you about muddy boots on the floor and dirty fish hooks in my sink," Paige promised.

Another round of chuckles went through the crowd and a couple of moments later the pastor said proudly, "I now pronounce you man and wife, you may kiss your bride."

While Paige and Jake shared their first kiss as husband and wife, Sadie's heart raced in anticipation for what would come after the wedding for her and John.

Chapter Twenty-Five

As the night began to darken, the bulb lights strung in the trees illuminated and added a bit of magic to an already special night. The clouds in the sky churned, warning of the storm that was making its approach, but the wedding party paid no attention. Paige and Jake were dancing under the lights, cheek to cheek even though the song playing wasn't a slow one. The cake had been cut and Henry dragged Caleb over to claim a piece. Faith, Sadie, and Chloe danced happily together. Cora Rae stood under an oak tree with Dr. Patel, the first blooms of love in their whispers and smiles.

John stood along the fence lining the waterway and watched Sadie swaying to the music. The way she moved captivated him, but it was her carefree smile that had him smiling as well. It felt like it had been a long time since he'd seen her truly happy.

"They look like they are having a great time out there," Travis said as he walked up to John, holding out a beer.

John took the offered beer bottle and clinked his with the one Travis had gotten for himself.

"Thanks, man. Yeah, the ladies are definitely partying over there. Good for them," John answered.

The two men sipped their beers in silence for a few minutes, until John decided to ask Travis a personal question, something he didn't often do. "Can I ask you something?"

"I thought I saw those wheels turning. Shoot," Travis replied.

"How did you know Faith was the one?" John wondered.

"She told me," Travis answered without hesitation.

Both men laughed. "Sounds about right," John chuckled.

"Nah, it was the fact that I couldn't get her off my mind. Anytime something happened, good or bad, she was the first one I thought of to share it with. It's still that way. She's my best friend, my lover, my partner. We've been through some tough stuff, and we've made it to the other side every time. I couldn't imagine doing life with anyone else," Travis explained.

"I see," John said simply.

Travis did not push for more than that, it was one of the things John liked most about him. It didn't take a mind reader to know that John was thinking of Sadie and the path of their relationship. What Travis said about Faith resonated with how he felt about Sadie. She was constantly in his thoughts, and she was who he wanted to call whenever there was anything he wanted or needed to share. He wanted to know how her days were. He already considered her one of his best friends and he felt like everything they had been through was bringing them closer together. They weren't lovers yet, but as he watched her body move on the dance floor, the ever-present longing for that to change grew more insistent. He wanted her so badly it was a physical ache.

The fast-paced dance tune ended, and a slow song took its place. Faith made a beeline for Travis and pulled him off of the sidelines and onto the dance floor. They wrapped their arms around one another and held each other close. Travis whispered something in Faith's ear that made her blush and giggle. John was happy for them and a little jealous. He wanted what they had.

He looked around to find where Sadie had wandered off to and found her standing by the refreshment tables looking straight at him. He didn't hesitate; he walked toward her with every intention of getting his arms around her. As he passed by an empty high-top table, he set his beer bottle down so he would have both hands free to touch her. Sadie began making her way to him as well, both maintaining eye contact the entire way. As they came together amid the other couples, her arms went around his neck as his encircled her waist, bringing their bodies flush against one another.

"You looked so good dancing, I couldn't take my eyes off of you," he whispered in Sadie's ear.

"Oh yeah? Why didn't you come join us?" she challenged.

"I was enjoying the view," he replied.

"Hmmm," Sadie murmured. "And now?" she asked.

"Now I'm thinking I'm going to have to thank Paige for picking out this silky feeling dress for you to wear," he answered as he rubbed his hand across the smooth fabric covering her lower back.

Sadie's breath caught has he rubbed the tip of his nose along her neck to the bottom of her ear. Then he began to place little kisses along her neck and jaw as their bodies swayed slowly together to the music.

"Come home with me tonight," he said between kisses.

Before Sadie could answer, thunder boomed in the distance, indicating that their time was up. The storm had made its way to them.

"Alright folks!" Jake yelled, "That's our cue. For those of you who have a longer drive home, please head home now so I don't have to feel guilty for keeping you out in a hurricane. Those of you that are local and are able, if you'll help get the refreshments and the remainder of the cake in Paige's parents' car. The rental company is already on stand-by to get the tables and chairs."

Everyone quickly dispersed, some heading for their cars after congratulating the happy couple one last time, while others started packing up the drinks, food, and cake. Sadie and Faith quickly loaded gifts into Jake's truck. John helped Travis carry coolers that were heavy with drinks and ice over to the back of Paige's parents' SUV.

When everything was packed up and he had made sure Chloe and Henry were buckled up to go spend the night with their grandparents, John went to say goodbye to his newly married friends.

"Great wedding guys!" he cheered as he shook hands with Jake.

Pulling Paige in for a hug, he made sure to compliment her choice of bridesmaid dresses.

"They got to pick out their own, but I get what you're saying," Paige laughed.

Sadie joined them by Jake's truck to congratulate Paige and Jake. As the women hugged, Sadie handed something to Paige that John couldn't quite see. Paige pulled back with wide eyes, then smiled brightly and hugged her friend even tighter. When the best friends let go of each other, Sadie turned and walked toward John. She tilted her head towards the parking lot, indicating that she was ready to go. John fell in step with her and put his arm around her waist.

"What did you give Paige back there?" he asked.

"I gave her my car key in case she needs to move it out of the way since it is parked at her house," Sadie replied.

John grinned from ear to ear and his heart leapt in his chest. "I guess this means you are coming home with me," he said happily.

"You bet your sweet ass I am," she said, pausing to pull him in for a kiss as they reached the passenger side of his car.

The kiss quickly escalated from sweet to promising, but another round of thunder, one much closer than the last, interrupted the moment. John opened the door for Sadie, making sure the bottom of her dress wasn't going to get caught in the door when he shut it. He practically ran around the front of his car and hopped in. He sped out of the parking lot, trying to get home as quickly as possible.

"Careful there, Officer John, or one of your coworkers might have to give you a speeding ticket," Sadie teased.

John looked over and then up and down her body. "Totally worth it," he replied.

Sadie let out an excited squeal as John pressed down on the gas even harder. She couldn't wait to get him alone!

Chapter Twenty-Six

Meadow Oaks is a small town, so it didn't take them long to get from the parking lot of the park to John's house. Both were buzzing with excitement, and at the same time, nerves were kicking in. Their chemistry was undeniable, and both were eager to find out if that would carry over to the bedroom. Sadie had the additional excitement of getting to see John's house for the first time.

John's driveway wasn't paved, simply a little red dirt lane that ran between two columns of great big oak trees. His yard was substantial, and Sadie noticed a tire swing hanging from a tree about halfway down the lane. The house itself was more of a small cottage, but the cheery yellow painted exterior shown bright even through the rain thanks to the porch lights John had the forethought to leave on. The bamboo wind chimes hanging from the eave spun and clanked, making beautiful chaotic music. John parked as close as he could to the porch stairs, and they made a run for the cover of the porch. John's rocking chairs were banging up against the house due to the strong winds, so Sadie helped him turn them over.

When they had flipped the final chair, John grabbed Sadie's waist and pulled her body against his. She let out a sultry laugh as he brought his lips to hers. The kiss grew urgent and they fell into a rhythm that left no doubt where things were heading. John had a brief thought that he should take Sadie inside, but he couldn't make himself break contact with her. He mentally tried to figure out the logistics of making things work on the porch swing. He didn't get a chance to think about it long as the wind shifted direction and the rain started coming down sideways, making the cover of the porch inadequate.

Sadie shrieked as rain pelted her neck, and John quickly took his keys from his pocket and unlocked the door.

"You only have the lock on the doorknob? No deadbolt?" Sadie asked, bewildered.

"No need," John answered, "there isn't anything to take that can't be replaced and it's only me here and I can protect myself."

"Well, obviously," Sadie smirked.

"Now, come here woman," John said with a mischievous grin, pulling Sadie back into his body.

"But I want to explore your house," she giggled as he threw her over his shoulder and started carrying her down a short hallway.

"Plenty of time for that later," he replied, smacking her playfully on her butt. "We've waited long enough for this."

Sadie laughed happily the rest of the way, thinking she couldn't agree more.

***

While John lay softly snoring on the bed, Sadie quietly rolled off to the side after one more gaze along John's impressive body. She reached for the nearest piece of clothing, which happened to be John's dress shirt from the night before and she slipped it on. The power had gone out at some point during the storm, but the dawning sunlight seeping through the blinds and curtains gave her enough light to see by.

As she buttoned up John's shirt, she made her way through his house. His room was down a very short hallway off of the living room. Hanging down from the ceiling of the hallway was a pull string for an attic door. As she walked under it, she jumped up and hit it with her hand like she used to do to the one just like it at her childhood home. Smiling, she went into the living room and admired the red and brown brick fireplace. It looked like it was a gas fireplace, so if it hadn't already been so muggy, they would have at least had some heat should they need it. A door at the back of the living area led to the back porch and off to the side was a doorway that led to a small, yet cozy kitchen. Sadie peeked her head in and saw a well-used wooden table with four matching lovingly worn chairs. Everything was neat and tidy. Making her way back through the living room, she took in a navy-blue couch that looked like it was from a Rooms-To-Go catalog, simple and functional. An old scratched up wooden coffee table sat in front of the couch. There were built-ins around the fireplace, but she planned on saving that for last. She peeked her head in the open door across the living room from the kitchen and saw it was a small bedroom that John had turned into an office. He had taken two two-drawer filing cabinets and laid a finished wood slab on top. A laptop and printer sat on top with a pile of papers in a bin to the side. A set of dumbbells laid on the floor under the only window in the room, leaving a permanent imprint in the carpet.

Back in the living room, Sadie opened the curtains on the front picture window to let in more sunlight so that she could get a better look at the photographs on the built-ins. She paused a moment to take in the sight of debris littering John's yard. It would take some time to cleanup, but it could have been much worse. Turning back to the shelves, Sadie started to peruse what was on display. There was a stunning picture of John's mom, on stage in a night-club singing into a microphone. Abella's outfit was not that different from the one Sadie had worn on her birthday and she appeared to be in her early twenties. There were quite a few pictures of John and his parents throughout the years. Sadie smiled as she saw through pictures how John transitioned from a baby to a toddler to a school-aged child to a teen and finally to a man. In some of the pictures John wore a baseball or football uniform. One thing was consistent from picture to picture and that was the love between the three of them. They were a happy family.

The thought made Sadie a bit nervous. She had decided a long time ago that she didn't want children, but what if John did? It was too soon in their relationship to bring it up, but she couldn't help wondering if it was going to be a dealbreaker. She had seen how great he was with Paige's kids, Chloe and Henry, and how excited he was about Paige and Jake's pregnancy news. It made her assume he wanted to be a father someday and was part of the reason she had hesitated to start a relationship with him before.

As she stared at the photos and pondered her future with John, she heard soft footsteps behind her and then two strong arms came around her waist and lips trailed kisses along her neck. Sadie moaned in appreciation and leaned back into John's embrace.

"You're up early," he murmured as he continued kissing her gently.

"I actually slept so peacefully for the first time in a long time. I can't remember the last time I woke up feeling this rested," she replied contently.

"Hmmm, could that be thanks to me and my magical..." John began before Sadie turned in his arms and slapped his chest.

"Don't finish that sentence or I'll think you're some silly frat boy," she joked.

Laughing, they embraced and kissed in front of all of John's family photos and Sadie forgot her worries over the future. He picked her up and she wrapped her legs around him, molding herself to his body. Carrying her by her backside, John sat down on the couch, never breaking their kiss. "Time for round two," he said against her mouth, and John was nothing if not a man of his word.

Chapter Twenty-Seven

Monday morning, bright and early at six a.m., Sadie returned to work at the hospital for a seventy-two-hour shift. She felt refreshed and ready to face anything. It was a feeling she thought she'd never have again and the relief it gave her was immense. She stored her purse in her office and grabbed her white coat before making her way to the resident's locker room to make sure they were ready for the day. Upon entering, she noted that while Dr. Pope and Dr. Wu were reviewing case notes, Dr. Jones and Dr. Madison were talking intimately leaning up against the lockers. Dr. Madison had his hand on Dr. Jones's waist and had the look of a man smitten on his handsome young face. Sadie could not begrudge them their blooming love, but she could tease them.

"Dr. Jones, Dr. Madison, I suggest you follow the example of your peers if you want to get ahead in your careers," she said sternly.

"Uh, sorry Dr. Jennings," Dr. Jones stuttered as she backed away from Dr. Madison.

Sadie almost missed the angry look that flashed on Dr. Madison's face, it was so fleeting. She filed the incident in her head for later review.

"I'm only messing with you, Dr. Jones," Sadie replied. "It is a good thing to find a bit of happiness in this crazy world. Especially when you work with illness, injury, and death day in and day out."

Dr. Jones gave Sadie a shy smile and looked over at Dr. Madison, who returned her adoration with a winning smile of his own.

Turning to the other two residents, Sadie asked, "Which cases are you reviewing?"

"A twenty-two-year-old male came in by ambulance on Saturday; he'd had a heart attack. I assisted Dr. Montgomery," Dr. Pope answered first. She went on to describe the rare situation and how Dr. Montgomery handled it and explained the reasoning of his choices. The four residents discussed the case and Sadie watched quietly, admiring their intelligence.

"And you Dr. Wu?" Sadie asked the other resident once Dr. Pope had finished.

"I'm reviewing the Leann Rivers case, Dr. Jennings," he answered.

"Why? She is being discharged tomorrow," Sadie questioned.

"This may be the most interesting case we ever see in our careers; a young woman, stabbed in the chest, survives after receiving emergency surgery from one of the best cardiovascular surgeons we may ever work with. Then someone, probably the same person, tries to kill her by injecting insulin into her I.V. and she gets saved again. It's intense and fascinating," Dr. Wu explained passionately.

Sadie found herself spacing out while the residents had a lively discussion about Leann's ordeal. She replayed the events in her head, starting with Leann's stabbing and ending on the knowledge that the patient in question was currently in her hospital room preparing to go home the next day. Sadie felt the sudden urge to go check on her.

"Dr. Jones, come with me. Dr. Madison and Dr. Wu report to Dr. Montgomery. I believe you'll find him preparing to do rounds. Dr. Pope, Dr. Patel has asked for your assistance today," Sadie directed and headed out of the locker room with Dr. Jones on her heels. They walked in silence through the halls and to the staff elevator.

"Where are we going first?" Dr. Jones asked once the elevator started moving.

"To check on Miss Rivers," Sadie answered.

"I'm glad she is getting to go home. I can't even begin to imagine how she has been affected by all that has happened to her. It is a horrible reminder about how life can go from good to bad in a moment," Dr. Jones commented.

"Yes, it is," Sadie said simply.

They reached Leann's door and Sadie punched in the security code on the keypad and cracked the door open. She knocked and waited for an answer before opening it all the way.

Leann's mom appeared by the door and once she saw it was Sadie, she opened it wide and let the doctors in the room. On the cot Leann's mom had been sleeping on was an open suitcase filled with neatly folded clothes. Dr. Jones went over to Leann and started chatting while Sadie spoke with her mom.

"Some of her friends are going to pack up her apartment, and then her dad is taking leave to come rent a moving truck and pick up her things. He's dying to see her in person. We had talked about hiring a moving company, but we were scared that her attacker would somehow find out and he'd show up at our house as one of the movers. Kinda crazy, huh?" Ms. Rivers whispered.

"Everything about this situation has been crazy, so I completely understand your caution," Sadie reassured her.

"I just want my baby girl to be safe."

"Me too, Ms. Rivers."

Sadie's mind was at ease about Leann since she was finally getting far away from danger and would be staying with people who loved her and would protect her. It left her mind to wander to John and their magical time together. The residents were taking more active parts in Sadie's surgeries, so while one part of her brain was focused on following their movements and instructing when needed, the image of John sleeping next to her was a constant presence in her thoughts. It got to the point where she felt like she would burst if she didn't talk about it. Since it was the middle of the workday when she finally couldn't take it anymore, she went on the hunt for Jeff. She found him in a scrub room, cleaning up after a surgery. Dr. Madison was with him, so she waited for the resident to leave before discussing anything personal. After briefly reviewing the procedure that they had finished, Dr. Madison left, no doubt to go find whichever on-call room Dr. Jones had gone to catch a quick nap in.

"Jeff, I'm in love," Sadie blurted as soon as the door closed behind the resident.

"Ah, so Officer John closed the deal for good, did he?" Jeff replied good-naturedly.

"Yes, I can't fight it anymore, and I don't want to," she declared.

"Sadie, I'm so happy for you. Jealous too, but happy," he proclaimed.

Sadie, unable to contain her joy, threw her arms around her friend's neck and hugged him tight. He returned her tight embrace and laughed with relief at seeing her so happy. He had watched her go through so many hard times over the past few months and believed that she deserved for things to finally go her way.

"I better be invited to the wedding," he joked.

"Of course!" Sadie exclaimed.

Arm in arm, they left the scrub room and went to the doctors' lounge for a well-deserved break.

***

Later, in the early evening, Sadie decided to check on Leann and her mom again. She acknowledged that she would miss the young woman she had grown so protective over. Sadie had done some research on therapists and cardiologists in the Pigeon Forge area and wanted to pass the information along to Leann. She planned on making calls to the doctors if Leann said it was okay to get her set up with appointments for as soon as she got settled back in Tennessee.

Sadie entered the code to Leann's door and as she pushed down the handle, someone shoved her from behind, causing her to stumble a few steps into the room. Luckily for Sadie, Leann's mom had been approaching the door upon hearing the beeps from the door code being entered and caught Sadie before she fell face first on the floor. Whoever pushed Sadie rammed into her back, trying to force their way further inside the room, but Sadie wasn't caught off guard that time and quickly turned around to stand shoulder to shoulder with Ms. Rivers to block the path. Sadie and Ms. Rivers pushed back at the unwelcome intruder and after a couple of failed attempts to overpower the determined women, he or she gave up and ran away towards the door for the stairs.

Sadie and Ms. Rivers speedily shut the door to Leann's room. Sadie called security while Ms. Rivers checked on her daughter. Leann hadn't seen much; the door had blocked her view.

"All I could see were arms pushing at you guys, but you were totally badass not letting him by!" Leann exclaimed. "I recorded the whole thing!"

Sadie looked over to see that Leann had hopped out of bed and was waving her cell phone around.

"Let me see that," Sadie said, holding her hand out for the phone. Leann handed it over and Sadie played the video with Ms. Rivers looking over her shoulder.

Leann had started recording as soon as Sadie had been pushed into the room. Sadie and Ms. Rivers could be seen clearly, but like Leann said, all that showed of the intruder past the door were arms and hands. The person wore dark gloves, and the arms were covered by a dark gray sweater that was tucked into the gloves. Unfortunately, no skin showed to give them a clue of the person's identity.

"It doesn't show us much, but it's a start. Good thinking, Leann," Sadie said, hugging her patient.

A heavy knock on the door had the three of them back on alert, until Sadie heard the deep voice of the security guard. She slipped out of the room to talk to him, only opening the door wide enough to squeeze her body through. He let her know that Charleston P.D. was on the way and that the intruder had snuck away through an emergency side door out of the stairwell, setting off the alarm, but still hadn't been found.

"Freaking stairwells," Sadie muttered under her breath, thinking of Paige and her incident with Stacey in the stairwell at the magazine office.

She stepped away from the security guard to text John about what had happened and then returned to the room to wait for the police with Leann and her mom.

John must have driven all the way from Meadow Oaks to Charleston with his sirens blaring because before Sadie knew it, he was at her side. Charleston detectives and officers crowded the hospital hallway making the normally quiet floor chaotic.

Sadie was concerned for Leann's mental well-being, but she was holding up like a champ. When Sadie and John went back into Leann's room, she was questioning Detective Jenkins as much as he was her.

"Have you watched the security footage from the floor yet? Do you have any leads?" Leann asked vehemently.

"Honey, I'm sure they haven't had time to get that far yet," her mom cut in.

"Our people are reviewing the security footage as we speak," he answered. "Don't worry, we are going to keep you safe."

Leann's mom went over and sat on the bed and put her arm around her daughter. "I'm fine, Mom. Promise," Leann assured her mom and pulled her into a tight hug.

Sadie and John watched the loving scene unfolding before them amid all the drama going on around them.

"Detective Jenkins," John said and led his fellow law enforcement officer to the corner of the room and asked in a low voice, "would it be safer for Leann and her mom to leave for Tennessee as soon as possible? She was about to be discharged tomorrow anyway. This seems like it was a last-ditch effort by the assailant to get to her, and I think the further away they can get the better."

"I agree with your theory," Detective Jenkins whispered. "So far all signs point to the perpetrator being a hospital employee. He or she avoided facing the cameras, so all we see is basically what Dr. Jennings saw when she kept them from getting in the room."

"Maybe somebody cased the floor beforehand," John mentioned.

"I thought of that, but this floor has been restricted since she was moved to it, so there is no way an outsider could have done that." The detective paused a moment to think. "Unless it was a family member of another patient, but that seems unlikely since they have to show ID and sign in to get on this floor."

"That makes sense. Do y'all have a list of who accessed the floor tonight?" John asked.

"Working on that now," Detective Jenkins answered.

It was a couple of hours before they started getting a clear picture. The list of possible suspects included orderlies, custodial staff, nurses, and doctors including the two male residents. It was a lot to weed through, but they were all determined to figure out who the culprit was. The detectives took the people on the list to be questioned one by one. They used a counseling room meant for mental health patients because it had two-way glass like the interrogation rooms at the police station. Sadie and Leann's mom were asked to observe the interviews in the room with the Charleston P.D. profiler to see if they could recognize anything that would connect the people being questioned to the person that tried to get to Leann.

Sadie watched each interview closely. She noted every small movement and the mannerisms of each person. Leann's mom told the profiler that she was certain it was not a woman, but he informed her that they had to interview everyone on the list to be thorough. After hours of watching the same questions being asked over and over, early the next morning they had narrowed down the list to four men: Dr. Wu, Dr. Madison, Dr. Montgomery, and Hank the grumpy janitor.

"I know it wasn't Jeff, I mean Dr. Montgomery," Sadie insisted to the detectives.

"He had access to the floor and his physical build matches what you and Ms. Rivers described," Detective Fuller replied. "I understand that he is your friend, but he can't be eliminated from the suspect list at this time."

"Yes, he is my friend, and I have known him for a long time. I have physically been side by side with him in operating rooms. I think I would know if it was him physically assaulting me."

"You might be right, but we know he was in the vicinity of Leann Rivers the night she was attacked. He was attending your birthday party, was he not? So, until we can make sure he didn't leave the party at any point or that he didn't have the opportunity to commit the other murders, he remains a suspect," the detective answered calmly but firmly.

"What about the shoe size? Y'all know the shoe size of the guy from the foot chase with Officer John Avery when Leann was stabbed," Sadie persisted.

"I promise you, Dr. Jennings, we are looking into it."

Sadie was about to argue with the detective some more when a young officer in uniform interrupted their conversation.

"Detective Fuller, here is a list from the hospital of who accessed the floor with their badges," the officer said as he handed her a sheet of paper. She quickly scanned the sheet and nodded her head dismissing him.

"The log shows most of them had left the floor by using their ID badges to use the staff elevator. The three who hadn't used their badges to leave are Dr. Daniel Wu, Hank Walters, and Dr. Jeffery Montgomery," Detective Fuller said, handing the sheet to Sadie.

"Doesn't mean they didn't use the stairs or the visitor elevators," Sadie answered. "It's quicker if there are patients being transferred in the staff elevators."

"We'll keep reviewing footage. We'll get to the bottom of this, Dr. Jennings," Detective Fuller assured her.

"I still say it wasn't Jeff," Sadie insisted again as John and Detective Jenkins walked up to join them.

"Duly noted, Doctor," Detective Fuller replied with a small smile. "I know you know that people can be capable of violence and seem perfectly normal to those closest to them. I'm familiar with your friend Paige's case."

Sadie and John put their arms around each other at the mention of their friend's violent ordeal. To keep her focus on the case at hand and not go down the rabbit hole of what Paige and Cora Rae had endured she brought the subject back to Leann. "Ms. Rivers was supposed to take her daughter home later today; can she still do that?"

Detective Jenkins spoke up, "Officer Avery here asked that too. I don't see why not as long as she is reachable by phone. She should be safe if we get her away from Charleston. Unmarked police cars will follow to make sure she isn't tailed."

Leann and her mom made their way to the parking lot surrounded by a horde of police officers. Sadie put her arm around Leann's shoulders as John listed off a bunch of safety tips for her to remember while they are travelling and for when they get home as well. Sadie stood in the parking lot with tears in her eyes as she watched the taillights disappear in the distance.

"I'm worried about you," John said as he wrapped his arms around her waist and pulled her in close. "The whole Meadow Oaks crew is. You were attacked at the hospital; a place where you should be safe."

Sadie didn't say anything. She was sure what she was thinking would have him worrying more. *Haven't we learned by now that if a crazy person wants something, nowhere is safe?*

Chapter Twenty-Eight

She got away from him, and it made his blood run hot as lava. He felt cheated, his divine mission thwarted. He paced the floor with clenched fists, trying to calm his mind so he could come up with his next step. Should he track her down? It would take some time, but it wasn't completely out of the question. Or was the fact that she had escaped death by his hands twice a sign that she was to be forgiven for her sinful ways? He would pray on it.

If only that damned doctor had not interfered! he thought. That night in Charleston, in the alley by the bar, the doctor had saved her. If the doctor had minded her own business his mission would have been completed, and he could have moved on to the next sinful woman. Then she figured out what had been done in the hospital to the filthy slut. Lastly, she had the gall to put herself physically between him and his destiny. It's her fault, the doctor. She was working against his cause, preventing him from the glory that called to him. She was allowing women to engage in immoral behavior and get away with it. It was she who must be stopped.

That's it! That is my answer! Take out the doctor and I'll be able to peacefully resume my holy work and she won't be around to stop me!

Chapter Twenty-Nine

"So now I am a suspected serial killer because some guy has a thing for unaliving girls who dress skimpy and shake their asses at night clubs and I just so happen to work at the hospital one of them was taken to. It's bullshit!"

Sadie turned her head to her left where a little down the hallway her residents were standing around talking about the situation going on at the hospital.

"I am not appreciating Dr. Wu's attitude right now," Sadie said to Jeff who was standing at the nurses' station with her.

"The kid is a kiss-ass, and this situation is bringing out the douche bag side of him, but that doesn't necessarily make him a murderer," Jeff replied.

"How are you doing with being a multiple murder suspect?" she asked.

"I know I didn't do it and once they confirm my alibis for the other murders my name will be crossed off that list," he replied with false certainness.

"You're a lot calmer than I think I would be in your shoes."

"It's not going to do me any good to freak out like Dr. Wu over there. My lawyer knows what is going on and I pay him enough to know he's on top of it."

Sadie looked back over to the residents and wondered if Dr. Wu's attitude was because he didn't have the assurance of a high dollar lawyer like Jeff had. After a few mumbled complaints on Dr. Wu's part, he walked away from his colleagues in the opposite direction from Sadie.

The remaining residents made their way towards the nurses' station, talking about Dr. Wu within earshot of Sadie and Jeff.

"I am so happy I never hooked up with him. I had briefly been tempted when you two started bumping uglies, but luckily, I got over that right quick," Dr. Pope said to her two colleagues.

Sadie and Jeff exchanged a quick amused look and went back to filling out orders on their tablets, pretending not to listen to the young doctors.

"We don't know for sure that he is guilty," Dr. Jones argued unconvincingly.

"Regardless of his guilt, I would have regretted sleeping with him. Turns out he's sexist and kind of a giant tool," Dr. Pope retorted.

"Maybe he has a giant tool," Dr. Madison quipped.

"In his dreams," the two female residents said at the same time. The group were all chuckling as they walked up to stand with their attending doctors and await orders.

Jeff started directing the residents to their assignments while Sadie finished her paperwork. She tried to focus but was having a hard time. Her mind kept wandering to John who was somewhere in the hospital checking on security measures and finding any excuse to stay near her.

The Meadow Oaks Police Chief had given John permission to hang around on duty for the day to help follow up with the case. Birdie Duvall's killer was still out there after all. She didn't mind his overprotectiveness even though she didn't think she was in any danger. Leann was safely in Tennessee being watched over by the local police there. No one had tried to follow her as far as the undercover cops escorting them could tell and that would have to be good enough for Sadie.

She lamented that they hadn't been able to have a repeat of the steamy events that took place the night of Paige and Jake's wedding. She was also bummed she hadn't got to see her friends since then either. It hadn't been that long, but being around them when something stressful was going on was the best medicine for a tired and stressed mind.

When she finished updating her charts, Sadie tucked the tablet under her arm and headed towards the doctor breakroom to grab a cup of coffee before her next surgery. Dr. Jones would be assisting her, and she hated to admit it, but she was relieved it wasn't Dr. Wu or Dr. Madison. She needed a little time before she had to stand across a surgical table from one of them. The distraction of wondering if the person standing across an open chest cavity from her was a killer or not wasn't something she needed. In the break room, Sadie was happy to see John sitting on the couch in her favorite spot sipping his own cup of coffee.

"Hey, you! I'm glad I get to see you before my next surgery," she said cheerfully.

She sauntered over to him, the need for coffee forgotten, and sat down next to him. She placed her hand on his knee and leaned over to kiss him deeply, glad that no one else was currently occupying the room.

"I could get used to this," John whispered breathlessly when they broke apart for air. "I have to admit, I checked the surgery board and came here hoping you would need a caffeine fix before your next operation."

"Hmm, kiss me again and I think I could get my caffeine fix off your tongue," Sadie quipped.

"So, my coffee breath doesn't offend you?" John asked jokingly.

"Far from it, Officer John," Sadie said as she went in for another kiss.

John leaned forward to set his cup down on the table next to the couch and then wrapped both strong arms around Sadie and pulled her onto his lap. He had to remind his hands that they were at Sadie's place of employment, and it wouldn't be ideal for the Chief of Surgery to walk in on him feeling her up. It also wouldn't be great if he was sporting a tent in his pants, so he occasionally thought about non-sexy things to keep his hormones in check. He was beginning to lose the battle of wills with himself when Sadie's phone started chirping. She pulled away from him with a sigh.

"That's my alarm. Time to head to the O.R.," she explained as she reached in the pocket of her white coat and turned the noise off.

She gave John one last peck on the lips before she stood up to leave. Suddenly she chuckled and leaned down, grabbed his coffee cup and took a long swallow from it. "Thanks for the pick-me-up, Officer," she quipped and winked at John. She made her way towards the door, adding a little extra sway to her hips.

"Sadie," John blurted, "I almost forgot, the crew wants to get together for dinner sometime this week before Jake and Paige leave for their honeymoon Saturday. They want to celebrate your patient making it safely home. When are you off?"

"I get off tonight at eight p.m. and then I don't have to come back on until eight p.m. Thursday night," she answered. "So how about tomorrow night?"

"I'll let them know," he said as she walked out the door.

He smiled to himself and sat back down on the couch. He grabbed his cup off of the table and put his lips on the same spot she had had hers when she drank his coffee. He finished what was left as he came up with a plan to get her back in his bed. John wanted Sadie close, for all the right reasons and for all the naughty ones too.

At eight p.m. that night, he was waiting for her at the exit that led out to the staff parking area. Sadie gave him a big smile when she spotted him and that gave him all the courage that he needed to put his plan into action.

"Come home with me," he said as he took her hands in his. "Stay until you have to come back on Thursday."

"Well, it's Tuesday night, so what you are saying is you want me to sleep over for two nights, Officer John," Sadie replied in a sultry voice.

"Oh, I want more than just two nights, Dr. Jennings, but I'll take all I can get." John pulled Sadie in for a deep, mind-altering kiss. His lips moved from her mouth to her ear and trailed down her neck. He let out a deep moan that turned into a growl as he pulled away and grabbed her hand to pull her to her car. He had already pulled his into a spot near hers. "I'll follow you to your condo so you can get what you need and then you are riding to Meadow Oaks with me. I want to spend every moment I can with you," he said demandingly.

"I'm so freaking turned on right now," Sadie exclaimed as she let him lead her to the car.

"Then I guess I'll have to take care of you when we get back to your place instead of waiting until we get to mine," John answered, his voice deeper with his blood pumping hot with wanting her.

Sadie was very happy to learn that Officer John was indeed a man of his word and took very, very thorough and meticulous care of her when they arrived at her condo. Twice.

Chapter Thirty

John woke up to find his arm wrapped around Sadie, his hand gripping her breast and his lower body curved around her athletic butt. They had not made it to his house the night before. It was probably his fault for joining her in the shower when they stopped by her condo so she could get out of her scrubs and pack a bag. He wasn't complaining though and she didn't seem to mind. After the shower they took her bed for a spin and eventually passed out from exhaustion, or was it bliss? Either way, he was a happy man.

"Is that a taser in your pocket or you just happy to see me, Officer John?" Sadie mumbled into her pillow.

"I'm not wearing any pants, Doc Jennings," he whispered into her ear as he started running his hand up and down her smooth thigh.

"Food, John. I need food and then you can have your wicked way with me again." Her stomach let out a hungry growl right on cue.

The only thing John wanted more than to have Sadie again was to take care of her when she would let him, so he got out of her bed after one quick nip to her tight rear-end and started searching for his clothes.

"How about I drive us over to Meadow Oaks and I can take you to my favorite little hole in the wall diner. They have the best grits," he said as he alternated between getting dressed and watching Sadie slowly arise from the bed.

"Sounds heavenly. Places like that always have the best food. Maybe not the best for you, but definitely the best tasting," she answered.

Sadie went into her closet and came out wearing a yellow sundress that got John's blood pumping hot again. "Doctor, those are the type of sundresses that get men to do whatever a woman wants," his voice getting deeper as he grabbed her from behind and pulled her against him.

She turned around in his arms and gave him a quick peck before saying, "Feed me, John."

"Yes, ma'am," he replied. "See, told you. Y'all get your way every time."

Sadie chuckled and finished the task of packing her bag that she never quite got to the night before.

The drive to Meadow Oaks was pleasant. John held her hand most of the time and only let go when he couldn't resist holding onto her bare thigh. "Really liking this dress," he said with a wink.

"I thought you might. Beats the scrubs I normally wear," she responded.

"You look hot in those to me, too. I dig smart women. But honestly, I don't think the clothes have as much to do with it as the woman wearing them."

Sadie blushed and looked out the window being shy about being complimented, but John took the genuinely happy smile that she had been sporting all morning as a good sign. As they got into Meadow Oaks, John started pointing out all his favorite spots in town and some of the memories that went along with them. He really wanted her to like spending time there.

"Over there in that grassy area across from the row of shops, me and Jake were throwing a football around one time when we must have been about seventeen. We were just killing time, nothing special, when these two girls came out of Under the Oak Tree. They had graduated the year before, and I guess were home on Christmas break from college. Anyways, we had the great idea to do a little showing off and Jake told me to go long. Well, I did but he still overthrew it, I had to really haul ass to try to get to the football and didn't realize that I was running right towards that giant oak over there," he said pointing to a thick oak that was at least a hundred years old, "until I slammed into it with my shoulder. Jake ended up having to take me to the doc to get it put back in the socket."

"Ouch!" Sadie exclaimed. "Did the girls at least come check on you to make sure you were okay? Maybe give you a pity date? Something?" Sadie asked, laughing quietly.

"They didn't even notice we were over there, much less know we existed," John said as he laughed. "We weren't as smooth as we are now, bagging two hot babes like you and Paige," he joked.

"Their loss, our gain," Sadie said and leaned over to give him a kiss on the cheek.

John pulled the car into a gas station parking lot and parked down at the very end away from the entrance to the convenient store. He went around and opened Sadie's door.

"I can wait in the car if you need to grab something from the store, unless you really want me to go in with you," she said looking up at him from the passenger seat.

"We are eating here," he informed her.

"Huh?" Sadie asked confused.

John pointed to a side door that had "Clay's Diner open 6am. to 2pm." in small white lettering on it.

"Oh, okay." Sadie took his hand and got out of the car. "I feel a bit overdressed to eat at a place attached to a gas station."

"You're fine, city girl," John teased.

He led Sadie into the little diner, and he smiled as her eyes went wide with surprise when she saw that the place was packed on a Wednesday morning. All of the tables were taken so he steered her towards the counter where they sat at the last two available stools.

"Ooh, they have a hook for my purse! I love it when I sit at a bar or a counter and I don't have to awkwardly hold it in my lap the whole time!" Sadie cheered.

They both ordered big breakfasts with a waffle, hash browns, eggs, grits and sausage. John loved watching Sadie eat every single bite of her food. It brought him joy to see her enjoying herself, even if it was over something so simple as a good hearty breakfast. He cleaned his plate as well, having worked up quite the appetite the night before pleasing his woman.

That's what she was, his, and he couldn't be more thrilled over anything in the entire world. They had made it through their rocky times and came out the other side closer than they were before.

"Oh, my goodness, that hit the spot," Sadie exclaimed as she licked her fork clean. "I can already feel my arteries clogging."

"I'm glad you approve. I love eating here. It's why I have to run so much. Well, this place and my job," John said as he patted his flat stomach.

They finished their coffee and after paying the tab and tipping the waitress, they walked hand in hand to the door. John was so preoccupied with looking at Sadie that he almost ran into the couple coming in the diner door.

"Excuse me," he said kindly without really seeing who he was speaking to.

"Good morning, Officer Avery," a man replied.

Recognizing the voice, John's attention sharpened on who was in front of him. "Mr. Duvall, Mrs. Duvall, how are y'all doing today?" John asked.

He felt Sadie tense next to him as he greeted Birdie Duvall's parents. An unmistakable hush settled over the diner, the patrons' heads turning to the door. The gentlemen that had not already removed their hats to dine took them off and held them to their hearts as a sign of solidarity. A lot of the women held their hands over their hearts in a similar gesture of respect and caring.

"We're taking it one day at a time," Mr. Duvall said, putting his arm around his wife's shoulders. "We've both taken a leave of absence from work, just trying to function at this point," he paused, "any news on our girl's case?"

John hesitated a moment, shifting foot to foot. In a low voice so as not to be overheard by the entire place he answered, "As I mentioned before we have linked Birdie's case to others in Charleston. The most recent victim survived her attack, as you already know. Night before last, there was another attempt by who we think is the perpetrator to get to the young woman while she was in the hospital."

"Is she okay? Was the guy caught?" Mr. Duvall blurted, interrupting John's update.

John shook his head, "No, he was not caught, but the woman is okay. The good news is Charleston P.D. was able to come up with a short list of suspects thanks to security logs and the woman's and witness descriptions." John reached out and squeezed Mr. Duvall's arm and gave Mrs. Duvall a gentle nod. "We are getting closer to finding out who took your daughter away from you and I promise I won't ever give up until you get answers."

Mr. Duvall closed his eyes and nodded, trying to hide the sadness and despair that was just below the surface of the brave face he was attempting to show the world. He cleared his throat and moved to the side a little to let an older gentleman who was leaving pass by. The two men nodded at each other and Mr. Duvall turned his attention back to John.

"I'm sorry, where are my manners?" Mr. Duvall said trying to sound cheerful but falling a little short. "Who is this beautiful lady you have on your arm today?"

John pulled Sadie forward a little and slipped his arm around her waist. "This amazing woman is Sadie Jennings. She is from Charleston, but I've convinced her to slum it in Meadow Oaks with me for a couple of days," he joked, trying to lighten the mood.

"Dr. Sadie Jennings?" Mrs. Duvall asked, speaking up for the first time since entering the diner.

"Yes ma'am," Sadie replied nervously. "I am so sorry for your loss."

John gently squeezed her waist as a subtle reminder that he was there to support her. Her hand covered his and she gently squeezed back.

Before John knew what was happening, Mrs. Duvall launched herself at Sadie and enveloped her in a big hug. "You poor thing, having to witness all that violence. Just hearing about it is bad enough, but you have to see it day in and day out as part of your job. You're so brave." Mrs. Duvall leaned back, still gripping Sadie's arms. "Thank you for trying to save our Birdie," she said to Sadie with tears glistening in her eyes. Sadie's eyes teared up as well. At a loss for words, she simply nodded and brought Mrs. Duvall back in for another hug.

John looked around the diner, watching the scene in front of him was making him emotional and he needed to be strong for Sadie. Everyone in the place had stopped eating and had their eyes on Sadie and Mrs. Duvall, many with tears in their eyes.

After a moment, Mr. Duvall softly pulled his wife from Sadie and kissed the top of her head. "We've kept these young people in this doorway long enough, hon," Mr. Duvall said "Let's let them on their way."

With one more quick hug between the women and a handshake for the men, John and Sadie walked arm and arm out of the door and to his car.

"I had to get you out of there before the whole town wanted to meet you," John said as he buckled up. "Once word spreads, you'll be a hero here in Meadow Oaks."

"That was intense," Sadie murmured. At John's concerned expression, she went on, "I'm glad I got to meet them and give Birdie's mom a hug. I just wish we could have saved their daughter for them. They are lovely."

"That they are. How about we go to my house and take a nap? Between the big meal and the emotional run in with the Duvalls, I'm feeling a bit drowsy."

"A nap sounds perfect. We'll need to be energized for our get together at Faith's house tonight," Sadie replied.

John drove his woman to his house and got her comfortable in his bed. He wrapped his arms around her and pulled her in close, making sure he wasn't crushing her. He placed soft kisses along her neck and ran his thumb over her hand in slow circles until he heard her breathing even out and slow down. Only then did he let himself fall asleep. He vowed to take care of her, his amazing woman who wasn't scared to face the hard parts of life and fight back against death. He would be her peace.

Chapter Thirty-One

After the best nap of her life and a round of hot lovemaking with John, Sadie rode shotgun in John's two-door pickup truck over to Faith and Travis' house. They lived only a few streets over and John usually walked there, but the weatherman was calling for thunderstorms later in the evening. As they pulled up to the cute white two-story farmhouse, Sadie took note of all of the debris in Faith's front yard. Caleb was raking it into piles while his little assistant, Henry, was gathering up some of the smaller branches.

"Hurricane Ivey made a bit of a mess here huh?" Sadie commented.

"Yeah, Travis got called to help restore power all over the state, so he hasn't had a chance to do any cleanup. He only got back home last night," John replied.

"Faith said something about that when I spoke to her briefly the other day. She said she had a good bit of cleanup at the daycare and was too tired when she got home to worry about her yard."

They got out of the car and waved to the hardworking boys. Henry waved back enthusiastically and yelled out, "Hey, Aunt Sadie! Auntie Faith said to thank me for helping in the yard she would let me have two desserts tonight!"

"Good for you, buddy!" Sadie answered cheerfully.

"They are great kids," she said to John. He smiled in agreement, and they made their way inside through the open garage door.

Faith recently had her kitchen remodeled and she loved cooking in it. She hadn't allowed Sadie to bring anything to contribute to the meal, so instead she brought wine. She had also picked up some sparkling cider for Paige and the kids.

John brought his chainsaw to help with the giant tree that fell across Faith and Travis' backyard. John was more than willing to work for food, especially when Faith was cooking. He left it inside the garage while he went to greet the others.

Sadie made her way through Faith's small mudroom to the kitchen. Delicious aromas wafted up her nose, rich Cajun spices and a hint of citrus. Sadie had always been too busy studying to worry about learning how to cook.

Her mom was a talented cook, making even the most basic meals seem gourmet, but she encouraged Sadie to focus on her schoolwork. "Make enough money and you can have someone to do the cooking for you, and they'll do the cleanup after too!" she had said. Take out and plastic cutlery were as close as Sadie had gotten to that concept, but she appreciated her mom supporting her dreams.

"Faith, it smells divine in here," Sadie said as she went over and hugged her friend who was busy sautéing at the gas range stove.

Paige and Cora Rae were sitting at the breakfast table watching Jake and Travis out in the backyard. The two men were standing by the fallen tree with a beer in their hands, presumably coming up with a plan about what to do with the wood.

"I've been looking forward to this all day," John said as he peeked over Faith's shoulder to see what she was cooking.

"It'll be ready in about twenty minutes so grab yourself a beer and relax," she replied, not taking her eye off of the pan in front of her.

John greeted the other ladies as he grabbed a beer from the brand-new stainless-steel fridge and then made his way out back.

Sadie opened the wine she brought and poured herself a glass of wine, offering some to Faith and Cora Rae as well. She sat a glass of sparkling cider in front of Paige and asked, "How is married life treating you, Mrs. Bennett?"

"Well, it's only been a few days, but so far it's everything I dreamed it would be," Paige replied with a huge smile and a little pink flushing her cheeks.

"The wedding was so beautiful, wasn't it!" Cora Rae exclaimed. "I've already written up the article for the magazine! I can't wait to see the pictures the photographer took so I can pick which ones to use."

"I'm so glad you agreed to have your wedding featured. You are the Editor-in-Chief of the dang magazine for crying out loud. Your wedding should be in it," Faith insisted from her post at the stove.

"I don't think it was fancy enough. Most of the weddings we feature cost more than my house," Paige reasoned.

"It was beautiful and elegant," Sadie argued, "and the pictures will reflect that."

"You might be the first pregnant bride we've featured, but there is nothing wrong with that. I can't wait until you read the article! You are gonna cry, but in a good way," Cora Rae gushed.

"The widowed mother of two beautiful children marries the man some psycho almost killed her over. Pure romance," Faith said into her spatula as if it was a microphone.

"No, you just did not!" Cora Rae said shocked. Then they all cracked up in laughter.

"Glad we can laugh about this now, because the Good Lord knows, it's been a struggle," Cora Rae added.

"Don't ever say that in front of Jake, he still hasn't forgiven himself," Paige said in a low voice.

"I would never," Faith vowed, looking over at Paige.

"Wouldn't what?" Chloe said as she entered the kitchen.

All of the women looked at each other, trying to come up with something less traumatizing to say to the pre-teen. Sadie came to the rescue. "Faith was telling your mom that she would never use instant grits for shrimp 'n' grits."

"Oh, is that what we're having for dinner?" Chloe asked.

"Not tonight, sweetie, but I've been craving it, so we'll have it soon," Faith answered.

Chloe shrugged her shoulders and grabbed a banana off the top of the fruit basket on the table and walked out to the backyard to join her new dad.

"Sheesh, that was close," Sadie mumbled.

"Chloe has come to terms with what happened. Kids are resilient, but I do try not to bring up what happened unnecessarily," Paige said.

Faith looked over to the table with a guilty look on her face, but Paige waved her off with a smile.

Sadie looked around at her friends and a swell of pride came over her at what a strong group of women they were. Mentally and emotionally they have fought to overcome what had been done to them, and in her and Faith's case, dealt with what they had witnessed of the aftermath. Sadie hoped that Leann had the kind of unwavering support being offered to her that Sadie and her friends gave each other. Thinking of Leann reminded Sadie about what had happened at the diner earlier in the day.

"Oh my gosh, I can't believe it slipped my mind, guess who John and I ran into this morning," she began.

"Who?" Paige asked, with Cora Rae looking on expectantly.

"Birdie Duvall's parents."

"Those poor people, I can't imagine what they are going through. How are they doing?" Paige wondered.

"As you'd expect. Struggling to resume living their lives. Her momma hugged me and thanked me for trying to save her. It was heartbreaking," Sadie explained. "They were so sweet and kind. I can't help but wish we could have saved Birdie."

"Y'all did your best, Sadie. I wasn't there, but I know you did. You and Dr. Cutie Pie," Paige said, reaching over to hold Sadie's hand.

The group stayed quiet for a few minutes. Thoughts of Birdie's parents and horrific tragedies no doubt going through all of their minds.

Sadie turned and looked out the window to where John was standing by the fallen tree with the other men and Chloe. It was not lost upon her that she sought him out for comfort. He had joined the short, but vital list, of people who gave unwavering support to her. Sadie liked to think of herself as tough and independent, but it sure was nice to have someone to lean on, someone to get lost in when she needed to feel something good. John's strong arms and broad chest came to mind, but also his heart. He had given it to Sadie, and that made her strong. They hadn't said the words out loud yet, but there was no doubt in her mind, they loved each other.

"Speaking of cute doctors," Faith said, breaking Sadie's train of thought and lightening the mood, "how are things going with that oh so hot Dr. Patel, Cora Rae? I saw y'all getting all cozy at the wedding." Faith was twirling her spatula and making kissy faces at Cora Rae.

Paige and Sadie laughed and encouraged her to spill the beans on her budding romance.

Cora Rae's face turned a pretty shade of pink. "Y'all, he is just the sweetest. He texts me good morning every day and calls when he is on a break if I'm not at work. He is so thoughtful and it's really the little things like remembering how I take my coffee that really make him different from the guys I usually end up dating. Those guys never lasted long. And he is so good to his parents. Raj is so wonderful and his ridiculous good looks are only the tip of the iceberg," she explained dreamily.

Sadie and Paige sighed and held their hands to their hearts in a playful gesture at Cora Rae's heartfelt sentiments.

"Yeah, but is he a good kisser?" Faith blurted with a mischievous smile.

Cora Rae rolled her eyes but answered as she blushed a deeper pink. "The man has skills," she said coyly.

"Have y'all...you know...sealed the deal?" Faith questioned as she waggled her eyebrows at Cora Rae.

"Faith!" Paige exclaimed. "You are incorrigible!"

"Just trying to get to the juicy part!" Faith defended herself.

The ladies laughed and all eyes turned to Cora Rae to hear her answer.

"No, we are taking it slow. This could be the real deal. We are getting to know each other before jumping into bed. I will say it probably won't be much longer though. We can't keep our hands off each other when we are together. Lots of heavy petting as you ladies so elegantly put it," Cora Rae revealed.

"Yes!" Faith squealed as the others clapped with glee.

The men picked that moment to walk back into the house from the backyard. "Uh oh. What are you four up to now?" Travis asked good-naturedly.

"Cora Rae's love life," Faith answered her husband as he came over to peck her cheek while she turned the flame of the stove off and moved the pan to an off burner. Travis put his hands on her hips and watched her work her magic.

"You know, Cora Rae," Jake began, "we need to hang out with him to make sure he fits in with the group since you are one of us now."

Cora Rae looked nervously from Jake to John to Travis. "I'm sure you guys will get along with him. He's really sweet to me and he likes fishing," she went on frantically.

John walked over to Cora Rae and put his hand on her shoulder. "Easy Cora Rae, Jake's just messing. If you like him, we'll like him. We'll only threaten him a little to make sure he knows that if he hurts you, he'll have to answer to us," he reassured her.

Cora Rae let out a deep breath and glared at Jake, who chuckled in response.

Chloe entered the kitchen and rolled her eyes at her new dad and took a seat at the table next to Cora Rae. "Don't listen to Dad, he says the same thing about when I start dating, but he's a big teddy bear. He won't hurt anyone."

"Best believe I would if they hurt my girl," Jake replied, puffing his chest out.

"Easy slugger," John said to his friend. "I'd let you ride in the patrol car with me, and we'd scare the crap out of the little punk. That way we get revenge, and you stay out of jail."

Chloe rolled her eyes again but couldn't hide the smile she was sporting.

"Someone go get those boys and tell them to get cleaned up for dinner," Faith said as she started plating the food.

John headed toward the front door and Sadie followed. He walked outside and hollered to Caleb and Henry to get washed up before Aunt Faith's food got cold. Sadie stood on the front porch with John and held his hand as they watched the two boys take off their gloves and head towards them. She smiled at them as they walked by her into the house. Once they were out of sight, John put his arms around Sadie and kissed her neck.

"They are some really great kids," Sadie murmured.

"Yeah, they are," John mumbled into her neck as he left a trail of soft kisses.

"You ever think about having kids?" Sadie asked nervously.

The kisses on her neck stopped and John turned her around to face him. He seemed to be examining her face before answering. "I never really planned on it," he replied carefully.

"Me neither," she said relieved. "I'm happy being an aunt to Chloe, Henry, Caleb, and the baby on the way."

John nodded and kissed her long and hard. When they finally pulled apart, he took her hand and they went back inside to join their friends for dinner.

That went well. Nervous for nothing, Sadie thought. *It's like we were made for each other.*

Chapter Thirty-Two

John woke up once again with Sadie's tight backside pressed up against him and her feet tangled up with his. It was early in the morning, and a light rain pitter-pattered against the windows. Sadie's breathing was slow and even with a small hint of a cute snore. He knew he should let her rest, but he couldn't keep his hand from running up and down her smooth thigh and up to her hip. She moaned in her sleep and burrowed deeper into her pillow. On the next stroke up her leg, he squeezed her hip and ground himself against her. He couldn't help himself.

Sadie stretched languidly and looked over her shoulder to the sexy grinning man behind her.

"Gotta pee!" she chirped.

She sat up and grabbed John's t-shirt from the end of the bed and slipped it on. She stood and made her way to the bathroom. John loved how the shirt barely covered her bottom, and he got a little peek of cheek with every step she took.

John rolled over onto his back, putting his hands behind his head. He couldn't remember the last time he'd been so happy. He had the woman of his dreams in his bed, and they were on the same page about where their relationship was headed. The only thing left to make his life perfect would be to catch the guy who haunted Sadie's dreams. At least they had a list of suspects.

His thoughts shifted back to the present as Sadie came sauntering out of the bathroom. She sashayed her hips playfully as she made her way to her side of the bed, teasing John. She had his undivided attention as she removed the shirt and crawled back under the sheets. Facing him, she smiled mischievously.

"You brushed your teeth, didn't you?" he accused jokingly.

"Uh huh," she giggled.

"Cheater!" he exclaimed.

John hopped out of bed, giving her a nice view of his muscular backside, and went to brush his teeth.

He exited the bathroom feeling minty fresh and slid under the covers to pull Sadie in close.

"I had an idea," he began.

"Uh oh," Sadie teased.

Gripping Sadie's hip firmly he went on, "I think you should leave some things here. I'll make room in the closet and the dresser."

"Officer John, does that mean you want to have more sleepovers with me?" she questioned with mock innocence.

"Many, many more," he growled, kissing her firmly. Sadie squealed in delight and returned the kiss with fervor.

Before he could get carried away, he pulled back from the kiss and cupped her face with his hands. He meant to say something serious but got caught up looking over the features of her face and counting his lucky stars.

"Damn, you're beautiful," he said in awe.

Sadie put her hand over his and closed her eyes, suddenly overcome with a swell of love for the man next to her. John waited until she reopened them to speak again.

"I meant it about making room here for you. I know you can't be here all the time and have to have your place in Charleston to be close to the hospital when you're on call, but I want this to be a second home to you, Sadie. I want you to be here when you're not working and I want to be in Charleston with you when you are," he declared.

"I want that too, John. I'll make room for you too," she vowed.

He smiled and pulled her harder against him and kissed her softly, letting his lips convey everything he was feeling in his heart.

"I love you, Sadie," he whispered against her mouth.

"I love you too, John," she whispered back, feeling happier than she ever thought she could.

She kissed him back with gusto and rolled on top of him. She sat up and grinned down at him. "Let's make that room right now," she said joyously.

She scrambled off of John, the sheet getting tangled up around her legs. Once she got free, she opened up John's closet and started making herself a spot.

John rolled to his left side and pushed up on his elbow to prop his head up in his hand to watch her.

"Do you have a preference of where I put my stuff?" she asked over her shoulder as she started sliding hangers around.

"Not at all. I'm just enjoying the show!" John answered. "I can't believe this is my life now. A sexy woman in my house? I'm a lucky, lucky man."

"That you are," she said as she stood back from the closet, contemplating how she wanted to rearrange it.

"You can use the closet in the other room too if you need more space," he offered.

John watched her move his things around and take a few things out of her overnight bag to hang up next to his uniforms. He loved the contrast of his plain black police shirts and her bright cheery sundress and purple tank top. Watching her bend and stretch to rearrange things had him needing her back in his bed.

Knowing she would not be distracted from her task, he got up to help her to move the process along faster. He went over to his dresser and started emptying the middle drawer that held all of his plain white t-shirts he wore under his work shirts. He squeezed half of them into his underwear drawer and threw the rest in a pile on the floor to use as rags when he did work in the shed behind his house.

"Here's a drawer for your unmentionables," he called out.

Sadie brought her overnight bag over to the dresser and placed the clean underwear and pajamas she hadn't needed inside. She placed a kiss on John's cheek as she smiled from ear to ear.

"I've never had my own drawer at a man's house before," she told him.

"I am honored to be the first and the last," he replied, bringing her close for a kiss. As he kissed her, he took the overnight bag out of her hand and threw it on top of the pile of discarded white tees. "Now, back to bed, woman!"

After celebrating their first day of somewhat moving in together, Sadie and John went to the local drug store to get toiletries for Sadie to leave at John's house. She had put on one of John's Meadow Oaks Police Department softball shirts to wear with her leggings. John noticed all the stares they were getting from the other shoppers, and he beamed with pride that the beautiful woman wearing his shirt was his.

When Sadie finished getting all of her new items set up in John's bathroom, she stood back and admired her handywork.

"Now that I've made myself at home here, I don't want to have to go home to Charleston for my shift tonight," she said to John who was admiring her from the doorway.

"Hmm," he murmured, stepping in close to grab her by the waist. "How about when I take you home, I bring a few things of my own to leave at your place?"

"Okay, okay, I can get behind that," she teased. "Bring some more of these t-shirts. They're comfy."

"How about I do even better and spend the night. Chief just texted me to follow up with Charleston P.D. as soon as possible and he wants me in the hospital keeping eyes on our four suspects," John explained.

"Whatever came of the shoe size thing? Wouldn't that have eliminated at least one of them by now?" Sadie questioned.

"You'd think so, but all four men wear a size eleven, so unless we find the actual pair of shoes and match the treads, it doesn't help us at all," John lamented.

"That's weird that they all happen to wear the same size shoe," Sadie commented.

"It kind of makes sense if you think about it. They all have a similar build, so it's not that out of left field," he reasoned.

Sadie shrugged and helped John pick out some things to bring to her condo, including a picture of John's parents. Sadie loved his parents. She didn't know them that well yet, but she loved their love story.

They drove into Charleston holding hands and comparing their schedules for the next week to make plans. Both wanted to come home to the other as much as possible.

John pulled his Meadow Oaks squad car into the parking lot of Sadie's condo building. He figured since he was technically in Charleston on official police business, he should drive the official police vehicle. He got out of his side of the car and grabbed his duffel bag out of the back seat. Sadie's purse had spilled its contents into the floorboard, and she was bent over gathering the scattered items. John went around the car to sneak a peek at her amazing backside and to tease her when something caught his attention over the roof of the car further down in the parking lot.

"Sadie, get back in the car and call nine-one-one," he said urgently. He gently pushed her back into her seat and closed the door.

He looked around the parking lot and drew his gun. There didn't appear to be anyone nearby, so John quickly made his way down the sidewalk to where Sadie's dark blue BMW M3 was parked. The giant red painted "A" on her cracked windshield was what had caught his eye. He slowly circled the car with his gun still drawn to make sure no one was hiding inside or out. The windows, headlights, and taillights had all been smashed too. The back windshield was cracked, and a huge splatter of red paint almost covered it entirely.

It appeared to John that someone tried to slash a tire as well but must not have had the strength to actually pierce through. It was a lot harder to do than people thought. Most of the time people who attempt it end up slicing their hand when the knife gets stuck, but their momentum keeps moving their hand forward along the blade.

Sirens sounded in the distance, pulling John's attention away from Sadie's car. He glanced over to his squad car and could see that Sadie had climbed over to the driver seat to get a better look at what John was doing. He knew she couldn't see the total of the damage from inside the car, but she could see enough. He holstered his gun and pulled out his cell phone to call his buddy Officer Sanders.

"John, how are things over in Meadow Oaks?" Officer Sanders asked in greeting.

"Hey, man. Actually, I'm in Charleston at Sadie's condo building. Someone smashed her car up in the parking lot. She called the police, and I hear them coming, but I think we are going to need a detective or a senior officer out here. This has to be the work of our guy."

"Where does the doc live?" Officer Sanders questioned.

"Tides, building C," John answered.

"On my way."

As John hung up, two Charleston P.D. squad cars pulled into the lot and parked in the middle of the lane behind John's car. Two uniformed officers got out and came over to John hurriedly. Before he could say anything to them, they looked past him to the damaged car and the sense of urgency drained from their demeanor.

"We rushed over here for a simple destruction of property? You gotta be kidding me!" one of the officers exclaimed.

He looked to John to be fresh out of the academy and had a serious attitude problem.

Luckily the taller of the two seemed to have a bit more sense than his colleague. Before John could put the rookie in his place, the taller one spoke up. "No offense, Officer, but dispatch made it sound like something more serious was going on. They couldn't tell us exactly what, but we were expecting a stabbing or something. This seems like a domestic dispute, like a crazy ex or something."

"First of all," John began, "domestic disputes are serious."

"That's not what I meant," the tall officer interrupted.

"Second of all, "John said over him, "this could be connected to multiple homicides."

"Yeah right," the short rookie said. "You're just some small-town cop looking for some excitement and wasting our time."

John was about to lose his temper with the rookie when he noticed Sadie getting out of his car. He took a deep breath and turned back to the cops in front of him. "How long have you been a police officer?" he asked the short one.

"Well," the rookie hesitated, "about four months."

"So even if this is a simple destruction of property or a lovers spat, it still isn't below your paygrade, is it?" John questioned with only a hint of anger in his voice.

The rookie mumbled something unintelligible and wandered over to Sadie's car and started processing the scene. The tall cop smirked and followed his fellow officer.

Sadie had gotten a good look at her car while John had been debating with the young cops. He had been worried she would be scared, but she looked pissed. If the guy who did the damage showed up right then, John would be more worried for his safety than Sadie's. She looked like she could take on ten guys and not even break a sweat. He was about to try to convince her to go up to her condo when Officer Sanders pulled up.

Officer Sanders started walking towards John and Sadie but changed course when he noticed the two officers processing the car. He yanked his belt up as he headed over to the crime scene. John couldn't hear everything being said as he stood down the sidewalk with his arm around Sadie's waist, but he knew Officer Sanders was giving those boys hell.

When Officer Sanders was done chastising the young officers, he came over and shook Sadie's and John's hands. "The tall one's not so bad, but that other one has a serious ego problem. They hadn't called in forensics yet, so I had them do that. Guys around the station are calling our killer the Slayer Surgeon so now they are pumped about being on this case. I've been in touch with Detective Jenkins, and I'll keep him informed about what we find here."

"I really appreciate you coming out, Officer Sanders," Sadie said, trying to tamp down the anger she was feeling since it wasn't directed at the officer. She hated that the killer was getting a nickname and notoriety. *Plus, it might not even be one of the surgeons, it might be the janitor!*

"Of course, Dr. Jennings. It's part of the job, but I owe you too," he replied.

When Sadie gave him a questioning look, he went on, "Last year you saved my mother-in-law. She had been visiting for my son Luke's high school graduation when she had a heart attack at dinner. My wife was distraught, and my kids were scared, but you saved her, and my family is whole."

John felt Sadie's body relax next to him as Officer Sanders' words helped some of her anger dissipate.

"I'm glad she came through," Sadie responded.

With Officer Sanders there to take charge of the scene, John and Sadie went up to Sadie's condo. Watching John find a spot and put away the stuff he had brought to leave at her place had Sadie's mood lifting considerably. She would not let some maniac ruin what was turning out to be some of the happiest times of her life. They would catch him eventually and she would have regretted not enjoying the important moment with John as they merged their lives.

When John was all settled and Sadie had changed into her work attire, they headed back down to John's car so they could go to the hospital for Sadie's shift and so John could do some investigating of the four suspects. In Sadie's mind, there were only three suspects, but John knew even though Dr. Montgomery seemed like a great guy, a cop couldn't take anything for granted.

As they were pulling out of the parking lot, a black tow truck with "Kimball's Towing" in neon orange was pulling in to take Sadie's car to impound as evidence.

The tension returned to Sadie's brow and shoulders, and John vowed that he wouldn't sleep until they caught the "Slayer Surgeon" and Sadie could get some peace.

Chapter Thirty-Three

At the hospital, Sadie had to report the incident with her car to the chief. Anytime something out of the ordinary happened that could possibly affect a surgeon's performance Dr. Richards wanted to know about it. He knew his surgeons could handle day to day stress and work-related stress without distracting them from their life-or-death work, but at the end of the day they were only human. He had it worked out that if there were extenuating circumstances, there was always on-call emergency coverage available. It cost the hospital extra money, but he felt it was worth it to protect patients and his surgeons.

Sadie found him in his office, sitting behind his desk with a huge pile of paperwork waiting for his attention. She rapped her knuckles on the open door and took a few steps inside.

"Heard you had some excitement tonight," Dr. Richards said without looking up from his laptop.

"News sure does travel fast, huh," she answered as she came further into the office and plopped down in a chair across from him.

"The detectives are here sniffing around. I hate that whoever is doing this has been under my nose the whole time," he mumbled.

"Yeah, it is a bit disconcerting," she agreed.

Looking up from his work, he waited until Sadie was looking back at him before he spoke. "I'm sorry all of this is happening and that you've somehow been caught up in the middle of it all."

Sadie took a deep breath and nodded, thinking about all the implications of the situation. "What are we going to do about it, Chief?"

"Well," he began, pushing back from the desk and leaning back in his chair, "I've placed the janitor on paid administrative leave, the two residents are on paperwork duty, they won't be interacting with the patients, and I'm not sure what to do about Jeff. He is a suspect, but I am ninety-nine percent sure he is innocent. However, the public might not agree and therefore might not feel safe coming to our hospital for their medical needs."

He rubbed his chin as he pondered the situation, then continued, "Did you know they are calling the killer the Slayer Surgeon? Detective Jenkins just told me. Right now, that is only being said around the police station, but it's only a matter of time before that gets picked up by a reporter or someone posts it on social media; then I'll have no choice but to bench him. Slayer Surgeon. Ha! It might be the janitor and then they'll feel really dumb."

"I thought the same exact thing when I heard about it! How did Hank feel about being placed on leave because he is a murder suspect?" Sadie wondered aloud.

"Oh, he was fine with getting paid to stay at home or to go fishing. He said he's innocent and to call him when the cops figure that out."

Sadie nodded, lost in her thoughts. They sat in quiet for a few moments. Dr. Richards watched her closely. When he saw that while she had a lot to think about, she didn't seem to be in such a state as to not be able to do her job with the excellence in which she normally does.

"Go suit up, Sadie. I believe your first surgery tonight starts in thirty minutes," he said, bringing her back to the present.

"Thank you, Dr. Richards," she smiled and stood up.

Dr. Richards came around his desk and took one of her hands in his. "We'll get through this, Sadie. You're a strong woman and a brilliant surgeon. Don't let this bring you down. My door is always open to you if you need to vent or talk or just sit in silence."

Sadie pulled him in for a hug and after he got over being caught off guard, he hugged her back.

Feeling a bit lighter, Sadie headed to her own office to get ready to go improve a life. She was putting her white coat on over her scrubs when John knocked on the door and slipped inside.

"Detective Jenkins and Detective Fuller want to talk to you when you get done with this surgery. They said they'll meet us in Dr. Richards's office so they can update all of us at the same time," he explained.

"Do they have any news for us?" she asked.

"Maybe. Charleston P.D. has had people working around the clock pouring through fob logs and security footage. I'm hoping they've found something," John answered.

"Me too," she said as she clipped her I.D. badge to her coat. "Well, I'm off to do a double bypass. How about a good luck kiss?"

"I think I can handle that," John replied, putting his hands on Sadie's hips and pulling her flush against him.

They kissed deeply, the emotions of everything going on and their budding love pouring into the kiss, making it more intense than either of them had planned. Sadie involuntarily moaned in pleasure, and it was what she needed to make herself slow down and pull away.

"You're spending the night at my place tonight while I'm here, right?" she asked.

"No, afraid not," he answered.

"You're going home to Meadow Oaks later in the middle of the night?" she asked, disappointed that he wouldn't be there if she got a break to go home.

"No to that too," he said, smiling at her look of confusion. "I'm staying here. I'll come nap in your office if I get tired. I don't want to leave you here alone after what happened the other night."

"I don't even have a couch in here," she pointed out.

"Eh, that chair looks comfortable enough," he replied.

Sadie chuckled and started pulling away to leave for surgery. "How about this, I was planning on crashing in an on-call room after my second surgery as long as no emergencies come in. I'll have about two hours to nap. You can share my bunk," she said as she opened her office door and stepped into the hallway.

John followed her out and joked, "Okay, but no funny business. I've got a reputation to uphold around here."

Sadie laughed and walked with John to the surgery wing of the hospital. He left her at the door to the scrub room and went to find Detectives Jenkins and Fuller to continue their investigation. While she worked hard, so would he.

Dr. Jeff Montgomery was already in the scrub room soaping up when Sadie walked in.

"Looks like I'm your assistant tonight since Dr. Wu and Dr. Madison are benched and Dr. Patel has Dr. Pope and Dr. Jones is off," Jeff said in way of greeting. "I also think Dr. Richards wants to keep me away from the patients' families until this whole murder suspect thing passes."

"Oh Jeff, I'm so sorry," Sadie lamented as she joined him at the sinks.

He shrugged it off. "Honestly, it's not that big of a deal. You're my favorite person in this place, so it could be worse. Maybe I'll learn something," he smirked good-naturedly at Sadie.

"I'll try to not go too hard on you," Sadie teased.

"I appreciate that boss," he replied.

Sadie smiled to herself as she thought about how lucky she was to have such supportive people in her life. She had her best friends and their families in Meadow Oaks, a wonderful man, and the best coworkers, minus whichever one was a killer, of course. Her mood picked up even more as she walked into the operating room and saw her favorite nurse, Pearl, was getting the final preparations for the surgery ready.

He can try to scare me, smash up my car, try to get me where I work, but he, whoever he is, will never defeat me. I am Dr. Sadie Jennings and after I kick this surgery's ass, I'm going to meet with those detectives, and my man is going to catch this guy, and I'll get my happily ever after.

Chapter Thirty-Four

"We aren't done going through all of the surveillance footage yet, but according to the fob logs, it's looking like Dr. Daniel Wu is our guy," Detective Maxine Fuller said without hesitation when everyone was present for the meeting in Dr. Richards' office.

Sadie didn't feel the shock that she had expected to feel when Detective Fuller said Dr. Wu's name. If she were completely honest with herself, the list of suspects had been circulating in the back of her brain, and it had been a toss-up between the two male residents as to who she thought really did it. Hank, while grumpy, had never given her a bad vibe in all of the years they had worked together. The idea of Jeff being a murderer was inconceivable to her.

"What did the logs show?" John asked.

He was standing on Sadie's left with his right hand on the small of her back. While unnecessary, the comfort he offered her was appreciated.

"Hank Walters used his fob to access the floor at six o' four p.m. and was on the floor during the time of the attack, but what surveillance footage we have been able to review clearly shows him mopping a hallway down aways during the entirety. He's cleared," Detective Fuller explained. Detective Jenkins stood behind her, nodding his head in agreement.

"Dr. Jeffery Montgomery came onto the floor at roughly five p.m. with Dr. Daniel Wu and Dr. Todd Madison in tow. Footage shows them all getting off one of the staff elevators together. We watched them go from room to room doing evening rounds," the detective went on.

"Did they go into Miss Rivers' room?" John asked.

Sadie already knew the answer. She had reviewed Leann's chart for that day and there were exam notes from Jeff, and it was mentioned that both residents were present for morning and evening rounds. It gave Sadie the heebie jeebies knowing that Leann's attacker had been in the room with her, more than once over the entire time she'd been in the hospital.

"Yes, they did," Detective Jenkins answered, consulting his notes. He continued, "They were in the room for about ten minutes and moved on to the next patient. Then at six-twenty p.m. Dr. Montgomery and Dr. Madison take the staff elevator to leave the floor and Dr. Wu leaves via the stairwell."

"All this we've been able to confirm with security footage. However, at six-thirty-six p.m. Dr. Daniel Wu's fob is used to reenter the floor via the stairwell, but we can't find him on the footage," Detective Fuller adds.

Sadie, John, and Dr. Richards nodded their heads but didn't say anything. They were all lost in their own thoughts.

"What's next?" Dr. Richards asked after a moment of silence.

"We bring in Dr. Wu for questioning, try to figure out his motive, see if he has alibis for the nights of the murders. We have interviewed some of your neighbors, Dr. Jennings, and we have been able to narrow down a timeline of when your car was vandalized. We'll see if he has an alibi for that as well."

"Okay," Sadie replied to Detective Fuller, not sure of what else to say.

"We'll continue to have our people comb through footage from all over the hospital to make sure there isn't anything we've missed. This case needs to be rock solid," Detective Jenkins said.

After giving John's hand a meaningful squeeze, Sadie thanked the detectives for the update and had to leave to prepare for her next surgery. Jeff was going to assist again, and she figured she owed it to him to let him know what was going on. It looked like he was off the hook.

As she walked down the hallway, she heard the detectives talking as they came out of Dr. Richards' office. "We are heading straight to Dr. Wu's address to bring him in for questioning." Sadie looked back over her shoulder to see that it was John they were talking to. She smiled to herself knowing that while she was in surgery, she could rest easy knowing John was on the case.

***

After another successful surgery, Sadie and Jeff cleaned up at the scrub sinks. Sadie watched her friend as he spread the soapy suds up to his elbows. He was humming an upbeat tune and swaying a little side to side.

"That maze surgery put you in a good mood?" Sadie asked playfully.

Jeff turned to her and gave her a megawatt smile. "So maybe I had been a little more upset about being a multiple murder suspect than I had thought. I didn't realize it until I felt a weight lift off of me after you told me what the detectives found."

"I knew it wasn't you the whole time. Never crossed my mind that it was even a possibility," Sadie assured him.

"Thank you, Sadie. That means the world to me," Jeff replied sincerely.

They dried off their hands and arms, put the used towels in the bin by the door and made their way into the hallway.

"You want to grab some dinner? We have a little break before our next one," Jeff said as they headed to the breakroom.

"I would, but I promised a certain small-town cop that we could nap in an on-call room," Sadie said. She couldn't help but grin at Jeff.

"Uh-huh, nap, right," Jeff teased. "I guess I should go call my mom anyway. She's been pretty worried. She's been looking up the statistics of wrongful convictions and freaking herself out."

"Please go put Mama Montgomery out of her misery. And tell her I say hello. I just love that woman," Sadie said, nudging Jeff towards the door.

"She loves you too and here comes your boyfriend, so I'll see you later," Jeff said as he glanced behind her to where John was walking towards them and then he looked back at her and winked.

Sadie blushed and turned to walk down the hall to join John. The hallway was relatively empty at that late hour, so she didn't hesitate in taking his hand and leading him to one of the single on-call rooms. Most of the on-call rooms had bunks, but there were a few with only one small bed sprinkled throughout the hospital and Sadie had called dibs on the best one earlier that night. She couldn't wait to get off of her feet and snuggle with her hunky man. She felt silly thinking of him as her boyfriend. Was she too old to call him her boyfriend? They felt more serious than that. *Partner*, she thought to herself. That's what he was, a partner. Someone to go through life with and share all things, good and bad.

Without saying a word, they locked themselves in the room. The only light came from a small nightlight plugged in by the door. They simultaneously removed their shoes and set them side by side. Sadie removed her white coat and dirty scrubs. She had already stored some clean ones in the room and put those on. While watching her change, John took off his uniform shirt and placed it across the back of the single chair the room boasted. He was wearing a plain white tee underneath and Sadie thought it was the sexiest thing she had ever seen.

They climbed in the small bed together, John wrapping his strong body around hers. He reached around to her front and held her hand. Sadie breathed deeply, relaxing into him.

"Relieved to know your friend has pretty much been cleared of murder?" he whispered.

"Yes. I knew he didn't do it," she quietly replied.

John kissed the back of her neck. "As a cop, I couldn't take anything for granted, but I am glad for him. If I'm honest though, I'm happier for your sake because I wouldn't want anything to cause you pain."

Sadie with her eyes closed, smiled and brought their joined hands up to her lips and kissed his fingers. "I love you, John," she said simply.

"I love you so much, Sadie," he answered.

And with that they both drifted off to a peaceful sleep.

Chapter Thirty-Five

At the shrill sound of the alarm on Sadie's phone going off, Sadie and John woke up from their nap and went back to work. Sadie was feeling refreshed since there hadn't been any emergency pages to interrupt her slumber. She met up with Jeff to get ready for their next surgery.

John decided Sadie would be safe enough in the operating room with Jeff for a few hours and headed to the Charleston Police Station to see if he could catch the tail end of Dr. Daniel Wu's interrogation or at least read the transcripts if they were done. It was crazy early in the morning, four a.m., so he didn't expect to see his buddy, Officer Sanders. He asked the night desk clerk where he could find Detective Maxine Fuller and Detective Ben Jenkins. The officer led him through the station to the elevators and told him to take it up to the second floor and take a right to the homicide departments bullpen. The detectives were at their desks which were pushed together facing each other. They both looked exhausted as they sipped coffee from paper cups.

"How's the coffee at this place?" John asked jokingly as he approached the detectives.

"I've heard rumors that the Meadow Oaks station has better," Detective Jenkins replied, playing along.

"How's Dr. Jennings handling all this?" Detective Fuller asked John.

John took a moment to think back through the last twelve hours or so with Sadie before answering. "She's resilient. The incident with her car really pissed her off. I thought it would scare her, but there was no fear, only anger. She's relieved that Dr. Montgomery has pretty much been cleared because she never for a moment could fathom him being violent. I think she's ready for this to be over with, as we all are."

"Amen to that," Detective Fuller agreed.

"How did it go with Dr. Wu?" John asked.

"Haven't spoken to him yet," she answered. At John's confused look she went on, "He had already lawyered up, and they are coming in at seven this morning for his questioning. We couldn't drag him in here since we don't have enough to officially charge him yet. I tried to play it off like just a friendly chat, but he wasn't going for it."

John checked his watch and saw that he wouldn't have too long to wait. He shot off a quick text to Sadie for her to see when she got done with surgery telling her where he was and to stay close to Jeff at the hospital.

"Do y'all mind if I watch the interview? Sadie is working another forty-eight-hours, and I don't feel like going back to her condo without her today."

"Fine by us," Detective Fuller answered, shrugging and looking to her partner to make sure he didn't have any objections. When Detective Jenkins nodded in the affirmative, John pulled up a chair.

The three law enforcement officers discussed strategy for the upcoming interrogation and reviewed all of the evidence they had so far. No doubt Dr. Wu and his lawyer were going over alibis and what he should say or not say.

"What about the other resident," John paused to check his notes, "Dr. Todd Madison? Are you planning on questioning him too? Try to get some alibis?"

"He's coming in at nine. As far as we know he hasn't lawyered up yet. Our research on him shows he may not have the resources to afford one on his own. We'll offer him a public defender of course. If we are not done with Dr. Wu by nine, we'll divide and conquer," Detective Jenkins answered.

"Well, alright, we might have some answers soon!" John exclaimed.

He was hopeful that he would have something worth telling Sadie when he went back to the hospital later.

Chapter Thirty-Six

He paced and paced in his room, restless and angry. They were closing in on him, and he hadn't yet finished his divine work. He was already disappointed and frustrated by his failure to send the jezebel he stabbed and poisoned to meet her maker. Leann Rivers. Such an innocent sounding name for a woman with such loose morals. If he didn't act quick the doctor would get away with her part in aiding the survival of such a creature. Destroying her car was not punishment enough.

He always knew he would get caught eventually. Planned on it, actually. He had assumed it would be much later in life, but God worked in mysterious ways. But at least he would be able to tell his side of the story. The world would know that it was a divine calling that led him to what he had done. The Lord's message had instructed him to rid the Earth of those who were not worthy of the life they had been given. Some might argue that there were men also unworthy because of their sins, but he already had a rebuttal for them; the Bible tells us that woman led man to sin. His calling told him that meant it was the fault of the woman and therefore they should be the ones to be punished.

A single candle had been all the light provided while he paced trying to organize his thoughts, but he noted that the sky outside was starting to lighten. Beams of early morning sunshine were filtering in around the edges of his curtains bringing the objects around his room to life. He looked around and took note of his space. The bed was a mess from him tossing and turning after he got the call about having to go down to the police station to be interviewed. "A formality," the female detective had said. *How dumb do they think I am? They are on to me. Damnit! I'm not ready!*

He made his way over to his dresser. He reached out his hand and gently stroked the items perched on the top. A silver bracelet. A lock of hair with a neon pink hair tie wrapped around it. A keychain that said some nonsense about queens straightening each others' crowns. There were a couple of things he couldn't bring himself to touch or even look at, but knowing they were there gave him comfort. Lastly, he held a blue labeled lip balm in his hand. It was vanilla bean scented, and he had taken it off of Leann Rivers' hospital table during rounds one day when no one was looking. The items were his trophies. His inner voice said he didn't deserve to keep the lip balm, but he couldn't let it go. Having the items on display gave him a sense of pride, but he would have to hide them for a while until he was ready for the police to find them.

Shortly, he would have to put on the mask which was the face he showed the world and go answer questions about where he was the nights of his crimes. That is not the word he would use to describe his actions, but the police would, so he needed to get used to hearing the word and not reacting defensively. The last thing he needed was to give himself away by not playing by the rules of modern times. His day of reckoning would come, but it would be up to him when that day would be.

And that day would be the day that Dr. Sadie Jennings died.

Chapter Thirty-Seven

Looking through the two-way mirror to where Dr. Daniel Wu sat whispering with his lawyer, John wanted to punch the smug douche bag in the throat. Staying level-headed throughout the investigation was becoming harder and harder as he pictured the young doctor attacking his woman. If he was lead on the case, he would have to excuse himself. It was lucky Charleston P.D. was in charge and that Detectives Fuller and Jenkins were dead set on getting to the bottom of it as soon as possible.

Sadie had told him about Dr. Wu's comments about party girls and his attitude towards women in general, so he had relayed that information to the detectives. Their game plan was to have Detective Fuller have a go at him first. Detective Jenkins joined John in the little room to observe the interrogation. They watched as Detective Fuller entered the interrogation room. She had shed the suit jacket she almost always had on and undone the top few buttons of her shirt to show a tiny bit of cleavage. The top was tucked in tight to her pants to accentuate her figure. She had added mascara and lip gloss to her usual clean-faced look. Her more feminine appearance was part of her strategy. Dr. Daniel Wu would underestimate her at his own peril.

"Thank you for coming in so early to talk to me Mr. Wu," Detective Fuller began, intentionally addressing him incorrectly.

He was quick to correct her. "Doctor," he snapped.

"My apologies, Dr. Wu," she replied with a sweet smile, emphasizing his title of doctor. "I'll try not to waste too much of your time. Why don't we begin by running through your alibis. Let's start with where you were last night between six p.m. and seven-thirty p.m."

"I was getting ready to meet my parents for dinner," Dr. Wu answered.

"It takes you an hour and a half to get dressed for dinner?" she asked skeptically.

"My parents, particularly my father, are sticklers for proper appearance. He is a prominent lawyer here in Charleston and believes that if I appear uncouth, it will bring shame to him," Dr. Wu said through clenched teeth.

"Okay, let's move on," Detective Fuller said looking down at her notes.

As Detective Fuller took Dr. Wu date by date of each incident committed, John and Detective Jenkins took extensive notes. John was impressed with the detective's interrogation skills. She would be asking about one date and jump back to a date they had already gone over trying to trip him up. She was getting under his skin and making him angry and careless. A few times his lawyer had to rein him in when he would make a sexist comment to the detective.

"Look, I didn't do it. Am I sad that a few party girls met a violent and untimely death? No. Does that mean I killed them? Also no," he argued, looking down to Detective Fuller's cleavage and back up to her face.

John really wanted to rearrange Dr. Wu's facial features for him, but Detective Fuller was unfazed. She continued on with her interrogation questioning him about any personal knowledge of the victims. John continued with his note taking and reviewed them whenever there was a lull, seeing if anything jumped out at him that they might have missed. Some of his alibis seemed shaky, the others should be easy enough to follow up on and confirm.

"How do you feel about your supervisor, Dr. Sadie Jennings?" Detective Fuller asked Dr. Wu, bringing John's attention to a sharp point.

Dr. Wu turned his head side to side, taking a moment to answer carefully. "She's brilliant," Dr. Wu finally said.

Detective Fuller waited a moment to see if he would elaborate, but he stayed silent.

John eyed him carefully, looking for any clue as to his true feelings about Sadie, but Dr. Wu gave nothing away. There wasn't a single hint at a malicious opinion towards her. He had secretly been hoping for an eye twitch or a sneer. The desperation to make Sadie safe had made his impartiality non-existent.

Detective Fuller threw everything she had at Dr. Wu for a couple of hours before letting him leave with a promise from his lawyer that he would not leave town while they check up on his alibis.

"We didn't have enough to hold him. He's an asshole but we can't charge him with that," Detective Fuller said as she joined them in the small room and plopped down in a chair. She was going on thirty-two hours without sleep.

"I'll get you some coffee, Maxine," Detective Jenkins said holding his hand out for a fist bump. "You want some, John?"

"Thanks, that would be great," John answered.

"You're my hero," Detective Fuller shouted as the door closed behind her partner.

Detective Fuller rubbed at her eyes but then cursed when she remembered she was wearing mascara. She grabbed a tissue on the desk and walked to the two-way mirror using her reflection to fix her makeup.

"So, what'd you think?" she asked John as she swiped with the tissue under her eye.

"I think I want this to be over so badly so Sadie will be safe that I can't be impartial. I'm glad she has you to drill these guys. Are you going to use the same approach with Dr. Madison when he gets here in a few minutes?"

She nodded her head in the affirmative. "Whichever of these guys is the killer has a thing against women who go to bars and clubs and maybe dress a little sexy. Since we can't really recreate the bar or club vibe here, the closest we can get is me making my work clothes look sexyish."

"Smart," John commented. "Did you get killer vibes from Dr. Wu?"

Detective Fuller turned her head side to side, checking her makeup while she contemplated her answer. "He's definitely hiding something. Whether it's that he is a murderer or not, I'm not sure. He has the skill and seems to have a chip on his shoulder when it comes to women. He had access to Miss Rivers at the hospital. There were a couple of instances he claims to not remember what he was doing on a particular night, but we'll see what his alibis for the nights he does remember turn up."

Detective Jenkins returned with their coffees and Detective Fuller hurried to the door to take one off his hands. "Bless you, Ben," she said happily and sipped at the hot cup, needing that caffeine fix.

John also thanked the detective and sat down with his own cup.

"Dr. Madison is here. He doesn't have a lawyer, so I have one of the rookies going over his rights with him and offering him a public defender. I don't want anybody to say we coerced or intimidated this young man into admitting something he didn't do when he very well coulda done it," Detective Jenkins proclaimed.

They drank their coffee for a few minutes, waiting for Dr. Todd Madison to be led into the interrogation room. The door to the room on the other side of the mirror opened and the three law enforcement officers turned to look at the second suspect as he entered. John recognized the tall rookie cop from the incident the day before with Sadie's car. The young officer pointed to the chair facing the mirror and told Dr. Madison to have a seat and that someone would be with him shortly. Dr. Madison was closed in the room alone and the rookie poked his head in the observation room.

"He declined a public defender. Said he has nothing to hide," the rookie reported. He gave John a quick nod of recognition before looking back to the Charleston detectives for dismissal.

"Thanks," Detective Jenkins nodded to him.

When the door shut and it was only the three of them again, they turned to watch Dr. Madison. He sat straight up in the hard metal chair with his hands folded together on top of the stark metal table. He didn't fidget or squirm. He simply looked down at his hands and seemed to be in a sort of meditative state. It gave John the creeps. Most people aren't so calm when they are asked to come in for questioning, whether innocent or guilty.

Detective Fuller took her time finishing her coffee before going into the next room to question Dr. Madison.

"Good morning, Mr. Madison," she began. "Thank you for coming in."

He didn't correct her like Dr. Wu had. He simply nodded his head in acknowledgement.

"You didn't want a lawyer?" she asked.

"Don't need one," he answered.

"And why is that?" she asked in a friendly tone.

"Didn't do anything," he shrugged.

"Okay, I'll make this quick then," she said sweetly.

She went through each incident one by one, and his response was "I might have been working or I was home alone," for each one.

"You live alone?"

"Yeah. My mom and sister took off a while ago."

"Where to?"

"Dunno. Not my concern."

"Fair enough," Detective Fuller conceded. "Let's talk about the victims."

She went through each victim with him, and he denied any connection to any of them. He didn't say anything derogatory about them or offer any more than that he didn't know them.

John was getting frustrated with his lack of responses and couldn't tell whether or not the guy really didn't know anything or if he was simply being uncooperative.

"I can't tell with this guy," John said to Detective Jenkins.

"He's a calm one that's for sure," the detective admitted.

"I was telling Maxine earlier that I've seem to have lost my ability to remain sensible with this case because of Sadie's involvement," John confided.

"Makes sense. The woman you love is being threatened. That's enough to make any man crazy. It's why we don't work cases that involve our loved ones. Don't beat yourself up about it. You're only human and your instinct to protect Sadie is more powerful than wanting to have a rational mind."

"You're right. It's the first time this has ever happened to me though. It has me feeling really off kilter," John replied.

"We'll get him. Trust in that," Detective Jenkins assured John, walking over to firmly squeeze his shoulder.

John nodded solemnly and turned his attention back to Detective Fuller grilling Dr. Madison. She was throwing everything she had at him, changing the wording to try to trick him up, but he kept playing ignorant. Frustrated, Detective Fuller stood up and faced the mirror. She shrugged her shoulder and let Dr. Madison leave. On his way out, she reminded him to be available in case any more questions popped up.

John hurried out to the hallway so he could get a last look at Dr. Madison as he left. He barely missed barreling into the young doctor, who made eye contact and smirked at John. Dressed in his street clothes, John had a hard time reconciling the image Sadie had painted of a talented upcoming surgeon with the grungy kid he saw before him in the middle of a police station. Dr. Madison didn't slow his stride, and John watched his back as he made his way out of the police station. John would be keeping an extra close eye on him.

Chapter Thirty-Eight

Sadie was a little annoyed that Jeff seemed to be sticking to her like glue, but at the same time she figured her friend was doing it for the companionship as much as trying to be a macho protector. It had taken a bit of arm twisting to get Jeff to admit that John had asked him to look after Sadie while John was at the police station watching the interrogations.

"I would have done it anyways," Jeff insisted.

"I don't need a babysitter. I'm a grown ass woman and I've already fought this guy off once. Maybe I should be the one protecting you!" she exclaimed haughtily.

Jeff was starting to get nervous. "Since when have you minded my company?"

"Since you tried to follow me into the bathroom!" Sadie shrieked.

Jeff scoffed. "I wasn't trying to go in with you; I just wanted to check it out first to make sure that no one who wasn't supposed to be in there wasn't lurking in the shadows waiting for you."

Sadie threw up her hands in mock frustration; she loved getting him all riled up. "Oh my God, Jeff, you are so dramatic!"

"A murderer is on the loose and it's somebody we work with!" he yelled. "If there was ever a time to be dramatic, now would be the time!"

Sadie noticed the vein that had popped out on his neck and decided to put him out of his misery. She laughed softly until his look went from worried to incredulous and then she couldn't hold back and let out a full belly laugh. She had to clutch her side to keep it from cramping, she was laughing so hard.

"You're wrong for that," Jeff said, shaking his head. A slow smile was creeping up on his face. Sadie's laughter was becoming contagious.

"You make it too easy," she squeezed out between belly shaking guffaws.

Soon they were both bent over in laughter. Dr. Richards walked by and looked at both of them like they were crazy and went off mumbling something about "Only those two would be laughing at a time like this."

The rest of Friday continued much the same with the two surgeons attached at the hip during their scheduled surgeries. The only times they were apart was when they had to divide and conquer two emergencies that came in minutes apart from each other. Around midday, she had a few minutes to breathe and checked her phone. John had sent her a text.

> John: I came by hospital, but you were busy in surgery. Going to report to my chief. Be back soon. Love you

She smiled at the phone and quickly texted back.

> Sadie: Love u too!

Sadie did a little happy dance to dispel some of the happy energy flowing through her. She practically skipped down the hallway to the doctors' lounge to grab a protein bar before her next surgery. Jeff had beat her there and was already scarfing down his own snack and chasing it with coffee.

"What did you have?" he asked her with his mouth half full of food.

"Fifty-two-year-old male suffering from a heart attack. Did a CABG on him. He should recover and live a long time if his wife can get him to lay off the fast food and go for a walk a couple of times a day," she reported. "What about you?"

"Smoker experiencing heart failure. Put in a LVAD," he answered.

"Nice! We have Mr. Sorenson up next," Sadie said, taking one last bite of her chocolate protein bar and throwing her trash away on the way out the door.

Jeff took one last swig of his coffee and followed her out, disposing of his paper cup in the same trash can.

Dr. Jones reported back in for her shift and was assisting the two surgeons. As they scrubbed in, Sadie was concerned by the way the young resident was staring off into space while she soaped up.

"Penny for your thoughts, Dr. Jones?" Sadie said.

Dr. Jones jumped, startled like she forgot where she was and that she wasn't alone. She settled back down and rinsed her hands and forearms off before answering. She grabbed a clean towel to dry off and handed one to Sadie as well. Jeff made himself scarce by entering the operating room, leaving the two women in the scrub room alone. Dr. Jones propped her hip against the big sink and sighed.

"I guess I am a little shook up about Todd being called in for questioning about the murders. My boyfriend is a murder suspect and even though I don't think he could have done it, it's starting to freak me out a bit," she lamented, looking to Sadie for guidance.

"I can understand that. Dr. Montgomery in there is my best friend at this hospital and it seemed unreal that he was a suspect too. He's the kindest man who really cares deeply about people. He's not a doctor for the status or to play God, but to really help improve peoples' lives," Sadie said, looking through the window to where Jeff was conferring with Pearl.

"Exactly! That's how I feel about Todd!" the young surgeon exclaimed. "He's so sweet and tender when he is with me. Never raises his voice. He's so patient and understanding about how my career has to come first right now. I've really been falling for him. He can't be a serial killer!"

Sadie wanted to pull the young woman in for a hug, but then they would have to re-scrub in, and they didn't have time for that.

Instead, she asked, "Are you okay to be in the surgery or do you need some time. It would be completely understandable if you needed to step back until the case is solved."

Dr. Jones shook her head from side to side vehemently. "No, thank you. My career is my main focus right now. It has to be. I'll be fine."

True to her word, Dr. Jones buckled down and assisted brilliantly during the procedure. She asked intelligent questions of Sadie and Jeff and impressed them with her smooth stitching when they let her take over.

Sadie inwardly hoped for Dr. Jones' sake that Dr. Madison was not the killer. *It usually is the boyfriend;* Sadie shook off the intrusive thought, blaming Paige's obsession with the movie SCREAM as the source. *That's when they are trying to kill their girlfriend,* Sadie argued to herself. She chuckled out loud absently about the ridiculousness of her inner debate. Jeff gave her a questioning look, but she shook her head and went back to watching Dr. Jones competently completing the procedure.

It had crossed Sadie's mind to ask Dr. Jones if she had heard anything from Dr. Madison about how his interview with the detectives went since she hadn't had a chance to talk to John about it yet, but she didn't want to upset Dr. Jones again. Sadie wasn't sure if Dr. Madison would have called Dr. Jones if they ended up charging him with something and arresting him. *Doesn't he get one phone call? Or is that something else from the movies?* Sadie pulled her attention back to the matter at hand and didn't let it wander again until the operation was over.

When they were cleaning up after the surgery, Jeff let Dr. Jones finish up first so he could talk to Sadie in private.

"What was all that about before the surgery?" he asked Sadie.

"She was freaking out about her boyfriend being a murder suspect," she answered.

Jeff groaned. "It is a bummer. Does she think he did it?"

"No, she doesn't. Says he is too sweet and tender," Sadie replied with a little smirk on her face.

"Imagine that! The bad boy of the resident group is a sweetie pie," Jeff joked.

"Maybe to her," Sadie said, shaking her head in slight disbelief. "I'm going to wait and speak with John about how the interrogations went before I start forming an opinion. For me, right now, it's a toss-up between the two residents."

"When will we be seeing the good officer? Shouldn't he be back by now?" Jeff teased.

Sadie shrugged. "He had to go back to Meadow Oaks to report to his chief. I guess it depends on what the chief needs him to do next that will determine if he comes back here or has to do a shift there. He's supposed to be off later tonight, but I don't know if I'll see him."

Jeff smirked at her. "Oh, I'd bet on seeing him. I've seen how he looks at you. He's not going to be away from you for long, regardless of whether or not there is a serial killer on the loose."

Sadie felt her face heat up. It did not surprise her that Jeff noticed the spark between her and John, but she did wonder if it was as obvious to people who didn't know her so well. The chemistry they shared was something she had never experienced before or even knew was possible.

"Yes, it is obvious," Jeff said, as if he read her mind. "I only hope that someday I am as lucky."

"You're too great not to be as lucky in love, Jeff," Sadie assured him.

The two friends exited the scrub room into the hallway. Sadie was hoping to run into John, while Jeff was pondering a shared future with a woman not yet known to him.

***

Sadie did in fact see John later that night after his shift. He was waiting for her in the hallway across from the doctors' lounge, a bag of takeout in his hand.

"Oh, my hero!" Sadie happily exclaimed.

John blushed and lifted the bag up with a shrug. "Figured you could use some real food."

"Too right you are. I've eaten like five protein bars today. We've been swamped," she replied.

"Lead the way," John said, gesturing with his free hand towards the door to the lounge.

Sadie entered and immediately went to the cabinets to get paper plates and plastic forks. "Do we need knives or spoons?" she asked.

"I think they put some in here," he answered, walking over to one of the three round tables. He set the bag down and started taking cartons of food out of the bag. "Yep, there are some in here."

Sadie glanced at the plastic silverware the restaurant provided. "Ugh," she scoffed, "that's the cheap stuff that breaks as soon as you stick it in your food. I got the good stuff right here."

John smiled. "Hope you like Peruvian. Cora Rae suggested this place."

"Yum! I love it. Please tell me you got some of the yellow sauce," Sadie questioned as she grabbed a couple bottles of water out of the fridge.

"Sure did. Cora Rae made sure to tell me to get extra."

"Gosh, I love her!" Sadie said as she started dishing out rice and chicken onto a plate.

They loaded up their plates with the delicious food, breathing in the scent of spices that had been rubbed all over the chicken. A few doctors came in to grab a cup of coffee and walked out again without a word. At first Sadie and John kept the conversation nice and light, discussing how good the food was and other restaurants they needed to try. Sadie loved planning a future with John. She reveled in the feeling of certainty that they loved each other and the sense of peace that gave her.

When the room was empty and they were helping themselves to seconds, Sadie brought up the interrogations. "Anything exciting happen at the station when they questioned Dr. Wu and Dr. Madison?" Sadie asked.

John took a few seconds to chew his food and then answered, "Dr. Wu is an arrogant douche bag. He had a lawyer who did his best to keep him from saying things he shouldn't. Dr. Madison declined the offer of a public defender and didn't really give us anything. I saw him in the hallway after and he kind of gave me the creeps."

"Huh," Sadie said, pondering the situation. "Which one do you think did it?"

"I'm really not sure, Sadie. We have a bit more digging to do into their alibis, but Charleston P. D. is keeping a close eye on both of them in the meantime," John explained.

"Maybe it really is Hank framing the two guys and he'll end up coming after us with a hook or something," Sadie joked.

"Hmmm, that would be pretty crazy," John laughed.

Under the table, John reached for Sadie's hand. They had been knocking knees throughout the meal. Sadie felt like a schoolgirl getting giddy over every little touch.

"What did your chief have you do after you reported to him about the interrogations?" Sadie asked absentmindedly. She was more focused on the way John's thumb was tracing slow patterns on her knee.

"He had me patrol for a while and answer a few service calls. It was nice being on duty at home, but I worried about you the whole time."

"You don't have to worry about me, John. I'm tough," she reassured him.

"I know you are. I can't help it. I love you and even the remote possibility of losing you scares the crap out of me," John admitted.

Sadie leaned forward and kissed John to ease his mind as much as hers. "I love you too," she whispered against his lips.

"I'm going to go sleep at the condo tonight since Jeff seems to have you covered and when you get off tomorrow morning, I'm going to make you breakfast," John said as he placed kisses over her lips and cheeks.

Sadie made an appreciative hum and then John started kissing down her neck. "And then I'm going to take you home to Meadow Oaks so you can sleep in my bed while I work. I'll be checking on the house regularly to make sure my lady is safe. When I get done and you've gotten enough rest, I'll show you how much I thought about you all day and then we'll have our friends over for burgers on the grill to officially celebrate my house being your house now too."

Sadie pulled back a little so John would look into her eyes. He gave her a questioning look, suddenly unsure. She could feel her eyes filling with tears and John's face turned from unsure to worried.

"You make me so incredibly happy, John," she stated, her voice full of conviction.

John let out a deep sigh, "You had me worried for a second there."

Sadie giggled and went back to kissing her man.

Chapter Thirty-Nine

Sadie woke up and stretched languidly in between the cozy sheets of John's bed. Well, her bed too, it seemed. The reminder that her life had taken such a wildly romantic turn had her smiling before her eyes even opened. She lay there replaying all of her favorite moments with John in her head, picturing every smile, every touch, every sweet word. She stayed in bed until nature called and could be ignored no longer. She scurried to the bathroom. As she washed her hands, she looked into the mirror to see her face staring back at her, well rested and happy.

Feeling chipper, she made her way to the kitchen to find a snack. That was where John found her when he got home from his shift. She was in his t-shirt that he had given her to sleep in, and she was bent over in front of the fridge, digging in the bottom drawer. Sadie could sense him watching her from the doorway, so she made sure to take her time picking the perfect apple to munch on.

"Enjoying the view, Officer John?" she asked, peeking over her shoulder to get a glimpse at her sexy man in uniform.

"You know it," he replied.

John spent a few more seconds admiring the view and when Sadie straightened up, he made his way over to stand behind her and put his arms around her waist. He kissed her neck and breathed her in.

"Did you sleep well?" he asked as he nibbled on her ear.

"I can't remember the last time I slept that well. Oh yeah, it was the last time I slept in your bed," she answered, snuggling back into him.

"I like you in my bed," he replied. "Why don't you eat your snack in bed while I eat mine?" he asked devilishly.

"What's your snack?" Sadie asked.

"Oh, you'll see," he answered.

He spun Sadie around and picked her up and threw her over his shoulder. He carried her out of the kitchen, down the hallway to their bedroom. John gently tossed Sadie on the bed. She squealed in delight, apple still in her hand.

***

"Oh Sadie, I love what you've done with the place!" Faith cooed mockingly as she walked in the front door.

"Hardy-har-har," Sadie responded. "I haven't had a chance to add my touches yet, but don't you worry, I'll make my mark soon."

"I bet the lovebirds have been too busy making their mark in the bedroom," Paige teased as she followed Faith into the house.

"Why did I just get a visual of dogs peeing?" Jake asked, bringing up the rear with Travis.

"My mind went there too," Travis agreed.

"You know what I meant," Paige said, playfully swatting Jake on the arm.

Sadie laughed as Jake put his arm around Paige and walked her further into the house. Faith and Travis followed, whispering happily together about how Jake saying that made her think she needed a puppy, a girl one, of course. Travis had his arms full of food containers, as usual. Sadie watched the two couples as she closed the front door. She was so used to being a single, but not anymore. She was part of a couple. It seemed so crazy and so natural all at the same time.

In the kitchen, Faith directed Travis as to where to set down all of the food she brought. Once she was satisfied, Travis and Jake went out the sliding glass door to the backyard to stand by the grill with John.

"They can have that. It's way too hot for me out there," Paige said as she sat down in one of the chairs by the kitchen table and rubbed her round belly.

"Oh, my goodness! Your belly popped while you were on your honeymoon!" Sadie declared. Sadie jumped into her hostess role. "Let me find something for you to prop your feet up on," she said, walking quickly out of the kitchen.

"I'm fine, Sadie," Paige hollered, but Sadie was on a mission.

Sadie looked all around the living room and thought about stacking some throw pillows on top of one another to make a tall enough prop for Paige to put her feet on. *Maybe as a last resort,* she thought. She decided to check John's home office-gym combo to see if there was anything in there that would be better. She found the perfect thing and carried it to the kitchen and set it down by Paige's feet.

"Oh my gosh!" Paige exclaimed. "That is the cutest thing! I want to get one made for the baby!"

Sadie smiled down at the hand-carved wood stool. JOHN was painted in a light blue color and there was a police car, a badge, and a police hat hand-painted on the top as well.

"We'll have to ask John who made it. It is precious," Sadie replied.

Faith, who had been setting out appetizers and desserts for later, came over to peek at the stool. "Oh, his daddy made that."

"How would you know that?" Paige asked.

"Because my parents bought a few things he made back in the day. It was a hobby for him, but he was very talented. Still is, I reckon," she shrugged.

"Huh, learn something new every day," Paige commented.

Sadie went over to look at the food Faith brought and made herself a plate of appetizers. She never did get to eat that apple. She piled cucumbers, tomatoes, and carrots on her plate with a big healthy dollop of ranch dip. The crockpot held meatballs slow cooked in barbecue sauce and the smell hit Sadie's nose as she lifted the lid, making her salivate, so she threw a few of those on her plate too.

"What kind of barbecue sauce is this?" she asked over her shoulder. "It smells divine."

"Sweet Baby Ray's, of course," Faith answered.

Sadie took another big inhale before she put the lid back on the crockpot. She glanced over at the cookies, and while she normally didn't eat sweets, she was really hungry. She grabbed an oatmeal raisin and turned to go sit down. Faith and Paige were both staring at her with huge grins.

"Hungry?" Faith asked sweetly.

"Leave her alone, Faith. I bet I'd be hungry too if I spent the afternoon working up an appetite with a hunky man," Paige teased. "Oh wait, I did. Move over and let me at the food!"

Sadie and Faith laughed, but gently nudged Paige back to her seat when she tried to stand up. "Sit down pregnant lady. I'll make you a plate," Faith said lovingly.

"Where is Cora Rae tonight? Wasn't she supposed to be here?" Sadie asked.

"She has a hot date with Dr. Patel," Paige shared cheerfully. "She thinks tonight is the night that they'll...you know!"

The women all hummed appreciatively. Faith came over to the table and set a plate down in front of Paige that matched Sadie's. Paige looked up at her and grinned mischievously.

"So, Faith, Cora Rae is about to be getting it on, Sadie is getting it on, I'm clearly getting it on, " Paige said as she rubbed her pregnant belly, "what about you? Huh? Travis still revving your engine?"

Sadie giggled as Faith gave a fake shocked face and held her hands to her head like she was about to faint.

"You mean old married me?" Faith asked in a thick southern drawl. "How dare you ask such a thing!"

Sadie and Paige couldn't hold back the laughter at Faith's shenanigans. Faith carried on with her pretend swoon and twirled prettily until she landed in an empty chair and joined in the laughter.

"Ladies," she began, "it's still like we're on our honeymoon!"

They all let out feminine hoots and cheers, which drew the attention of the men outside the sliding glass door standing by the grill. Their simultaneous looks of wonder had the ladies laughing even harder.

"If they only knew what we get to talking about," Paige said between chuckles.

As Sadie made eye contact with John through the glass door, she once again reveled in the giddy feeling of being part of a couple. It had never fazed her before to not be part of one and knew in her heart it was because she hadn't been with John yet.

She looked over to Paige and thought back to when Jake came barreling back into Paige's life and all of the craziness and love it had brought. With all that, Jake also brought John into Sadie's life. For that, she would always be grateful.

"How was the honeymoon, Paige?" Sadie asked.

"It was wonderful!" Paige gushed. "The Blue Ridge Mountains are gorgeous and the log cabin we stayed in had the best view! We took a few easy hikes to see waterfalls and drove around a lot to take in the views. And of course we took advantage of having some privacy for once."

Faith snorted. "Where are your kids anyways? Didn't y'all get home last night?"

Sadie felt her attention being pulled back outside to where John was. He was so dang fine standing by the flame of the grill. The way he gripped the spatula had the muscles of his forearms popping out in the most delicious way.

"They're still with my parents. We'll pick them up tomorrow," Paige replied, not that Sadie heard her.

"Sadie," Faith began, bringing Sadie's attention back to the conversation, "what's the first thing you plan to change around here? This is a bachelor pad if I've ever seen one."

Sadie looked around her. She hadn't really thought about it yet. The early days of love were keeping her too distracted. She hoped to be too distracted by John for a long time. Between her work schedule and them not being able to keep their hands off one another, redecorating was the last thing on her mind.

"There are still some touches here and there from when his fabulous mama lived here," Paige argued.

"Where?" Faith questioned, skeptically.

Paige slowly rose from her chair and started poking around. Having no luck in the kitchen, she wandered out to the living room. Faith and Sadie smirked to each other.

"Aha!" Paige exclaimed. "The curtains!"

Faith made her way to the living room to check out the curtains while Sadie stayed put at the table, finishing her appetizers and peering out the glass door to watch John man the grill while he drank a bottled beer. *Domestic bliss,* she joked to herself. It was a sight seen in thousands of backyards all the time, but it didn't make it any less special to her. Finally, it was her backyard and her man.

"Ok, so the curtains are feminine," Faith was saying as she walked back into the kitchen. "And John's mama had excellent taste for the nineties, but they need to be updated."

"Aye, aye, Captain! I'll get right on it," Sadie said dutifully, saluting Faith.

"Let's go shopping tomorrow!" Paige shouted excitedly. "We can invite Cora Rae, and she can tell us all about her date and hopefully breakfast with Dr. Patel!"

"Tomorrow is Sunday," Sadie said.

"So what? Get up, go to church with us if you want and then we can shop. The stores all open at noon on Sunday anyway," Faith insisted.

Before Sadie had a chance to answer, the sliding glass door opened and the men came piling in, bringing with them the scent of grilled meat. John carried a platter covered with burgers, some covered with cheddar, some covered with provolone, and some plain. Jake followed with a plate of bacon and Travis with toasted buns.

Faith had brought over tomato slices, lettuce, and onion slices. She went to the fridge to bring out the container holding the fixings. Sadie nudged in with her and took out mayo, ketchup, mustard, and pickles.

"I have chili and slaw too if anyone wants a Carolina burger," John said.

The kitchen was crowded, but the friends didn't mind. They moved easily around each other preparing their burgers and scooping out the potato salad Faith set out. Paige stayed put at the table and Sadie watched as Jake made her a plate without even having to ask what she wanted. *That will be us someday,*

Sadie thought as she sidled up next to John by the counter to put a little mayo on her bun.

"I wouldn't think a heart doctor would eat mayonnaise," John whispered to her.

"Guilty pleasure," she whispered back.

"Hey, John," Faith said as she sat down at the table next to Paige with her full plate of food.

John finished putting the lettuce and tomato on his burger and placing the bun on top before turning to Faith. There were not enough chairs for everyone to sit, so John leaned against the counter to eat standing up.

"What's up, Faith?" he asked before taking a big bite out of his cheeseburger.

Faith looked up at him and grinned. Sadie wondered what in the world she was up to.

"How would you feel about us ladies taking Sadie shopping tomorrow so she can put some personal touches on y'all's house?" she asked sweetly.

John looked over to Sadie and smiled, making sure to keep his lips closed as to not show her a mouth full of food. He finished chewing and answered Faith's question while never moving his gaze away from Sadie.

"I would love that," he said proudly. "You can put whatever you want, wherever you want."

Faith and Paige smiled at each other in approval and the six friends went on with their meal happily discussing their day to day lives and plans for the future. There was no mention of the murderer on the loose in Charleston or the heightened security at the hospital. In the small kitchen that belonged to Sadie and John, those thoughts didn't even enter her mind. All that occupied her was what was right in front of her, good food and the people she loved most in the world. *This is the life,* she thought blissfully.

Chapter Forty

He risked a peek around the small garden shed that he had been hiding behind while the three men were huddled around the shiny gas grill. He had listened to them discuss their upcoming plans for the remainder of the weekend. Extra special attention was paid to what the man he'd seen with Dr. Jennings had to say.

It wouldn't be long before the police would figure him out and then he would have to flee or risk being taken into custody. He wasn't built for prison. He had hoped it wouldn't have to end like that. He had planned to live his two lives for a long time, but his mission was more important.

In his eyes, the only thing standing in his way from taking out the woman doctor who had put him in the position to be caught before he was ready was the man the other two men called John. He couldn't lie to himself and deny that it wasn't a little intimidating that Dr. Jennings' lover was a police officer. He would have to be especially careful and play it smart. But he'd have to be quick, the clock was ticking.

Soon. Very soon.

Chapter Forty-One

Sadie entered Under the Oak Tree with Faith and Paige. She had never been in there before and looking around, she didn't know how she would ever leave. The store was so inviting and cozy. Every item had been placed with care. There was a section of really cute clothes. The summer selections were on a sale rack, and the new fall clothes were displayed along the side wall. The women walked past the clothes and the jewelry counter and started perusing the home section.

"What should we look for first, Sadie? Furniture or knick knacks?" Faith asked. "Or maybe some cute organization containers for around the house?"

Sadie glanced around to decide where to start. "Well, I need a small desk for the home office, but I don't see any furniture for sale. I guess I could just work at the kitchen table."

Faith let out a little laugh. "All of the tables and cabinets displaying the smaller items are actually for sale too."

"Ahh," Sadie replied and started paying closer attention to the pieces that the tea pots, candles, statues, and other home decor sat upon.

Paige had slipped away to peruse a hutch that displayed all sorts of dragonfly decor. Sadie smiled remembering how Paige's dorm room had been covered in dragonflies, the comforter, the lampshade, a really pretty glass statue, and even dragonflies hanging from the ceiling. Her gaze focused on the hutch itself; she really liked it. It was hand painted sage green with daisy wallpaper covering the back of the shelves. The honey oak accents gave it a warm glow. *Maybe I'll get it and turn it into a tea and coffee station in the kitchen,* she thought as she pictured how it would fit in the small space.

Sadie made a mental note to come back to it and started looking for a small desk. There were so many cute things in the store that she kept getting off task and admiring items that would add homey touches. A beautiful tea set caught her eye. It was bone white China with daisies and dandelions. The vision of her tea station was starting to come together perfectly!

"Faith! So good to see you!" A pleasantly plump older lady exclaimed as she approached the section the three friends were shopping in.

"Ms. Shirley!" Faith answered. "How are you today?"

The lady embraced Faith in a warm hug. "I'm good, sweetie. What brings you in today?"

Faith gestured to Paige and Sadie. Paige greeted Ms. Shirley with a small wave. "Ms. Shirley, this is my other best friend, Sadie. Her and Officer John are living together now, and we are helping her find some pieces to give John's bachelor pad a woman's touch."

The lady slowly looked Sadie up and down before giving her the biggest smile and walking over to squeeze her in a big hug.

"It is so nice to finally meet you, dear. I was so happy when John told me he had a special lady friend," Ms. Shirley gushed. "How did you like the hair pin he got you?"

Sadie blushed at all the attention. "I absolutely loved it. It was perfect," she answered.

"How much help did you give him picking it out, Ms. Shirley?" Faith teased.

"Oh, absolutely none! He found it all on his own," Ms. Shirley insisted.

Faith gave Sadie a sly wink and started browsing again. Ms. Shirley let out a relieved sigh and swatted her hand at Faith for teasing her. Turning her attention back to Sadie, she got down to business. "So, honey, what did you have in mind to make John's home your home?"

Sadie turned to face the hutch where Paige was piling her arms full of stuff. "Well, I think I'll start with that hutch that Paige is conveniently clearing off for me," Sadie grinned as she pointed to her friend. Paige looked up guiltily but then shrugged it off and smiled.

"And I would like this tea set as well," Sadie said, pointing to the tea pot, cups, and saucers on the nearby shelf.

"Ooh, those will be perfect together," Ms. Shirley cooed.

"Also, I need a small desk. Do you happen to have one of those?" Sadie asked, looking around trying to spot one.

"Hmmm...I think I am down to one. It is back in that corner Faith is headed towards. I believe there are some vases and picture frames on it. I'll start wrapping up the tea set while you take a look at it," Ms. Shirley said. The lady gently took the tea pot from the shelf and nudged Sadie in the right direction.

Faith waited for Sadie to catch up to her and together they found the desk Ms. Shirley had told her about. It was a dainty old fashioned women's writing desk with a new paint job. It was bright white with bronze hardware on the drawers. It was exactly what she needed. She did most of her work at the hospital, but she liked to research the latest surgical techniques and read about new medical studies in the comfort of her own home. She ran her hand over the top and opened all of the drawers to make sure they slid in and out smoothly.

"You like it?' Faith asked.

"Yeah, I really do," Sadie answered.

"Now, we just need to find you a chair for it," Faith mumbled, looking around. "Aha!"

Sadie watched as Faith sped walked over to a high-backed white wood chair that had curlicues carved along it. The seat was heavily padded and Faith plopped down to check the level of comfiness. Sadie slowly walked over to join her, enjoying the show of Faith bouncing on the chair and twisting her butt around on the cushion.

"What's the verdict?" Sadie asked jokingly.

"Laugh all you want. I say it's comfy, but not so comfy you'll fall asleep reading your boring online medical journals," Faith said.

Sadie scoffed, "They aren't boring to me."

"Whatever," Faith mumbled. "Let's see if it's the right height for the desk."

Faith stood up and carried the chair over to the desk, carefully avoiding any breakable objects. She set it down and looked to Sadie. "Come sit," she instructed.

Sadie obliged and took a seat. She scooted the chair up under the desk to make sure her legs would fit. They did.

"I'm kind of used to having a rolling chair," she pondered aloud.

"I think a rolling chair would mess up that thick carpet y'all have in your home office," Faith replied. "I just love saying that, y'all's home office in yours and John's home."

Sadie smiled and looked at her friend. "I love hearing it and I think you're right about the carpet."

Faith clapped her hands together in victory. "Ms. Shirley, we'll take the desk and this chair too!" she hollered through the store.

They made their way to the front where the register was. There, Ms. Shirley was ringing up the armful of stuff Paige had decided on.

"Good thing Jake doesn't mind my dragonfly obsession," Paige said sheepishly to her friends.

"These are gorgeous items, Paige," Ms. Shirley reassured her. "This pink stained-glass dragonfly would hang beautifully in the window of a baby girl's room."

"That's the plan," Paige cheerfully replied as she handed over her credit card.

"Wait! It's a girl?" Faith and Sadie shrieked at the same time.

Paige nodded the affirmative and the three women clapped and cheered in delight.

"Awe! A baby girl!" Faith said joyfully.

"Congratulations, Paige. That is just precious!" Ms. Shirley said, handing over Paige's bag of purchases. "I wrapped that glass in bubble wrap, hon."

When it was Sadie's turn to check out, Ms. Shirley grabbed a notepad and started writing down the pieces of furniture Sadie wanted. "You wanted the hutch and if I heard Faith's hollering correctly, the desk and which chair?"

"The white painted one with the curlicues and the yellow cushion. We left it over with the desk," Sadie answered.

Ms. Shirley nodded as she wrote it all down. She pulled a silver bell from under the counter and gave it a couple of rings. Sadie wondered what that was all about, but Ms. Shirley didn't explain, and her friends seemed unfazed by it. She pulled her wallet out of her handbag to get her credit card ready as Ms. Shirley started ringing her up.

"You rang?" a dry male voice said from behind Sadie.

Sadie turned around to see a tall older man with silver hair. He appeared to be in great physical shape and even though his tone of voice implied annoyance at being summoned, his blue eyes sparkled with playfulness.

"Sadie, this is my husband, Carl. Carl, this is Officer Avery's lady, Sadie," Ms. Shirley said, making introductions.

Carl looked from Sadie to his wife and back to Sadie. He leaned forward with his hand outstretched. "It sure is nice to meet you, Sadie. The town has been abuzz with the news that John is finally settling down."

Sadie's eyes widened at learning that she was the talk of the town. Carl noticed her look of discomfort. "Small towns," he shrugged, "better get used to it."

"Carl," Ms. Shirley said to regain her husband's attention, "Sadie is buying that green hutch over there and that white desk in the back left corner. There is a chair with it, bring that too." Then she looked to Sadie. "Is John coming to pick up the furniture or would you like Carl to deliver it?"

"Uh, I haven't thought about it. Just a moment," Sadie said and took out her phone to text John.

"I think all the guys are hanging out watching baseball. The Braves have to beat somebody or other to make the playoffs," Faith informed her.

Sadie's phone chimed. "Yup, John and Jake are on the way. Travis is going to hang back and finish watching the game. It's tied in the bottom of the eighth, whatever that means."

Faith shook her head and chuckled, "That man."

The three friends stood around chatting with Ms. Shirley while they watched Carl haul the furniture pieces to the front of the store.

"So why didn't Cora Rae come today? I was looking forward to hearing all the juicy details about Dr. Patel," Sadie wondered.

Paige waggled her eyebrows suggestively. "She's still at his place! She snuck me a quick text. Apparently, breakfast turned into some kind of sexy foreplay involving maple syrup, and he had told her he had no intention of letting her leave his bed anytime soon!"

"Way to go, Cora Rae!" Faith cheered. "That's my girl!"

A little while later, as the women were playing a friendly guessing game about Dr. Patel's attributes, the bell over the front door chimed as John and Jake came walking in.

"I brought the truck," Jake said as he made his way over to kiss his wife on the cheek. "Find anything good?" he asked her.

"You know it," Paige answered.

Sadie admired the view of John walking towards her and held out her arms in anticipation of touching him and the excitement of wanting to show him what she picked out for their home.

John wrapped his arm around her shoulders and whispered in her ear, "And you? Find anything good for our home?"

Sadie pulled him over to where Carl had set the desk and the chair. "For me for our home office and then that hutch over there where Carl is clearing off the couple of remaining items with dragonflies that Paige didn't buy."

"I already have them," Paige commented.

Jake pulled her into him and rubbed her belly while whispering something in her ear privately.

"I also got a tea set that matches the hutch," Sadie went on.

"Oh yes, it is in this box on the counter. I bubble wrapped everything," Ms. Shirley said.

"Great!" John said, clapping his hands together. "Let's start loading it up."

He gave Sadie a quick forehead kiss and him and Jake each took an end of the desk to carry it to the truck. When they came back in the store, Carl had the hutch cleared off, so the three of them took it out to the truck. They came back in for the last load, Carl taking the chair, John grabbing the box with the tea set, and Jake relieving Paige of her bag.

"Be careful, some of it is fragile!" Paige shrieked.

"I got it! I got it!" Jake assured her.

"Yeah, Jake, be careful not to break the thing she got for your baby girl's room!" Sadie teased.

Jake beamed ear to ear like the proud papa he was.

The ladies said their goodbyes to Ms. Shirley and Carl and went outside to see what the guys were up to next.

"We'll go unload this stuff at the house and then grab some lunch," John said, looking over to Jake for a nod of approval. "Where y'all off to next?"

Sadie thought about it for a few seconds before responding, "Probably Target or somewhere like that to get some towels."

"What's wrong with my towels?" John asked in mock offense.

"Not fluffy enough," Sadie answered, pulling him in for a hug and goodbye kiss.

"Mmhmm," John murmured against her lips. "Don't forget, I got called in to work a few hours tonight, but I'll probably see you before I have to head out and I should be home in time for bed."

"Cut it out lovebirds. We have shopping to do, " Faith teased from beside her car. "Let's get to it!"

Sadie and Paige said their goodbyes to their men and climbed in Faith's sedan. As they pulled away, Sadie watched John and Jake finish tying down the furniture. She didn't notice the guy watching them from across the street.

Chapter Forty-Two

It was hot and muggy, and the mosquitos were eating him up. He slapped his neck as another one tried to take a bite of him. "Damned bloodsuckers," he mumbled.

He turned his attention back to the sickeningly cheery yellow house. Last time he was there, he watched from the shed in the back. He chose the woods that ran along the front side of the property for his current stakeout. There was no need to hear anything, only to see when the good doctor got home from shopping. Such frivolity. It disgusted him.

He checked his watch to try to gauge how much longer he would have to wait in his uncomfortable perch. The cop had told his buddies that he would be going into work for a few hours. That would be his time to strike; better to take on the doctor by herself.

He circled his head around, trying to ease the crick he was getting in his neck. His ears perked up at the sound of an engine approaching. He ducked behind a thick tree and watched a silver sedan turn into the drive. He snuck a peek and saw Dr. Jennings in the passenger seat singing along to whatever ridiculous song he could hear blaring through the windows. Her blond friend was driving, but there was no sign of the pregnant one. They must have dropped her off already. Hopefully blondie won't stay long. No doubt the doc will want some alone time with her lover before he goes to work.

"Slut," he muttered.

A few moments later, he got his wish and the blond left. He sat down between the trees to wait for the cop to leave.

"I hope y'all make your goodbye count as it will be your last," he proclaimed, an evil smile mutating his normally handsome face.

Chapter Forty-Three

"Honey, I'm home!" Sadie announced joyfully as she opened the front door. She was still really excited about sharing a home with John. It made her feel giddy and light.

Faith followed her in; both ladies had their arms laden with bags filled with housewares. "Where do you want them?" Faith asked, lifting her arms to indicate the shopping bags.

Sadie looked around the entryway and the living room, contemplating where the best spot would be to have them easily accessible but not in the way. "The couch, I guess," she answered.

They both plopped their bags down onto the navy-blue couch, completely covering it.

"Those red throw pillows you got are going to look great with this couch," Faith commented.

"Yeah, I think they'll work. I really wanted those buttercup yellow ones, but the red ones were less feminine. I don't want to completely take over his house," Sadie responded.

"You honestly think he would care? That man is so crazy for you that you could paint this whole house neon pink and have all flowery fabric furniture, and he would still be thrilled that you are here," Faith joked.

Sadie chuckled. "I wouldn't go quite that far."

The man in question joined them in the living room and looked at the impressive amount of shopping bags covering his couch. "Y'all leave anything for the other shoppers?" John teased.

"Well, your woman here did elbow some old lady right in the nose over a lamp. There was blood everywhere. Then she ended up not even wanting the lamp," Faith told him in a serious tone.

John turned his shocked face to Sadie. "She's joking, right?"

The women laughed good-naturedly at him and he shook his head.

"Y'all got me on that one," he said joining in on the laughs. "The scene I just pictured in my head was wild!"

A phone chirped with an alert, and they all simultaneously pulled out their cell phones.

"It's mine," Faith announced. "Travis is wondering where I am. He's missing me. The Braves lost in the ninth inning and he's needing some comforting."

Faith hugged Sadie and John goodbye and headed towards the door. "Ahh! I'm so happy for you guys!" she said excitedly on her way out.

John grinned and pulled Sadie in for a kiss. "I'm so happy for us too," he murmured against her lips.

"Alright, alright, stud," Sadie said, pushing back from John while giggling happily. "I want to get these towels I bought in the wash so we can start using them."

John followed her over to the couch where she started pulling out huge fluffy teal towels. "So, these are the towels that are so much better than the ones I already had?" he questioned teasingly.

"Oh yeah. These bad boys are going to be so snuggly when we get out of the shower. And they'll add a pop of color to your boring gray bathroom."

John kissed her cheek. "I love them."

He helped her carry the half dozen towels, hand towels, and wash clothes to his washing machine. His house was an older one and had been built before the time of everyone owning automatic washing machines and dryers. When the original owners of the house got a set, they added on to the master bath and put them in there. John still had the same appliances that his parents had bought when they upgraded in the nineties. He showed Sadie the cabinet where he stored the laundry detergent and the vinegar to keep the towels soft. He measured out the liquid detergent, added in a little vinegar and started the machine.

"Those things are dinosaurs," Sadie commented as she followed him out of the bathroom. She plopped down on the bed to watch John get dressed for work.

John turned to face her while taking a black uniform shirt off of a hanger. "They still work like champs though," he retorted.

"Why do you have to cover for someone for a few hours? I forgot to ask earlier," Sadie questioned.

"Officer Doug's kids are singing in a church concert tonight. I told him I'd cover for him so he could go," John answered.

"Well, aren't you a sweetie pie," she teased. *Aren't I lucky to have found such a considerate man,* she pondered to herself.

"Hmmm...I prefer small-town hero," he quipped. He leapt on the bed and playfully tackled her, covering her face and neck with butterfly kisses before settling in for some serious making out.

Before things could get to the point John would have to start completely over getting dressed again, Sadie rolled over to sit on top of him.

"If you don't get something to eat Officer John, you'll have to go to work hungry," Sadie chastised playfully, looking down at the gorgeous man beneath her.

John flirtatiously smacked her butt. "Well, then you better feed me, woman!" he jested.

In the kitchen John made BLT with avocado sandwiches while Sadie threw together a Caesar salad.

"I'm going to check up on you periodically while I'm driving around on patrol. We need to think of a secret signal, so I know you're okay when I drive by," he said before popping a piece of bacon in his mouth.

"How about a simple text?" Sadie asked as she took a couple of bowls out of a cabinet.

John looked at her in disbelief. "How am I supposed to know for sure if it's you texting back? Huh? You could be tied up, or unconscious and some maniac could be texting me, 'yeah babe I'm fine'," he said incredulously.

"Would I ever call you babe?" Sadie questioned, breaking out her signature eyebrow move.

"I wouldn't want to risk it," he replied.

He thought for a few moments while he ate his sandwich. Sadie watched him with interest as the wheels were turning in his head.

"I got it," he began, "I'll text you to say I'm out front in the street and you flicker the front porch lights off and on. Then I'll know for sure that you are safe."

"We couldn't just use a code word?" she suggested.

"Too risky," he determined.

Sadie chuckled at his over-protectiveness, but inside it made her heart flutter. It felt good to be so important to someone that they planned out secret safety measures. They took a few bites in silence before John's attention shifted to the new sage green hutch behind Sadie.

"I like that hutch you picked out. It looks good in here and fits perfectly," he complimented. "I had been a little worried at the store that it might be too big. This kitchen isn't very spacious."

Sadie turned around to admire their new hutch and smiled. Her mouth was full of a big bite of lettuce, crouton, and shaved parmesan cheese so she simply nodded in agreement.

John went on, "I left the tea set in the box over there on the counter. I figured you would want to unpack it and set it all up yourself. Also, if you don't like where Jake and I put your desk in the office feel free to move it or wait until I get home and I'll move it anywhere you want."

"Okay, I will see if I'm satisfied with where my delivery boys put my new desk," Sadie replied mischievously after she swallowed her food.

After dinner, they put their dishes in the dishwasher and John went to brush his teeth. Sadie opened the box to the tea set but then decided to save setting up the tea station for last; then she would reward herself with a nice relaxing cup of tea when she was done. She heard John walking towards the front door and went to say goodbye. They snuck in one more long deep kiss before having to part.

"Oh, I forgot to mention the gun safe. It's in my closet on the floor right inside the door. The code is ten-twenty-four-eighty-three. It's my parents' wedding anniversary," he informed her.

Sadie felt a bit uncertain. She didn't want to even think about holding a gun. "Thanks, but I'm more comfortable with knives," she countered.

John smiled at her indulgently and stole one more quick kiss. As he was walking through the threshold the washing machine dinged.

"That was fast," Sadie remarked, looking down the hall towards the sound.

John stepped out onto the front porch and turned around. "Yeah, no high efficiency crap here. Those old school appliances use a ton water so it doesn't take as long."

Sadie laughed and went out on the porch to kiss him one more time. She couldn't get enough of him. She wondered if it would always be like that.

"Don't forget, when I text you, flicker the front porch light off and on," he reminded her before pulling away.

He gave her little wave before he got in his squad car and drove off to report for duty.

Too bad he didn't see the man hiding in his woods.

Chapter Forty-Four

Finally, the damned cop was leaving! The cop pulled out of the long driveway after saying goodbye to his slut like a dozen times. If he had to watch anymore lovey-dovey crap he was going to puke.

Instead of rushing right up to the house, he waited for a few minutes to make sure the cop didn't return in case he forgot something, or heaven forbid wanted to kiss the soon to be dead Dr. Sadie Jennings again.

When the coast seemed to be clear, he stepped out of the dense woods and made his way down the driveway, using the huge oaks that lined it as cover. He crept up by the wide stairs of the front porch and crouched down for a few breaths to make sure he hadn't been seen by the doctor inside the house.

He took the porch stairs slowly, staying low. Once on the porch he crept up to a window. He stole a quick glance inside the house through the big picture window. There was a dark blue couch covered in shopping bags in a small living room. The coffee table was old and worn with scratches. He could see through to the back door and there was an opening that from what he could remember from his earlier spying led to the kitchen. There was a small hallway on each side of the living room. All that he could see, but no sign of the doctor he was looking for.

He crept to the other side of the porch past the front door to another set of windows. The blinds were slatted open, but the curtains behind were drawn so he couldn't see inside. He put his ear up against the window and at first he couldn't hear anything. Suddenly there was a slam, like that of a door closing. Then he heard what sounded like the hum of a dryer start up.

He made his way back to the window that peered into the living room and sure enough a few seconds later, his target came into view. She bent over the couch and looked through the bags before picking a few of them up and carrying them down a hall which he guessed led to a bedroom.

He creeped over to the front door and inspected the lock. He was amused at finding that there was only a lock on the doorknob. He had expected at least a deadbolt to contend with. *How convenient for me.*

Time to end this.

Chapter Forty-Five

John pulled his squad car into the parking lot of the Meadow Oaks Police Station to check in before going out to patrol. He sat at his desk to check his messages then decided to give Detective Jenkins a call to see if there were any updates.

The line rang a few times and right when John was about to give up, Detective Jenkins answered. "Good evening, Officer Avery. Care to guess where I am right now?" Detective Jenkins queried.

John sighed. "Please, tell me there hasn't been another murder," he pleaded.

"No, thank goodness. We got a judge to sign off on warrants today to search the homes of Dr. Daniel Wu and Dr. Todd Madison," he informed John. "I'm at Dr. Wu's right now and Detective Fuller is currently at Dr. Madison's place."

"How is it going at Dr. Wu's? Anything interesting turn up?" John asked eagerly.

"Hold on a sec," Detective Jenkins paused.

John could hear him excuse himself to someone and move to somewhere with less background noise.

"Okay, I'm back. Dr. Wu is clearly OCD. There doesn't seem to be a thing out of place. Every shoe slot in the closet is filled with shoes that are immaculate. As far as the forensic team can tell, none of the treads match what we got the night you chased the guy. But if he was smart, he would have gotten rid of them that night anyways."

"That's a shame," John muttered. "Anything else?"

"He's got a lot of nice clothes. Whoever does his laundry uses so much starch that his shirts and pants are stiff as a board. The man even has his t-shirts ironed," Detective Jenkins commented.

John heard Dr. Wu's lawyer pipe up from next to Detective Jenkins, "His dad expects perfection from his son."

"Damn, nosy lawyer," Detective Jenkins mumbled. "Listen John, we just got started and still have a long way to go. I'll give you a call when we are finished and this soulless bloodsucker isn't hovering over me."

John heard the lawyer scoff.

"Thank you, Detective Jenkins. Talk to you later," John replied and hung up.

Instead of leaving to patrol he decided to make a quick call to Detective Fuller to see if her search of Dr. Madison's residence was going any better.

"Fuller here," she answered on the second ring.

"I hear you are searching Dr. Madison's house right now," John said. "How's it going?"

"This place is a dump. He has a two-bedroom in a shitty apartment building. You know, the kind of place where bad people can do bad things and no one would bat an eyelash. The place is trashed so I'm going to have to call you later. This is going to take a while," she lamented.

John hated having to wait on news and not be there to assist in the searches, but he didn't work for the Charleston Police Department so he would have to try to keep himself busy in order to help the time go by faster.

He stood up from his desk to go start patrolling when Alice, the nine-one-one dispatcher, approached his desk.

"Hey, Alice. You changed your hair. I like it. It's feisty," John complimented.

Patting her newly dyed fire red hair, Alice shrugged. "It was time for a change. Anyway, Widow Barnes called in, says she heard something rooting around in her garbage cans outside. Probably just a critter. Can you check it out?"

"Of course," John answered. "I'll head there now."

John left the police station grateful that he had something to keep him occupied, at least for a little while.

***

Leaning down into the washing machine, Sadie pulled out the last wet towel and tossed it into the dryer. She turned the ancient dial to set the cycle but remembered before she started it that she had bought new wool dryer balls to use instead of the dryer sheets John had. *Much less toxic.*

Back in the living room, Sadie reached over the back of the couch and dug through the bags until she found what she was looking for. A movement outside by the big oak tree with the tire swing caught her eye. She walked over to the big window to get a closer look at what was going on outside. She shrugged when she didn't see anything unusual and went to start the dryer. The dryer balls were loud at first, bouncing around in the dryer as the drum turned round and round. Sadie wasn't bothered by it, *once they get tangled up in the towels it won't be so loud,* she reminded herself.

She returned to the living room, the list of all the things she wanted to do running through her mind. After a glance into the bags to make sure she was grabbing what she wanted, she carried a few into her home office to set up her new desk. She had also bought a new yoga mat, so she went back to the living room to get it. She figured she should take advantage of the country quiet and take up yoga and meditation.

John and Jake had put her desk in front of the double window, next to his dumbbells. *Probably going to move those later.* She sat her bags on the ground in front of the weights and opened her laptop to fire it up. She put the yoga mat in the closet for the time being. The house was a little too quiet, besides the hum of the dryer, so she pulled up her playlist on her computer that she liked to have going in the background when she read medical journals.

The blinds behind her desk were closed, so she stood up to pull the string to turn the slats open to take another look at the huge oak with the tire swing. She couldn't believe that she had such a beautiful front yard. The sun was starting to set and the sky above and behind the trees was a pretty orange and pink color. She could look at the view of the majestic trees all day which could end up being a problem on days she really needed to get her work done.

Tearing her eyes away from the outside, she sat back down on her new yellow cushioned chair and bent down to retrieve the items she had purchased for her new desk. Singing along to some old school Toni Braxton, Sadie piled paperclips, staples, pens, highlighters, and Post-it notes on the desk. She pulled out a pink ceramic container that said BOSS LADY on it and plopped the pens and highlighters in it. The other items went in the top drawer of the desk. A stack of legal pads went in the bottom drawer.

When all of the office supplies were put away neatly, she rummaged through the bags trying to decide what to put out next. She pulled out a Sea Salt and Orchid scented candle, bringing it to her nose to take a deep inhale of the scent. Still holding the candle to her nose, she reached down to feel around for the lighter she bought to keep in her desk to light the candle. She hated having to go rummage around in kitchen drawers anytime she wanted to create a cozy ambience. She found the lighter and set the candle down on the desk to free her hand to rip open the packaging.

Behind her, the floor squeaked.

"Good evening, Dr. Jennings," a familiar voice said in greeting.

Chapter Forty-Six

With the racoon safely taken care of at the home of Widow Barnes, John went back out on patrol. He set the plastic container of thank you cookies she had rewarded him with in the passenger seat, excited to share them with Sadie when he got home later. Widow Barnes made the best snickerdoodles.

John decided to cruise down Main Steet before heading out into the neighborhoods. He passed by Under the Oak Tree, which was locked up tight for the evening. Frankie's Jazz Club was closed on Sundays, but he could see lights on upstairs in Frankie's apartment. The bookstore owner was locking up for the night, and John gave him a friendly wave.

His cell phone began to ring, and the caller ID let him know that it was Detective Fuller. John pulled over into a parking space across from the town square so he could give the detective his undivided attention.

"Detective Fuller," he greeted, "get anything good?"

"Um, this guy is a little strange," she commented.

"What do you mean?" John queried.

"It looks like the place was either ransacked or maybe he packed up some of his belongings in a hurry, but we did find this notebook with weird rantings in it," she said.

"What did it say?" he wondered curiously.

"At first glance, it just looks like affirmations which isn't necessarily weird. Trust your inner voice, God will show you the way, you have been chosen for greatness, stuff like that. But then along the margins in shakier handwriting there are scribbles about the unworthy inhabiting the Earth. It's a little difficult to read."

John scratched his chin while he pondered what the detective had described to him. "That is a bit strange. Anything else?" he asked.

"There seems to be items missing from the top of his dresser, I can tell because of all the dust. There are clear outlines where they used to be," she explained. "One outline is circular, like maybe there was a bracelet laying there. It might be difficult to determine what the other ones might have been, but forensics has taken their photos, so maybe someone in the lab can figure it out."

"What about shoes? Did y'all find any that matched what we had on file from the night Leann Rivers was attacked?" John questioned.

"No, there aren't any shoes here at all. Technically there isn't anything here that we can use. I called the hospital to check his schedule, but he's not due in until the morning. With the way his apartment was left, I asked them to call me right away if he doesn't show up. Sorry I don't have more for you yet," Detective Fuller said.

"No, thank you so much for filling me in," John replied.

"How is Dr. Jennings doing?" she asked.

"Oh, Sadie is a trooper. I'm hoping this is all over soon so she can heal and move on. Her best friends went through something similarly crazy to this a few months ago, so she's still trying to process that too," John answered.

"Yeah, I heard about that case from Officer Sanders. That had to be some rough shit," she responded.

"Yeah, Sadie is at our place in Meadow Oaks tonight. I think I'm going to go check on her, just to put my mind at ease," John said.

"I'll let you go then. I'll call you if something comes up," she promised.

John hung up the call and sat for a minute replaying the information Detective Fuller had given him in case anything would stand out in his mind. There was something he was missing, something that would make everything click together and break the case wide open. When nothing seemed to jump out at him, he backed his squad car out of the parking space and headed towards home to check on his woman.

***

At the sound of the voice coming from behind her, Sadie took a deep breath in and steeled herself for what was to come. Slowly, she turned sideways in her chair, her feet next to her shopping bags and John's dumbbells on the floor.

"Dr. Madison, to what do I owe the pleasure?" she asked calmly. She squeezed the back of the chair tightly to keep her hands from shaking.

She looked him over head to toe. His dark hair was unruly, like he had been pulling at it a lot. He had on a camo long sleeved shirt, even though the temperature that day had been in the low nineties with seventy percent humidity. His brown cargo pants had plenty of pockets to hide weapons, but at least he didn't have any in his hands. His black sneakers were covered in dust and dirt. Pulling her attention back up to his eyes, she noted he had dark circles and his eyes were bloodshot, making him look tired and a bit deranged.

When he didn't say anything in response, she tried again to get him talking.

"I didn't hear a car pull up, Todd," she commented. She remembered reading something in an article about using first names when someone is threatening you to remind them of any familiarity you may have with them if you happen to know them.

"I parked on the next street over and walked here through the woods," he stated. "I've been watching the house, waiting for your boyfriend to leave."

He walked over to John's desk, turned the chair to face Sadie, and sat down. He didn't say anything else, only sat and stared at her with a grim look of determination on his face.

"Why are you here, Todd?" she asked.

"Because Dr. Jennings, you have to die," he told her.

His tone came off as nonchalant, which scared Sadie more than it would have if he had sounded angry. *Would killing me mean so little to him?* she fretted.

Sadie's heart rate went into overdrive, but she didn't let it show on the outside. Remaining as calm as possible, she decided to try to keep him talking to buy her some time to come up with a plan.

"Why do I have to die, Todd?" she queried, trying to match his tone of nonchalance.

"Because you helped her," he said simply, like it should have been the most obvious thing in the world.

"Helped who, Todd?" she asked, even though she already knew the answer.

"The whore from outside the bar. Leann Rivers," he said her name with a sneer.

"Why do you assume she was a whore, Todd? Did you know her personally?"

"I didn't need to know her personally. Any woman who spends their time in places like that is a whore."

Sadie frantically searched her mind for all she knew about Dr. Todd Madison in an attempt to come up with something to change his mind about wanting to kill her. Then it dawned on her, the probable root of his psychosis. Thank goodness she liked to read medical journals for fun. Maybe she could recall enough information from one to help her.

"Dr. Madison, Todd, what happened to your mother and sister? You told the detectives that they had moved away. Is that true?"

"Kind of. They got sent to Hell where they belong," he answered, sounding bored.

"You killed them," Sadie stated.

"They deserved it. For years, my mom barely held down shitty jobs because she was too busy chasing men in bars that she thought were going to take care of her. Meanwhile she was sending me to school hungry and in dirty clothes. Those men saw her for what she was though, and she never got one to take her seriously."

"I understand, Todd. And your sister? Why did you feel you had to kill her?"

Dr. Madison shook his head in disgust and closed his eyes briefly. Sadie took the opportunity to look around frantically for something she could use to protect herself or to fight back with. *Why couldn't I be one of those people with a fancy knife-like letter opener?* she chastised herself.

"My sister, Breanna, was an amazing big sister to me for most of my childhood. She was only two years older than me, so we were very close. We had different dads, but we never thought of each other as anything other than full-blooded family. It was us against everything and everyone else. Then one day when she was fourteen and I was twelve, she went crazy over some boy. He was seventeen and it wasn't too long before he defiled her and then got her hooked on drugs. She stopped caring about me so much after that," he said, anger starting to seep into his voice.

"I'm so sorry, Todd. That had to be really hard on you, so young going through so much," she sympathized.

"Yeah, well, he dumped her when she got all strung out and wasn't so pretty anymore, but she didn't clean up her act. She started hopping from guy to guy like our mother, spending her time in bars and clubs chasing the next high. I tried for years to help her, but about six months ago, God sent me a message."

"What did He say, Todd?"

"He said that she would be better off dead. That they both would."

"How did he tell you that?"

"He spoke to me. His voice was in my head. I did as He bid me and I took care of them in their sleep with a kitchen knife. My mom woke up after the first stab and started to scream, so I had to put a pillow over her head, but my sister was so drugged up that she never knew it was happening. She just laid there and died." He sounded a bit disappointed.

"What did you do with their bodies, Todd? With the others you left them where they were killed, but I never heard anything on the news about your mom and sister." She had to keep him talking.

"Luckily for me, Dr. Jennings, the shitty apartment building my mother rented for us, the one I imagine the police will be searching soon, if they haven't already, is a place where people don't ask questions. Everyone there has secrets, so they mind their own business. I wrapped my mom up in the shower curtain and my sister in a blanket; and since neither of them weighed very much due to their hard way of living, I carried them right out in the middle of the night to the trunk of my piece of shit car. I drove out to the middle of nowhere, I'm not even sure exactly where, I just drove until there was nothing around and a bit of swamp. I poured gasoline all over them and burned the bodies. Fitting since their souls are burning in Hell."

Sadie nodded like she understood, but inside she was freaking out. The young man had lost his mind. Childhood trauma and some kind of mental breakdown had him actually thinking that what he did was directed by God. Sadie's church attendance record was spotty at best because of her crazy work schedule, but she had gone every Sunday as a child, and she didn't remember anything like that being in the preacher's sermon.

"What about the other women, Todd?" she asked. "Why kill them?"

"His voice told me I had done a great job with Mom and Breanna and that He was proud of me. He told me I passed the test and had been chosen to rid the Earth of all the sinful women who did not deserve to inhabit it."

For a moment, Sadie and Dr. Madison simply stared at each other. Sadie was trying to think of something else to say to keep stalling, but her mind was reeling with everything he had told her. The images of Birdie Duvall and Leann Rivers after their attacks clouding her mind. *Those poor young women.*

Chapter Forty-Seven

John pulled up to the end of his long driveway and put the squad car in park. The sky was losing the last of its light for the day, so he could see that there were lights on in the house, but he couldn't see inside. The house was a little too far away and there were the big oak trees blocking his view as well.

He grabbed his cell phone out of the cup holder and opened his text messages. It was easy enough to find the thread with Sadie as she was the last person he had messaged that day.

> John: Hey babe ❤ I'm outside.

John looked up from the phone to watch the porch light for their signal. He waited patiently for a couple of minutes, but when nothing happened, he started to get nervous.

"Come on, Sadie. Come on," he mumbled.

He tapped his fingers on the steering wheel uneasily while he waited another moment.

Maybe she's in the bathroom?

***

Sadie's cell phone chirped and buzzed noisily on the desk. *Maybe John is here!* she thought in relief.

However, the noise startled Dr. Madison out of the staring contest he was having with the woman he was there to kill, and it brought his attention back to his task.

"No more talking," he proclaimed and pulled out a knife from the big pocket on the right leg of his pants. He took the leather sheath off of the five-inch steel blade and stood up to move towards Sadie.

Sadie blindly reached down towards the floor and wrapped her left hand around the closest of John's dumbbells, never taking her eyes off of Dr. Madison. As he approached her, she switched the weight to her right hand and came up swinging with all of her might. The side of the dumbbell caught Dr. Madison on the left side of his head at his temple as Sadie tried to deflect the deadly sharp knife he was bringing down on her with her other arm.

***

John inserted his key into the front door lock of his house and as he was about to turn it, the radio on his shoulder went off loudly with a message from dispatch.

"Call from forty-two Deer Run Lane, intruder on site, ambulance requested," the voice squeaked.

Once John heard his address being said over the radio, he turned the lock and threw the door open so hard it hit the spring door bumper and came back at him. He ran down the short hallway to his bedroom, but Sadie wasn't in there or in the bathroom. He ran back out into the living room and ducked his head in the doorway to the kitchen, but she was not there. He noted the box with the tea set was open but still on the counter.

"SADIE!" he yelled, already heading for the other hallway that led to their home office.

He found her standing in the middle of the floor, the crumpled form of Dr. Todd Madison beneath her. In one hand she had one of his black and silver dumbbells by her side and in the other she had her cell phone up to her ear.

"Yeah, he's here," she said to whichever dispatcher was on the other line. "Thank you so much."

Sadie hung up the call and practically jumped into John's arms. He caught her with one arm and with the other he took the dumbbell from her.

"Twenty-pounder, huh?" he teased with relief as he held her tightly.

"Knocked his ass right on out," she responded, her voice shaking only a little.

"That's my girl," he whispered, kissing her neck.

John and Sadie held each other close, both not wanting to let go. All of the nerves that Sadie had been able to push aside to remain calm in front of Dr. Todd Madison came rushing to the surface and her whole body started to tremble. John began to rock side to side to try to soothe her.

"I got you, Sadie," he whispered in her ear. "You're safe. You beat him, baby. I got you."

He held her and whispered reassurances over and over while sneaking peeks down at Dr. Madison to make sure he didn't regain consciousness and catch them off guard. The sound of sirens coming down the street brought Sadie out of her panic, and she tried to pull herself together. She didn't want anyone other than John seeing her like that.

John carried her out to the living room and gently set her down on the couch among the remainder of her shopping bags. The dryer buzzed in the background.

"Sounds like your fancy towels are dry," he teased cautiously. He leaned down and kissed her cheek. "I'll be right back."

Sadie curled her legs underneath her on the couch and John walked back down the hallway to their home office. The sirens were almost to the house and Sadie could see the headlights of the police cars as they pulled into the driveway and raced down to stop in front of their porch. She looked over to the front door to see if she needed to open it for them, but John had left it open when he came home. She was relieved, she didn't know if her legs would hold her up yet. The adrenaline coursing through her left her shaky.

An officer she'd never met in a Meadow Oaks uniform poked his head through the door, gun drawn.

"Good evening, Miss. I'm Officer Tate," he said, "dispatch said the intruder was unconscious, is that correct?" he asked taking a few cautious steps into the house.

"Yes, Officer John Avery is back there with him," she responded, pointing in the direction of the office.

The officer walked to the entry of the hallway and hollered, "Yo, John, you got him secured?"

"He's handcuffed and still knocked out," John shouted back.

Officer Tate walked back over to the front door and Sadie's eyes followed him. He gave a signal to someone outside and then went to join John in the other room. A moment later, a pair of EMTs made their way through the front door with a stretcher and a medical bag.

Sadie sat up straighter on the couch. "I'm a doctor, do you want help with him?" she asked.

One of the EMTs came over to Sadie and squatted down in front of her. "I recognize you from the hospital, Dr. Jennings. My name is Sarah," she said. "How are you feeling? Are you feeling any distress, any shock symptoms?"

Sadie did a rapid mental run through of her entire body and assessed it as if she were examining a patient. "I have some adrenaline still trying to work its way out of my system, so I feel a little shaky," she admitted. "My arm hurts a little where I knocked his arm away when he came at me with a knife. I'm fine though. I'm not going to go into shock."

The EMT looked at Sadie's arm. There wasn't any swelling and there wasn't any worry about a broken bone. She flashed a pen light in Sadie's eyes and was reassured by what she saw. "You seem alert and your pupils are normal. Rest and stay hydrated, Dr. Jennings. Have one of your colleagues check you out if you have any concerns."

"Thank you, I will," Sadie responded.

"You're welcome. Now, where is this asshole you knocked out?" the EMT questioned with a smile on her face.

"Back there," Sadie directed, pointing out the way.

The EMTs squeezed the stretcher through the narrow hallway and Sadie could hear them talking to John and Officer Tate. A knock on the open front door brought her attention back behind her. An older gentleman in khakis and a maroon USC polo was standing in the doorway.

"Dr. Sadie Jennings?" he asked, running his fingers through his graying hair.

"Yes, that's me," she answered.

The man walked over to her and shook her hand. "I'm Chief Atkins of the Meadow Oaks Police Department. It's nice to finally meet the woman John won't shut up about. Sorry it's not under more pleasant circumstances."

"Nice to meet you too, Chief," she replied, giving him a small smile. It was all she had the energy for. The adrenaline was wearing off, and exhaustion was threatening to take over.

"I'll just go help my boys process the scene," the chief said, excusing himself.

Sadie closed her eyes and rested her head on the back of the couch. When she woke up, she found herself in John's bed. She checked her cell phone to see how much time had passed and saw it had only been a little over an hour since John had carried her out of the office. She could hear through the closed door of the bedroom that a bunch of commotion was still going on in the rest of the house. She went into the closet and grabbed one of John's sweatshirts to throw on, feeling chilly despite it being warm outside. She wandered out into the living room and when John saw her, he rushed over to check on her.

"Hey, I didn't expect you to wake up so soon," he murmured as he looked her over.

"Did you carry me to bed?" she wondered.

"I came back out to the living room to see how you were and you were fast asleep sitting up on the couch. Figured you'd be more comfortable in the bed."

Sadie nodded and looked around at all the people milling around their house. Detective Jenkins came down the hall, followed by Detective Fuller. They walked over to talk to Officer Tate and Chief Atkins who were waiting for them a few steps away from the opening of the hallway in the living room.

"Where is Dr. Madison?" Sadie asked John.

"The ambulance took him away. He had regained consciousness by the time they got him loaded up on the stretcher, but he wasn't talking yet," John informed her.

"Did they take him to MUSC?"

"No, they took him to a small county hospital. Figured it might be a little hard for your colleagues to treat him medically after he tried to kill you," John explained.

Detective Jenkins and Detective Fuller made their way over to John and Sadie. Detective Jenkins shook Sadie's hand and then Detective Fuller pulled her into a hug. "Glad you're okay," she said.

"I'm glad it's over," Sadie replied.

"I think we're about done processing everything and should be out of your hair shortly," Detective Jenkins said. "Any chance you know how he got here?"

"He told me he parked his car one street over and walked through the woods," Sadie remembered.

"Great. We'll wrap up here and go find it," the detective replied.

John led Sadie to the kitchen and had her sit in one of the chairs at the table. He went over to the box with the tea set and pulled out the tea pot, a cup, and a saucer. Sadie watched as he cleaned and dried each item. He filled the pot with tap water and put it on the stove. He turned the knob to light the flame. While he waited for the water to boil, he put the cup on the saucer and went to look through Sadie's stash of teas. Just watching him move around the kitchen had a peaceful feeling washing over her. He carefully read each tea box and finally made a selection. Pulling a tea bag out of the chosen box, he placed it in the cup, hanging the string over the lip.

"John, come sit with me," Sadie urged.

He complied and took the seat next to her. He reached over and took her hands in his, rubbing her knuckles with his thumbs. He loved the feel of her smooth skin.

"I love you, Sadie," he vowed. "I don't know what I would have done if I had lost you."

"And you don't have to know," Sadie reassured him. "I'm not even hurt, John. I was pretty shook up, but I'm already feeling better."

The tea pot let out a whistle and John rose to turn off the flame and pour her tea. "I don't really know what I'm doing here," he muttered as he placed the saucer in front of her. "Do you need sugar or anything?"

Sadie sniffed at the tea. "Chamomile, perfect choice," she said approvingly. "No, I don't need anything with it. Thank you."

Once John was convinced that she was okay, he grinned at her devilishly.

"What's that all about?" she demanded playfully.

"You better drink your tea and rest up. Our phones have been blowing up with messages from our friends. You're going to have a lot of questions to answer young lady," he teased.

"Oh Lord. Is Faith having a heart attack yet?" Sadie pondered.

"I'm surprised she's not banging down the door. I bet Travis is having to hold her back."

"I'll drink this tea and give her a call. Might as well do a video call with the whole gang."

Sadie sipped her hot tea with one hand and held John's hand with the other. It was finally over and everything was going to be okay.

Chapter Forty-Eight

The next day, Sadie woke up to the sound of her alarm telling her it was time to get up and get ready for work. When she picked up her phone to quiet it, she saw a text from Dr. Richards informing her that he had heard about Dr. Madison and to take another day off. She put her phone back on the nightstand, snuggled back up to John's warm body, and went back to sleep.

When she awoke again, John was no longer in bed with her and the sun was shining brightly through the blinds and curtains. She checked her phone and saw that she had slept until lunchtime. It was very unusual for her to do so unless she had gotten off of work in the wee hours of the morning. All of the drama the night before had worn her out.

After getting cleaned up in the bathroom, she threw on a pair of black yoga pants, a sports bra, and purple tank top. Her back was stiff from staying in bed so long and she planned to lay out her new yoga mat in the living room and do some stretching.

Her plan was thwarted when she saw that her friends were in her kitchen. Surprised, she went to join them and saw that their significant others were outside in the backyard with John.

"Sadie! You're awake! Come sit down," Faith urged when she spotted Sadie in the doorway.

Paige and Cora Rae looked her over as she took a seat at the kitchen table with them. There were lines of worry etched all over their pretty faces.

"Stop looking at me like that. I'm fine," she insisted.

Paige burst into tears. "How can you say that? Someone tried to kill you!"

Sadie reached over and took ahold of her pregnant friend's hands. "He didn't make a very good show of it, Paige. All I got is a small bruise on my arm."

"Sometimes the mental trauma is worse than the physical," Cora Rae advised.

"I'm not going to say it doesn't give me the heebie jeebies that Dr. Madison wanted to kill me. But at the end of the day, he didn't succeed. Leann can have some peace now that he's definitely not coming after her and I have my very best friends to help me process the whole ordeal," Sadie replied.

"Damn skippy," Faith hooted.

"Faith, what are all of those containers on my counter?" Sadie asked, taking in the scene of her kitchen counters behind Faith.

Faith shrugged and gave Sadie a nervous grin. "I was up all night panic baking. I knew you were fine after our group video chat, but I still couldn't sleep. I hope you're hungry!"

"Starved," Sadie admitted.

Faith wouldn't hear of Sadie getting up to fix her own plate even though Sadie insisted that she was perfectly capable. When Sadie lost that battle, she watched the men milling around outside. Everyone must have called out of work today. She asked her friends for confirmation.

"How are y'all here in the middle of the day on a Monday?" she questioned. "Not that I'm not grateful, of course," she added.

"Cora Rae and I are working from home today," Paige explained. "Jake rescheduled his surveys to later in the week."

"And I'm my own boss and can do whatever I want," Faith contributed.

At Sadie's raised eyebrow, Faith amended her statement, "Well, every once in a while, I can. Travis had a bunch of comp time from Hurricane Ivey, so here we all are."

"Raj sends his regards. He's at the hospital today. He was so shocked when I told him who had come after you," Cora Rae relayed. "He told me he did a few surgeries with Dr. Madison and would have never guessed he would be capable of intentionally harming anybody."

"I bet his girlfriend, Dr. Jones, is struggling with wrapping her head around it too," Sadie mentioned.

"You think you know a person," Faith added, shaking her head.

About that time, John noticed Sadie was up and in the kitchen. Without a word to Travis or Jake, he headed inside. Guessing what had pulled their friend's attention, they followed him through the sliding glass door.

John went around the table to where Sadie was, and she stood up to embrace him. They held onto each other while their friends found other things in the kitchen to occupy their attention for a moment.

"I didn't want to wake you. You were sleeping so deeply," John whispered.

"Thank you. I guess I needed it," Sadie murmured back.

"Now that we are all together, maybe y'all can tell us what this guy's deal was?" Faith proposed.

Sadie sat back down and John stood behind her with his hands resting lightly on her shoulders.

"He confessed to all of his crimes this morning, so there won't be a trial. But to be on the safe side, anything said in this room stays between us, got it?" John requested.

When everyone nodded their assent, John looked down at Sadie to see if she wanted to start. She took a deep breath and shared with them what Dr. Todd Madison had told her the night before when he had come there to kill her.

"He had some sort of psychotic break, brought on by his childhood trauma caused by his mom and sister. He said that God spoke to him through an inner voice and that when he passed the test of killing his mother and sister God charged him with the task of eliminating other women with loose morals," Sadie shared.

"Makes me so mad when people use the Lord's name for hate instead of love," Faith said heatedly.

"Yes, Dr. Madison was full of hate," Sadie agreed. "It's such a waste. His story should have been about overcoming the odds and breaking the cycle, but instead it's a tragedy with a handful of innocent victims left in his wake."

"They found items belonging to the victims in his car. He had kept trophies. He kept them on his dresser. When Detective Fuller searched his place there were dust outlines where he had removed them to take with him when he ran. His plan was to kill Sadie and disappear," John revealed.

"How did he get back on the hospital floor we were keeping Leann on that night he tried to bust in the room behind me? He didn't use his badge according to the fob logs. How did he manage it?" Sadie wondered aloud.

"Detective Fuller asked him the same thing this morning. In an attempt to frame Dr. Wu, he snatched Dr. Wu's badge off of him when they met up in the resident locker room and then used it to access the floor by way of the stairwell," John explained.

Sadie thought about that for a moment. "But wouldn't the police eventually find Dr. Wu on the cameras somewhere else during the time of the attack and know that it couldn't have been him?"

"Maybe, if he left the locker room during that time. It would have at least bought Dr. Madison some time while the police did all that leg work, which it did," John reasoned.

"What were you feeling while you were facing him down, Sadie? Were you scared?" Cora Rae wondered. "I sure was scared of Stacey's crazy ass."

Sadie looked around at each of her friends in the room before answering. Her eyes lingered on Paige a few extra seconds to make sure her friend was not getting overwhelmed by the topic of conversation. When she saw Paige was wary but not struggling, Sadie turned her attention back to Cora Rae.

"Yeah, I was terrified, Cora Rae. I had to call on my training as a surgeon to remain calm on the outside. Inside I was freaking out, trying to come up with a plan. I kept him talking and kept using his first name to remind him that I wasn't just some stranger. I thought if I made him think about the times we had spent together as coworkers or the times I encouraged him as a surgeon it might save me. In the end it didn't work. But no matter what I wasn't going down without a fight. I wasn't letting him take away this life I've built. I have a job I love, friends I love, and a man I love," Sadie declared vehemently.

"A love to fight for," Cora Rae praised.

"Yes, exactly," Sadie replied, smiling at her dear friend.

"So, Faith, you ready?" John questioned.

Faith was about to take a bite of a vanilla cupcake with yellow buttercream frosting and her hand stopped in midair, John's question catching her off guard. Everyone looked to John with confused expressions.

"Ready for what?" she queried.

"Paige and Cora Rae had their psycho killer experience, now Sadie has had her turn," John began before getting smacked in the arm by Sadie.

"Don't you dare wish that on her, John!" Sadie shrieked, absolutely shocked.

John chuckled and grabbed his arm, "Ouch! I'm just playing. It was getting so tense in here."

"Good luck to 'em," Faith declared boldly.

"Yeah, I wouldn't mess with the little blond tornado," Jake agreed.

"Tiny but mighty," Cora Rae added.

As her friends discussed the stupidity of messing with Faith, Sadie stood and hugged John close. When they pulled apart, she stayed next to him, their arms still wrapped around one another.

"Time for our happily ever after, my love," John whispered in her ear.

"Sounds good, Officer John," she said, kissing him quickly on the mouth. "I love you so much."

Epilogue

A few months later...

Sadie was walking down the hallway of the hospital with an iPad in one hand and a travel mug of coffee in the other. She was reviewing a chart on her way to the doctors' lounge. She had a couple of hours before her next scheduled surgery and was determined to catch up on all of her paperwork so when she got off later that day, she could give John her undivided attention.

As if her thoughts had summoned him, John came hurriedly around the corner looking for her. He was looking awfully handsome in his uniform as usual. Sadie let out an appreciative sigh.

"Paige is in labor!" he announced excitedly. "I just escorted her and Jake here with the squad car. She waited until the last dang minute!"

"Here, take this," she said handing him the travel mug of coffee. She tucked her iPad under her arm and took off running for the labor and delivery wing.

A nurse directed her to Paige's room and Sadie hurried to the door and went inside. Another perk of working at the hospital was that she got to be in the room when her new niece was born. She went over to the sinks and washed her hands thoroughly before joining her friend at the hospital bed.

Jake was at the head of the bed, cheering Paige on and letting her squeeze the crap out of his hand. Sadie took her other hand and was extremely impressed by her friend's strong grip. Half an hour later progress was being made.

"Push! Push! Push!" the doctor instructed from where he was sitting between Paige's open legs. "I can see the head."

"You're almost there Mrs. Bennett!" the nurse encouraged from her post behind the doctor, looking over his shoulder.

"Yes baby, you're doing so great," Jake cheered as he kissed his wife's sweaty forehead.

Paige let out a primal yell as she pushed with all her might and Sadie snuck a peek down below to see if her friend's efforts had paid off.

"Okay, the head is out. One more big push with the next contraction and she'll be out, Paige. You got this!" Sadie cheered.

Her best friend took a deep breath and pushed again with all her might when the next contraction hit and screamed at the top of her lungs. Sadie heard the cries of the newborn and saw Jake's bewildered excitement at seeing his daughter for the first time. Jake cut the umbilical cord and took the baby from the doctor and laid her on Paige's chest.

Sadie went over to talk with the doctor by the sink to give the new family a moment alone.

"Any concerns I should keep an eye out for, Doctor?" Sadie asked her colleague.

"Nothing out of the ordinary. Mom and baby look great," he answered as he scrubbed his hands in the sink after removing his gloves.

Sadie made sure to thank all of the nurses who had helped and were now straightening up the room, getting things ready to move Paige into a recovery room.

"Little Clara Rae, you're so perfect," Paige cooed to her daughter.

Sadie thought it was so cool that Paige and Jake had decided to name her after Cora Rae since she was the one who helped save Paige and her unborn child that horrible day in The Hideaway Cottage.

Sadie walked back over to the bed and smiled down at Paige. "I'll go out and tell everyone she's here. I am sure they are anxious." She bent down to the little bundle of joy and said, "Welcome little one."

The waiting room was filled with Paige and Jake's loved ones and Sadie felt honored to be able to announce, "It's a girl!"

Faith and Cora Rae squealed and hugged each other at the joyous news. Chloe and Henry jumped up and down and cheered. Caleb high-fived his little brother and sister. The sight warmed Sadie's heart. Paige's parents smiled at each other and hugged, then went over to congratulate Jake's parents. Sadie watched as John shook hands with all of the men and hugged all the ladies, saving Sadie for last. They hung back while everyone else went over to the nursery window, waiting for a chance to see the new baby.

"Did witnessing the miracle of childbirth change your mind about not wanting one?" John questioned.

"It was very beautiful watching my niece being born, but no. I am still okay with not personally experiencing it for myself," Sadie assured him.

She stole a quick kiss from her man and when Jake came into view holding little Clara Rae in the nursery, Sadie and John joined the others at the window. The proud daddy held up his baby for his family and friends to see. He had happy tears streaming down his face.

John pulled Sadie into his side and kissed her cheek. They had each other and their loved ones and lived each day as the blessing it was.

About the author

This is Jen McGee's second novel. She is an avid reader and loves coming up with her own stories. Jen is married with three rambunctious children and one yappy dog. In her spare time she enjoys reading, yoga, puzzles, and coaching little league softball. The Carolinas have a special place in her heart as she was born in South Carolina and was raised and currently resides in North Carolina.

Acknowledgements

Once again there are so many people I need to thank for helping to make this book happen. First, my husband and kids who had to put up with me hiding in the bonus room to write, especially in the last few weeks leading up to the release. Thank you to Jessica, Hope, Amber, and Trysh for reading pages over and over and for giving great constructive feedback. An extra thank you to Amber for making the cover so beautiful and updating my website! Also, a huge thank you to my parents, siblings, in-laws, Ms. Gail, and other friends and family for spreading the word about my first book, which really helped to encourage me to continue my writing journey. I would like to give a special shoutout to Rebecca from the East Regional Library for taking a chance on an unknown author that she randomly met at a town Christmas tree lighting! From the bottom of my heart, thank you so much to everyone who reads this book. You have no idea how much it means to me.

www.ingramcontent.com/pod-product-compliance
Lightning Source LLC
LaVergne TN
LVHW041912070526
838199LV00051BA/2591